in hovering flight

in hovering flight

JOYCE HINNEFELD

UNBRIDLED
BOOKS

Unbridled Books
Denver, Colorado

Library of Congress Cataloging-in-Publication Data

Hinnefeld, Joyce.
In hovering flight / by Joyce Hinnefeld.
p. cm.
ISBN 978-1-932961-58-4
1. Mothers and daughters—Fiction.   2. Terminally ill—Fiction.
3. Birds—Fiction.   4. Women—Fiction.   5. Family secrets—
Fiction.   6. Maine—Fiction.   I. Title.
PS3558.I544815 2008
813'.54—dc22
2008018616

1   3   5   7   9   10   8   6   4   2

Book Design by SH • CV

First Printing

For my parents, Wilma and Lynn Hinnefeld

Whatever it was I lost, whatever I wept for
Was a wild, gentle thing, the small dark eyes
Loving me in secret.
It is here. At a touch of my hand,
The air fills with delicate creatures
From the other world.

—James Wright (from "Milkweed")

Occasionally my parents themselves said to me, "There are also cheery things in life. Why do you only show the dark side?" That I could not answer. It held no charm for me.

—Käthe Kollwitz

I

field notebooks

one

ACCORDING TO JOHN JAMES Audubon, there was once a species of bird in southeastern Pennsylvania, the Cuvier's kinglet, *Regulus cuvieri,* or, as Audubon liked to call it, Cuvier's wren. And according to Addie and Tom Kavanagh, the mysterious bird may have magically appeared again nearly two hundred years later on a ridge near their home, seventy-five miles north of Audubon's original sighting.

Audubon claimed that he had discovered this "pretty and rare species" on his father-in-law's plantation, Fatland Ford, northwest of Philadelphia, in June of 1812. As was his custom, he shot it in order to draw it, thinking at first it was the more common ruby-crowned kinglet. "I have not seen another since, nor have I been able to learn that this species has been observed by any other individual," he wrote in his famous *Birds of America.*

But Audubon wasn't known for his honesty. He claimed to be the son of a French admiral and a beautiful Spanish Creole woman from the islands, but his father was actually a French merchant, slave dealer, and naval lieutenant, his mother an illiterate French chambermaid. And surely it was a practical move, this naming of a bird (real or not) for Baron Georges Cuvier, the famed French naturalist and one of Audubon's earliest patrons.

Consider, also, the "joke" Audubon played on a naturalist named Constantine Samuel Rafinesque, when Audubon and his wife, Lucy, hosted Rafinesque at their Kentucky home in the summer of 1818. For his guest Audubon described—and drew—ten species of imaginary fish that he claimed were native to the Ohio River. Rafinesque included accounts of these fish (including something called the "devil-jack diamond fish," described as between four and ten feet long, weighing up to four hundred pounds, and covered with bulletproof scales) in several articles and eventually a book.

There has been no single sighting of a Cuvier's kinglet in the two hundred years since Audubon claimed to have shot one. Unless, that is, one believes the Kavanaghs, the bird-artist-and-ornithologist team who published the environmentalist and antiwar classic *A Prosody of Birds*—an odd blend of delicate artist's plates and dense poetic scansions of birdsongs—in 1969. Actually, only Addie claimed to have spotted the Cuvier's kinglet, one morning at dawn. It was an overcast morning in May 2001, and she was on a routine excursion into the field, on the ridge above her home along the Nisky Creek, near Burnham, Pennsylvania. Though he wasn't present at the time, Tom has never disputed his wife's claim. But, strange as it may seem to question the veracity of a serious scientist and teacher like Tom Kavanagh, there are reasons to doubt both him and Addie.

If what Addie saw that morning was not a Cuvier's kinglet but a ruby-crowned kinglet—a mistake neither Addie nor Tom would be likely to make—then she had her reasons for such a mysterious lapse. Addie always had her reasons for every outlandish choice she made. And Tom loved her deeply through all of them.

Tom and Addie's daughter, Scarlet, has always loved birds too, though not with the nearly fanatical passion of her parents. She has loved them enough to write about them, off and on, since she was a child. But now she is less concerned about whether or not the Cuvier's kinglet suddenly, magically, reappeared in southeastern Pennsylvania than about the instructions her mother presented to her and Tom two weeks ago—for what she wished them to do with her body: clear orders for a brazenly illegal burial. There is no easy way to handle such a request, as far as Scarlet can see. And it's hard to say what Tom is thinking.

Now it is early May 2002, the beginning of the spring migration through the northeastern United States. Scarlet and Tom are in Cider Cove, a sleepy, off-season town on the New Jersey shore, in the rambling old house, now a bed-and-breakfast, of Addie's dear friend Cora. Scarlet would have expected her mother to choose to die in her own ramshackle cottage in Burnham, windows open to each morning's raucous dawn chorus. But the Burnham cottage is a place filled with much history, and in the last ten years or so, even birdsong seemed, at times, to make Addie angry, or sad, or both.

Last night Scarlet left Addie, who was clearly drawing her last breaths, alone with Tom. She couldn't bear to be there for the actual moment when her mother died. She curled up on a wicker divan on Cora's screened porch, watching the stars, listening to the wind and the pounding of the waves at the end of the long slope down from Cora's house. When Tom roused her a couple hours later, a filmy light was slipping through the purple clouds, and the hospice worker was packing her bag.

"Addie's gone, Scarlet," Tom said. "I'd like you to help me move her body down the street." And so Scarlet followed him into Cora's studio, fitted for several weeks now with Addie's hospital bed. Cora had been there through the last days too, along with Lou, Addie's other good friend. Now both of them were crying silently, busying themselves with straightening the bedclothes, tidying vases of flowers; they seemed desperate to find something useful to do. Tom tucked a blanket around Addie's body, as if to keep her warm. Every move, every gesture like this one seemed to Scarlet both funny and heartbreaking. She watched as he lifted her mother's tiny, weightless body in his arms.

Tom tucked Addie in carefully once again when he lowered her onto the cot in the walk-in cooler of a restaurant several doors down from Cora's house. This was Cider Cove's only seafood restaurant, owned by a trusted and discreet friend of Cora's and open, in the off-season, only on weekends. Tom had told Cora that they might need a few days to work out "the arrangements," and within fifteen minutes she'd arranged this access to the restaurant cooler with her friend.

Neither of them wanted to leave her. But, Tom said, it was surely better to have her body there, not worrying them all back at Cora's while they tried to figure out what to do next. Scarlet was quiet and compliant as they moved and arranged Addie's body; she felt like a child again, relying on her father to handle everything, particularly everything involving her puzzle of a mother.

Addie looked like a child herself. Scarlet held her mother's hand for a while, but eventually that felt forced to her, as though she were trying to play the role of the grieving daughter instead of actually being one. She had already had her moments, her real moments, with Addie: first, two nights before, when Addie had seemed suddenly present and clear, herself again, when Scarlet had spoken with her alone. And then just moments ago, following her father down the street, below the familiar Cider Cove streetlights, watching how tenderly he cradled Addie's body, his face buried in her neck, breathing her in one last time.

They locked Addie into the cooler at last and walked back to Cora's in silence as dawn broke around them. Tom went inside to gather his binoculars and scope and headed out in search of birds. Scarlet got her notebook and returned to the porch. Cora and Lou were nowhere in sight.

And so Scarlet started writing. Some years ago she'd had a moment of success as a poet, success that was complicated by its connection with her mother. Two of the better-known poems in her one published book were, indirectly but clearly, about Addie. They were also, in some ways, about birds. That book had won a small literary prize in 1995, at the peak of Addie's fame—or notoriety, depending on one's outlook. This was a year after Addie had run afoul of some people in Washington over an installation involving, among other things, two crucified gulls.

For years Alex, Scarlet's editor, has been pushing her to write a memoir. "It's a logical step for you, with all this awareness of your mother, her presence in your poems, all the connections," he has told her repeatedly. "And frankly," he seems always to add, "it's the only way you're going to make any money as a writer."

But, as she has told Alex many times, Scarlet has no idea how one goes about writing a memoir. Sometimes she has tried to imagine telling the story of their lives as a play. Now, as she sits on Cora's sunporch in the pink-gray light of dawn, she thinks about beginning with the cast of characters assembled nearby:

The husband, Tom, barely visible at the far southern end of the beach, his scope trained on a plover's nest a hundred yards away.

The two friends from Addie's college days, Cora and Lou, offstage doing who-knows-what. Probably Cora is baking something. Maybe Lou is shopping.

And then there is Dustin, the young man at work outside Cora's studio window, sawing, planing, hammering old pieces of barn siding, shaping these into some semblance of a coffin. A more logical addition might surely be Addie's brother, John. But he is in Scranton, probably at work. Scarlet wonders whether Tom will even call him. She hasn't seen her uncle since her college graduation. Instead of a brother and an uncle, she thinks, her family has Dustin the coffin-maker.

Finally there is Scarlet herself: a sometime poet, wrapped in a sleeping bag on the chilly porch where she spent the night because her room upstairs holds too many memories. Scarlet, fighting the urge to seize one of the cigarettes Lou has left behind, not even drinking coffee, scribbling madly in a notebook, leading the others to imagine that she is penning eloquent, mournful poems.

When in fact she is trying to envision a memoir. Which, unlike the poems she wishes she was writing, feels to Scarlet like a kind of betrayal—of Addie, of Tom, of them all. How could she possibly pull together the scattered threads of all these lives?

So far she has managed only a list of possible titles. One is *Zugun-ruhe*—the term in German for the migratory restlessness of birds, and Tom's affectionate name for the last twelve years of Scarlet's life, spent making her way down the eastern seaboard, finally landing in New York. A migration punctuated with brief stays on the coast of New Jersey— a place that suddenly, once again, has begun to feel like home.

But that is Scarlet's life, not Addie's, and it's Addie's life that Alex, and others, are really interested in. The years of Scarlet's migration, through the decade of the 1990s up to this cool and puzzling spring of 2002, were relatively quiet ones for Addie. Had her mother somehow been holding her breath, reining herself in, waiting to see how far south, and now how near to this overdeveloped coastline, Scarlet would fly? Had she been watching for those final fledgling years to pass before her next—and last—great scheme?

One thing Addie was doing in those years was handling her first bout with cancer in the most conventional of ways: two rounds of chemother-apy, a bit of radiation. Not many people know this. Far more people have heard about the second, far more invasive cancer, the one she chose not to fight.

There is another possible title for a story about Addie Kavanagh: *Field Notebooks.*

Scarlet has access to all of her father's and nearly all of her mother's notebooks from the field, all neatly penned in black ink on 15.2-by-24.1-centimeter loose-leaf paper, one side only, red margins penciled in an inch and a half from the left, bound in three-ring binders (20.3 by 25.4 cm). All of Addie's coded to correspond with carefully compiled portfolios of her drawings and studies for paintings. All—except for their content— in accordance with the conventions established by Professor Joseph Grinnell at Berkeley in the early decades of the twentieth century. "No notebook this day, no sleep this night!" were Grinnell's famous words; he also urged his students to view their notebooks as public documents, re-cords designed to educate their readers, to add to the store of knowledge of all who might one day encounter them. Tom Kavanagh presented Grinnell's field notebook conventions, in painstaking detail, to Addie and the other students in his May-term Biology of the Birds class at Burnham College in the spring of 1965—that notorious 1965 class, the one that might have gotten him fired. The class that prompted a year's leave, which led to his only book and to Addie's first rough but moving paintings of birds—and, ultimately, to Scarlet.

Scarlet has all of Addie's notebooks save one, her first, the one from that five-week course in May, spanning the spring migration through the woods and rivers of eastern Pennsylvania. The notebook with which she seduced Tom. It will be Scarlet's, he has told her, when he dies—leaving her to imagine, for now, what Addie might have written there.

There are times, despite her mother's long and maddening silences, when Scarlet feels certain that she can.

Journal—Field Entry

6 May 1965
Thursday

Sunday Woods, Burnham, Bucks Co., PA (1–2 mi. from Burnham College campus, via Ridge Path behind the Hall of Science)

Time: 05:20–06:30—Plum Pond; 06:40–07:30—Large meadow SE of
Plum Pond
Observers: Burnham College Biology of the Birds class (20 students +
Prof. Kavanagh)
Habitat: Tall grasses at the muddy edge of Plum Pond, a small freshwa-
ter pond in a natural basin at the center of pine and scrub woods;
meadow ½ mi. SE of pond—a former home site (foundation visible;
18th century?); vegetation includes yellow wood sorrel, fiddlehead

ferns, and rue anemones (or windflowers, as Cora Davis says her
mother calls them)

Weather: Temp. 58 degrees F; Dry, with variable winds

Sun, with drifting clouds—30% cloud cover, according to Professor
Kavanagh (I am not sure how this is determined)

Remarks: Several of the girls were ridiculously underdressed, one in
sandals; half the group seemed to be sleepwalking, others more alert.

SPECIES LIST

Canada Goose, *Branta canadensis*   25

Mallard, *Anas platyrhyncho*   8

Great Blue Heron, *Ardea herodius*   1

Downy Woodpecker, *Picoides pubescens*   1

Tree Swallow, *Tachycineta bicolor*   20+

Cardinal, *Cardinalis cardinalis*   2 (M & F)

Black-Capped Chickadee, *Poecile atricapilla*   1

Scarlet Tanager, *Piranga olivacea*   1

Purple Grackle, *Quiscalus quiscula*   4

Tufted Titmouse, *Parus bicolor*   1

Red-Eyed Vireo, *Vireo olivaceus*   1

Gray Catbird, *Dumetella carolinensis*   4

Mourning Dove, *Zenaida macroura*   7

Number of Species: 13; *Number of Individuals:* 76; *Time:* 2 hrs., 10 mins.

Comments: Two students, Karl being one of them, are enviably skilled in
recognizing birdsongs; now I at least begin to understand Cora's
attraction to him! None, however, can approach Prof. Kavanagh's
skill.

6 May—Where do I begin? Do you wonder why students take this class?
Perhaps you're aware of your reputation? "He recites poetry while you're
climbing the path up from Sunday Woods." "If you make it past the sec-

ond week, some days he'll take you out in the woods and play his fiddle and lead a sing-along instead of lecturing!" "He's also *gorgeous!*" (I imagine you're aware that the girls speak this way about you, and of the reputation your class has among some jealous college boys.)

But much as I do look forward to poetry and Irish folk tunes, my reasons for being here are different.

I am in love with birds, and I don't quite know what to do about it.

I'm afraid I've come to this love too late. According to all the stories you've been telling us, all the great lovers of birds—John James Audubon, Louis Agassiz Fuertes, Roger Tory Peterson, and you—discovered their passion at an early age. Some important person handed them a pair of field glasses or a field guide or a stuffed dead bird and that was it; they were hooked.

But I'm twenty-one years old.

And do I need to mention that they were also always *boys?*

None of their experience applies to me. It feels sometimes like I never even saw a bird until last fall, when I went to England to study. What was I doing before that? I don't know, reading poetry, going out, listening to music, staying up late talking to my roommates. Then one dreary day in early October, when I was to read a paper on Keats's "Ode to a Nightingale" in my tutorial, my tutor, Miss Smallwood, brought in her personal collection of three Audubon plates, including one of a nightingale—not the English one, of course, but the American hermit thrush.

"Let's talk about these today instead," she said. "Aren't they *marvelous?*"

And they were. They were maybe the most beautiful things I'd ever seen.

The following Saturday I joined Miss Smallwood and her "Oxbridge Birder" friends on a ramble in the Cotswolds. We had tea in a shop in Stratford-upon-Avon decorated with silhouettes of Shakespearean characters. I was the only one there under sixty-five. For the rest of the term Miss Smallwood and I read Audubon's *Journals* instead of Romantic poetry. (Don't tell anyone in the registrar's office or the English Department—ha ha.)

On weekends I traveled all over Britain with the Birders' Club. I have drawn since I was a child—nothing special, pictures of my family, the animals on my father's farm, some friends in high school and here at Burnham. I never took it very seriously and never studied at all, beyond my high school art classes and Drawing I here at Burnham, when I was a freshman. There wasn't room in my schedule for any more art classes (up until last semester, I planned to be an English teacher).

But I started carrying around a sketch pad when I went places with the Oxbridge Birders, and eventually Miss Smallwood introduced me to Clive Behrend (Do you know him? His illustrations are quite well-known in Great Britain), who let me sit and sketch with him in his hide in the woods outside Oxford and encouraged me to start painting. With no training! He just let me loose in his studio one day.

I knew by December that I had to take as many art classes as I could when I got back to Burnham. So I abandoned student teaching last semester and signed up for four.

My parents still don't know this, exactly. I've told them I'm going to graduate and be an art teacher instead, and they believe me, poor souls.

Of course I'm going to graduate, instead, prepared to do nothing at all in the "real" world. A girl, no less. A girl who discovered birds, and painting, far too late, if you believe all the stories. A girl who's going to graduate in a month and, probably, have to look for a job as a secretary in Scranton.

But do you know what? I don't care. Because I've found something that *matters* to me, for the first time. And I'll work as hard as I have to to get this right. I think I'm burning up with the same thing Audubon was burning with. I feel like him somehow, like some kind of out-of-place mongrel from Pennsylvania who almost faints when she's near a living bird.

He achieved his first real success after a trip to England, you know.

That sounds vain, I realize. All I really mean to say is that I *have* to find a way to show what I see, and how I feel, when I look at a bird. It's all I care about now.

Which is why I'm in this class. And which brings me to a problem. I need to find a way to have *time* with these birds. With the class there's too much movement, too much hurrying on to the next bird, too much rushing to make a longer species list. There is no way for me to draw like this, and drawing, then painting, is the only way for me to get this out of my system, if you understand what I mean.

I've never had to share the experience with so many people. Even with Miss Smallwood and her group, I was never in a hurry to keep finding *more*. I'm concerned about whether this is going to work for me. (They shot and stuffed them for a reason, I almost want to say. But of course I don't mean that.)

Yes, I'll be out on my own as often as I can. But now I have to confess my worry about this: How will I find them? I'm able to wait very patiently. But I struggle so to recognize their songs! This is what I most need help with. I think I have a tin ear; I wonder if I can really learn.

I know "personal asides have no real place in a scientific field notebook"—unless they pertain to the field of study, in this case our "quest to know these marvelous creatures." I hope the things I've written here seem to you to pertain. Either way, I guess I needed to tell you all this.

The thing I most want from this class (you did ask us to write about this) is the ability to hear a bird's song and know it instantly, as you do.

Already I've forgotten the song of the wood thrush. On Monday, when we heard it during class, I thought it was the most glorious sound I'd ever heard. Now I'd give anything to recall it, but it's gone.

two

TYPICALLY, MORE WOMEN THAN men were enrolled in Biology of the Birds, which was thought to be a function of Tom Kavanagh's allure; it was affectionately known, among the students, as "Birds and Chicks." For all its appeal, though, the handsome Irish instructor and the strange blend of science, music, and poetry he was famous for bringing to this unusual class also scared many students away. There was the poetry, for one thing; "What does this have to do with biology?" science majors had been known to ask. And there was also Tom Kavanagh's fervent insistence on the tenets of evolutionary theory, as notorious among the more religious and conservative students at Burnham as the required five A.M. field excursions, every weekday for the entire five weeks of the term.

Cora and Lou had signed up for the course as well. Cora, a biology major, had been saving the course for her final term at Burnham. Lou, always the curious flirt, had different reasons; throughout her four years at Burnham she'd admired Tom Kavanagh from a distance—his wiry, muscular skill on the basketball court at intramural games, his accomplished fiddle playing with a group of local musicians. And now she wanted a closer look.

Addie had her own reasons for taking the class. She had been longing to take it since the previous fall, her full-scholarship semester abroad in Great Britain, a time when she was to have been awash in Shakespeare, Milton, Wordsworth. And when she had, instead, immersed herself in Turner landscapes and the works of John James Audubon.

How could she have known that she would feel so at home, so comfortable in her own skin, maybe for the first time—in her icy room in Oxford, on the gray streets of London, tramping along sodden paths in the Lake District or through fields of grazing sheep in the Cotswolds? And discovering, remarkably, that she had a real talent for drawing and for painting.

Back in Pennsylvania in December, she'd told her parents nothing about her change in plans. She'd also said nothing to her college boyfriend, though she'd known since October that she would break up with him at the first opportunity when she returned to campus. Still, she did worry at times that she'd be foolish to give him up. They had talked, vaguely, of marriage after graduation. And what *would* she do now, with no teaching degree to back her up?

"Work as a waitress and live in Greenwich Village and meet fabulous, sexy artists like Willem de Kooning," Lou—who was an art major herself, and from a wealthy family from Philadelphia—said when the three friends were together again in January. "Get a job as a secretary in Philadelphia and take night classes in art until you have enough credits to become an art teacher" was Cora's alternative. They were still the only ones who knew of Addie's plans. While she was abroad she had longed for them as if they were lovers, her beloved roommates, the only people who understood her.

At home, in her parents' house over the Christmas holidays, there'd been no one who could understand. She'd returned from Britain thinner than she'd been in years, no longer setting and teasing her dark-blond hair. Her mother watched her worriedly, urging more food on her at every meal. But Addie could barely touch the eggs, the fried potatoes, all the foods of her childhood. She only sipped some coffee and nibbled at a piece of her mother's homemade bread. She also found it nearly impossible to draw. Each day she bundled herself in a rag wool sweater and tattered tweed coat, both purchased for pennies in a tiny secondhand shop in London, then pulled on her mud-splattered Wellingtons. These had left a layer of dust and grime at the bottom of her suitcase, where it remained because it was English dirt and she could not bear to part with it. And each day, though she feared it would be no different from any other since her return, she took along her sketchbook and a pencil.

At the frozen pond down a country road from her parents' house, away from the smells of mud and manure and her mother's daily baking, away from her childhood bedroom and, in the barn, the mournful, cheated-looking eyes of the cows—only at the frozen pond could she catch a glimmer of what she'd felt on the banks of Grasmere or walking in the shadow of Westminster Cathedral, notebook in hand, sketching furiously. But not the rippling lake and not a flying buttress; what she drew, obsessively, religiously, with the devotion of a pilgrim, were the ruffled wings of a magpie, the dusty breast of a wood pigeon. Creatures that seemed to be moving through their lives as randomly and fitfully as she.

By March, Addie was drawing and painting furiously again. And Cora and Lou had adjusted to the changes in their friend, who, on her return from England, wore black tights and flats with wool jumpers and let her hair grow long and straight. Now, instead of tending to her hair and nails and baking cookies for her boyfriend on the weekend, Addie took the train into New York City with Lou as often as she could afford it. They would start at the Metropolitan Museum or the Museum of Modern Art, eat sandwiches in Central Park while Addie sketched and Lou chatted with strangers, and step reverently into one of the galleries on 57th Street. Then, flush with the confidence that art always gave them, they'd ride the subway downtown to drink wine and smoke cigarettes at the Cedar Tavern or Max's Kansas City, eyes scanning the crowd in search of famous artists.

Once, lingering longer than they'd intended, hoping to sight, say, de Kooning or Robert Motherwell, they missed the last bus back to Doylestown and walked the streets of Manhattan until dawn, drunk for the first half of the night, sober and staring, entranced, for the second. When they returned at midday to the dorm suite they shared with Cora, she made them coffee in their illegal percolator. Lou went to bed and slept until her first class on Monday morning. Addie locked herself into her tiny studio in the crumbling old Art Department building, where she spent her time obsessively painting the pigeons she'd seen on the steps of the New York Public Library, finally sleeping for a few hours on the sofa in the student lounge.

By the last week of April, when classes ended for a one-week recess, Cora and Lou had grown accustomed to the new Addie; her English adviser, Dr. Curtis, had abandoned his efforts to persuade her to complete her teaching certification requirements; her boyfriend was a thing of the past; and the dean had granted her request to fulfill the science requirement by taking Biology of the Birds. At a small school like Burnham, radical changes in a student like Addie Sturmer were duly noted, and administrators eyed the budding artist nervously, happy to hurry her along to graduation.

She spent the April recess with Lou and Cora and Cora's boyfriend Karl, a studious engineering major, at Lou's family farm, riding horses, eating exotic "gourmet" dinners, and drawing constantly. Then, early on the third morning of May, the three young women walked up a sloping path through the damp patch of woods that separated the campus dormitories from the academic buildings. Slowly, each lost in her own thoughts, they approached the stately Hall of Science, a second home to Cora, foreign territory to Lou and Addie, for Tom Kavanagh's eight A.M. lecture.

As they walked through the edge of the woods to the building's side entrance, a bird chirruped in a towering oak above their heads. Its flutelike song was barely noticed by Lou, who, despite being barely awake after a night spent drinking wine along the river, had arranged her long dark hair in an artful chignon and whose slow, willowy walk was noted appreciatively by every sleepy-eyed male they passed. But Cora—newly engaged and deeply in love—thrilled at the sound of the bird's song, which she heard as a splendid echo of her own happiness on this crisp and sunny morning.

For Addie, who'd been wondering, at that moment, what in the world she was doing, this bird's song was a revelation. She paused, gazing up into the tangle of branches, hoping for a rustle of wing. She did not yet know that thrilling sound as the song of the wood thrush; for her, at that moment, it was nothing less than the voice of all her unnamed longing.

three

TOM KAVANAGH STARED AT the expectant faces that greeted him as he entered the room; this was the most alert they would be, he knew, for the next five weeks. It was a large group for Biology of the Birds: twenty brave souls. He wondered how many would fade away by the second or third morning's field excursion. Over half were majors, and most of these he knew; in a small program like Burnham's, he was sure to have had them in Zoology at least, maybe even back in the introductory course for majors. There was Cora Davis, a lovely girl, smart and reliable, cheerfully attractive; he gladly returned her ready smile, and it was then that he noticed the two next to her.

One, who could only be described as dark and sultry, with her long legs languidly crossed beneath her desk, was giving him a frankly suggestive look: expectant in a different way. It was a look he'd come to recognize, even expect, and, in past semesters, to deflect good-humoredly. Though now he wondered, momentarily, what might happen if he didn't smile back like a tolerant friend of their older brother's (he was, after all, only a dozen years older than most of them) but instead stared back with equal, or greater, interest. *Why don't you meet me in my office after class to discuss this further?*

Certainly it had begun to cross his mind, with things the way they were at home, Polly so restless and bitter, always furious at him, chafing at the role of "faculty wife," longing for a city, for a chance to pursue her singing with real seriousness.

"And what work would there be for an unemployed ornithologist in New York City?" he'd asked her last fall, gently at first, trying, but as always failing, to soothe her.

And then, after a few more glasses of wine, she'd begun to harp, there was no other word for it, her angry voice growing louder, filling the room. "There's nothing for me here. You don't care for me at all. And where is your illustrious career, stuck here in the sticks in Pennsylvania, teaching and tending to your little students all the time . . . what are *you* doing that's so valuable, you haven't written a word since your dissertation, there's no sign you ever will. . . ."

"So now I'm to sacrifice this job as well?" he had snapped back, unable to contain his fury. "Forget about my work here and follow you to New York, is that it? And what do you suppose we'll live on then—your coins from busking in subway stations? Or did I miss it when they called from the Metropolitan Opera to offer you a role?"

What was to stop him? he thought as he stared at the brazen girl next to Cora. Then he glanced at the one sitting on the brazen girl's other side. Long blond hair falling into her eyes and boiled-wool sweater slipping from her shoulder: bohemian clothes, but they didn't seem to fit her somehow. She was decidedly *not* looking at him but at an open notebook in front of her. From time to time she raised her eyes, carelessly brushing strands of her hair out of her way, and looked pointedly at the stuffed and mounted great horned owl he had placed on the desk in front of him. She was drawing it, and even from this distance he could see that the likeness was strong.

She saw him watching her then, and momentarily returned his gaze. Her own look was inscrutable. She was pretty, but there was something pained in her expression that might have prevented most people from noticing. She blinked once and returned to her drawing.

Not since his days as a teaching assistant had he felt flustered and distracted at the front of a classroom. For years now he'd felt completely at home standing before a room full of students—as confident in the work he did there as when he was in the field. But for just that moment, when she blinked as if he were distracting her from something much more urgent, she had unnerved him somehow. He looked down at his notes and gathered his thoughts; then he turned and wrote two things on the chalkboard:

Ontogeny recapitulates phylogeny. (Ernst Haeckel)

and

Sluggards! Spread the wings of your mind to the sky, and rise from
   the earth.
Strive not to catch but to become birds! (Petrarch)

"Here," he said when he had returned the chalk to the tray and turned to face the class, carefully avoiding the occasional gaze of the girl in the front and to his left, "are the two poles between which this class will string its tenuous wire. I am an ornithologist, and also a musician, and a lover of poetry. No study of these illustrious creatures called 'the birds,'" and here, as always, he began pacing the room, warming up, gathering momentum, "these marvelous creatures with their hollow bones . . . did you know their bones are hollow?" He had deliberately walked to the right side of the room, pausing there in front of the desk of a nonmajor, who stopped scribbling notes long enough to shake her head.

"It's true! Hollow bones. Imagine what this means. Strength *and* lightness. Flight and surety. They hover too magnificently between the practical and the whimsical, the rational and the exquisitely nonsensical, for any student of their physiology and habitat and history to dare to linger too long at either pole, the strictly 'scientific' or the purely 'poetic.'"

"And further," he went on, walking back to the chalkboard and pointing, "though Haeckel's theory of recapitulation is largely discredited now, evolutionary theory, my friends, decidedly is *not*, as our objects of study, of close observation, even, yes, of our *desire*," and he risked a fleeting glance at the two girls next to Cora Davis, sensing somehow that this last claim would reach both of them, "as these fascinating creatures make abundantly clear." Here he paused, as he always did at this point in introducing the course, suddenly standing still and lowering his voice. Pens and pencils stopped, as they always did, and waiting eyes all turned to him.

"Understand this," he said then, in a near-whisper; he would not disappoint them in their eagerness for the drama of this moment. "If you harbor any childish and ill-founded notions, which, one would hope, you surely will not, after even one year of a college education, about the 'evils' of the study of evolution, you do not belong in this class. Such an attitude will be a terrible detriment to you here. Every bit as problematic as an inability to rise at dawn to join the birds in their morning rousing and singing."

He paused then, trembling, as he always was by now. Even now, even ten years after leaving Ireland in 1955, in love with the music and the countryside but sore with the strain of suppressing his excitement over all he had learned—about the natural world, about the lives of the creatures he had watched, listened to, and cherished since his lonely childhood—even now he felt it. A tremendous rush of excitement, and maybe a trace of fear, when he laid it before his students so boldly: "The world is more ancient than a strict reading of the book of Genesis will allow; there is undeniable proof of this. Birds are, in all likelihood, evolved from prehistoric creatures, some of which did not even fly. They are soaring, melodic evidence, undeniable, all around us, impossible to ignore, of natural selection. *Please take note:* I embrace the music and poetry they inspire, but I will quell the slightest effort to twist their near-mystical beauty into religious dogma."

The power to proclaim this, to insist upon it, after his silent youth, after years of quietly absorbing the church's denial of all that his senses made clear to him, always, always, left him nearly giddy.

Having made his point, he returned to the podium and his lecture notes, to tease out the subtler points of the theory of recapitulation. All eyes were on him, he knew, all pens and pencils poised. All except those of the blond girl, who had continued with her drawing all this time. He plunged ahead with his notes as the pencils began their frantic scribbling.

He resisted the urge to laugh at this desperate note-taking, as if there were some way in which he might test them on the kind of knowledge he was trying to impart. As if he planned to give them any sort of exam. As if their performance in this course would ever be evaluated on any grounds other than the quality of their attention in the field, and the seriousness and probity of their field notebooks.

Then, to shift from the drier, if crucial, background from Haeckel and Darwin and Alfred Russell Wallace and to give them more to copy maniacally (and absurdly), he read them one of his favorite quotations, from the poet John Clare:

> For my part I love to look on nature with a poetic feeling, which magnifies the pleasure. I love to see the Nightingale in its hazel retreat, and the Cuckoo hiding in its solitude of oaken foliage, and not to examine their carcasses in glass cases. Yet naturalists and botanists seem to have no taste for this poetic feeling.

"Now. Take a good long look at this 'carcass,' " he went on, turning to the desk to lift the stuffed owl aloft, then setting it back down with a dramatic thud, "removed, for the moment, from its 'glass case.' This is a great horned owl, male, killed and stuffed right here in the valley of the Delaware River forty years ago, by none other than my predecessor at Burnham College.

"Take careful note, now. Record everything you see that might help you recognize this bird in the future." As always, the majors began writing immediately, while the nonmajors stared helplessly for a full minute or more before beginning to write some tentative notes.

All except the blond girl, "the artist," as he thought of her now, who sat quietly, her hands in her lap, staring at the stuffed owl, occasionally glancing at her drawing and making some small adjustment. Her bold friend, sitting next to her, pointed to her drawing and whispered something, to which the artist responded with a nod, then made some adjustment. The look on her face when she glanced up at the owl was completely unreadable to him. It was not, as far as he could tell, the absorption of someone who was studying a specimen carefully; it was something else, and though he couldn't quite place it, he began to believe it might be something like contempt. Not for him, not for the poor bird, but more for this exercise he had assigned the class.

It astonished him that he recognized that look on her face. Contempt for the practice of closely observing something that had been killed and stuffed was precisely what *he* felt. But in all his years of teaching, no student had ever failed to register surprise at what he did next. To audible groans from those who had only begun to notice some feature of the great horned owl that they might record in their notes, he grasped the owl at its base and returned it to the black case in which he'd carried it into the room.

"And that," he announced, "is the last time you will look at a stuffed carcass, in or out of a glass case, in my class." He glanced at the artist again, searching for even the smallest smile of complicity, but her head was down, her hair once again shielding her eyes.

"Tomorrow we enter the woods from the path behind this building at five A.M. sharp," he continued. "We'll return by eight, you'll have an hour to get breakfast, then back here for the day's lecture at nine. Afternoons and evenings will be for additional excursions of your own and tending to your field notebooks. In the words of the renowned ornithologist Joseph Grinnell, 'No notebook this day, no sleep this night.'

"Advice, by the way, that you'll do well to attend to—more so than to anything I've said to you so far this morning, which, I assure you, will at no time nor at any place appear on an examination." More groans then, along with a few gasps of disbelief. "I take it as a given that you are in this class because you wish to learn, deeply and meaningfully, about birds. If you have other reasons, you may wish to consider a visit to the registrar's office to see what other courses remain open at this point."

Here he found himself looking not at the usual lost-looking, gum-chewing sorority girl in the back row, nor at her boyfriend, the misguided young man who suddenly believed he should pick up some science classes and go the premed route, like his father, but instead at the frankly flirtatious girl in the front, between Cora and the artist. He was surprised by how much his feelings had changed over the course of an hour's opening lecture, surprised and a bit amused to see how undaunted she was, staring back at him readily. He suppressed a laugh, thinking about how valuable his work was when it came to sustaining his faithfulness to his marriage, crumbling though that marriage might be. He did, however, find himself once again avoiding the eyes of the artist.

He glanced at the papers on the podium, reaching now for the class roster. Resting a pair of horn-rimmed glasses on his nose, he began to call the roll. Hers was the second-to-last name on the list. Just as he read it— "Adeline Sturmer"—and she responded with "Call me Addie," a wood thrush trilled from the branches of the ancient oak outside the open window. All heads turned, and Tom Kavanagh laughed.

"That's a wood thrush, Addie Sturmer. Is he a friend of yours?" he asked, and when she looked back at him and smiled, then turned back to the window, clearly hoping to hear the bird again, there was no denying it: Something in his chest hurt, and it was a blissful kind of pain, of a sort he remembered from his lonely days on the hills of Donegal.

He forgot to call the last name on the list, that of a timid young man in the back row, who waited until the end of that morning's lecture to approach the professor and make sure his presence was noted.

four

WHEN HE OPENED HIS mouth to speak and she heard the first soft lilt of his Irish accent, she did not know what to do, or where to look; she could hardly contain her joy, the feeling of something bubbling up inside her. And so to keep herself from suddenly singing, or whooping, or hysterically laughing, she grabbed her pencil and began to draw.

That ridiculous, fusty old owl. She knew without thinking that he had brought it as some sort of joke; it bore absolutely no resemblance to a real bird.

So she drew it, realistically enough in outline and obvious detail, the large head with its tufted ears, the ringed eyes, the white bib with the bars below. But she gave it a recognizable, if caricatured, human face.

"Dr. Curtis?" Lou leaned over and asked in a whisper when Addie had nearly finished the bulging eyes below a receding hairline. She nodded, and then Lou wrote, on a page of her own notebook, "I'd rather draw HIM," finishing with an arrow toward the front of the room.

Addie smiled and went back to the shadows under her owl's eyes until Lou pinched her arm and pointed, again, to her own notebook, where she'd added one more word: "Nude."

Addie rolled her eyes, her standard response to Lou's excesses. She kept to herself the fact that while mindlessly sketching a moldering stuffed owl with human features, she was, in fact, memorizing the rich contours, the lines and shadows, of Tom Kavanagh's remarkable face, the thin nose and strong jaw, the large, dark eyes, all shadowed by a head of unruly black hair that showed some streaks of gray. Later, in the privacy of her student studio, she would do her best to reproduce some image of that face from memory. She would work on it each day, she decided, immediately after leaving his lecture.

And she would, just as he'd urged, devote her afternoons and evenings to more outings in the woods, and to keeping a careful field notebook. Not because she cared at all about how she did in his course, but because from the moment she'd heard the wood thrush sing, just as Tom Kavanagh had called her name, she had realized something powerful. What she wanted was not only to draw birds but to understand them, to come as close as she could to feeling what it was like to fly with hollow bones. To sit atop a warm and throbbing egg within a delicate bed that rests in the crook of a branch. To sing not from something like a human throat but from a place deep within the breast.

Tom Kavanagh's passion for birds did not frighten her. And she found evolutionary theory less threatening than sleep-inducing. But what he had, and what she wanted, was clear to her from that first morning: a passion for birds—for truly hearing, seeing, knowing them—that made everything else in life seem trivial.

Somehow, she felt that if she had his face in front of her all the time she could hold on to that possibility. So she planned to throw herself into the course as wholeheartedly as she knew Cora would. (Lou was a different story; surely Lou would be one of the ones who went in search of another course.) But Addie knew that in the midst of her attention to birds she would also draw him, secretly, from the memory of watching him each day.

Journal—Field Entry

12 May 1965
Wednesday
Riegel's Point, Plumville, Bucks Co., PA (Spit of wooded land be-
tween the Delaware Canal and the Delaware River, ½ mi. north of
Plumville)

Time: 06:00–06:30—Mouth of Kleine Creek, near intersection of
   Old Philadelphia Road and the river road; 06:45–08:00—Riegel's
   Point
Observers: Addie Sturmer. Alone.
Habitat: Pin oak, maple, and what, at home, we call an osage
   orange tree (with those odd, baseball-sized, brain-looking pods).
   Bluebells are blooming, and I saw more of Cora's beloved
   windflowers.
Weather: Temp. 65 degrees F
Overcast and still, after a heavy rain. Would this be considered 100%
   cloud cover? Or did I see a small (1%?) patch of blue for just a mo-
   ment at the turn in Kleine Creek at Haupt Bridge Road?
Remarks: I've taken your advice to cut class and *listen,* on my own.

SPECIES LIST
At mouth of Kleine Creek:
American Robin 3
Song Sparrow 1
Downy Woodpecker 1
Goldfinch 6
At Riegel's Point:
Spotted Sandpiper (I think) 2

Number of Species: 5; *Number of Individuals:* 13; *Time:* 2 hrs.

Comments: I heard—and recognized—the Robin and the Downy
Woodpecker. But the best moments were spent drawing a Sandpiper,
pecking at the mud like an irritable old man who's dropped all his
change.

I just can't keep writing all that Latin. I'm sorry.

12 May—I'm flattered that you're willing to take me out in the field alone
on Saturday; I look forward to this.

And I'm also flattered that you're interested in seeing my drawings
from England. Yes, I'll bring along some of these. But not the paintings,
no. They're absolutely awful; I don't think I'll ever let anyone see those.

If I'm feeling brave maybe I'll bring along a painting of a goldfinch
I've been working on. I drew it for hours one day in New York City, in
Central Park. Did you know the bird life there is incredible?

Well, that's silly. Of course you would know that.

As to the great horned owl I drew on the first day of class—no, I don't
think so. That was more of a caricature really, to be honest. Nothing I'd
want anyone to see.

And yes, it also has some of Louise's commentary. But believe me, it's
not critical of you. Hardly.

Please don't underestimate Louise (we call her Lou). It seems that
nearly everyone does, and I suppose it's her own fault. Honestly, though,
she's observing, and learning, more than you might realize—even though
she probably seems to be interested only in luring Mr. "I'm Premed Like
My Father" away from Princess "I Hate These Bugs!" (Lou can't resist a
challenge. The minute he takes the bait, she'll turn her attention to other
things and spit him out like cold coffee.)

Anyway, by now you've already seen what I mean about her in her
field notebook. She's a beautiful writer, isn't she? And she's getting really
good at spotting birds—almost as good as Cora and Karl. When I go out

on my own—which is better for the drawing, of course—I miss L and C's good humor.

Even those predusk excursions are getting crowded, though. Karl always wants to come along, of course, which usually means his friend Robert as well. And I understand Mr. Premed is to join them on Friday. I imagine there will be a bottle of brandy too, and a tipsy walk back up Rising Valley or over from Gallows Hill.

But they'll be watching and listening for birds too; they're completely hooked. It's all your doing, you know—you and your poems and that clever ruse of "calling out" the bobolink with your fiddle Monday morning. It's all "the Survivors" (as we've taken to calling the eight of us who've yet to miss a morning in the field, and don't intend to) talk about.

So, yes, it's all your fault that the trails and fields and creek banks all around Burnham Ridge are crowded with insect spray–wearing, field glasses–wielding "birding loons" (our other name for ourselves) at the best hours for sightings, Monday through Friday.

So as I've said, I look forward to listening quietly, with only you, on Saturday morning—when all the Survivors will be sleeping off their birds and brandy.

five

PENNSYLVANIA, DEPENDING ON ONE'S outlook, is either all subtlety or a long lesson in contrasts, quiet and nuanced or screaming with too much history. It can feel—on, for instance, a drive from New York to Chicago—like an endless pelt of brown and gray, broken by a dramatic river and a bit of industry now and then, plus the requisite cheap and ugly overdevelopment of late-twentieth-century America. This was Scarlet Kavanagh's view of Pennsylvania throughout her twenties.

But settling for that abstracted, through-a-car-window view, she eventually realized, was to miss some significant points of difference. The famous Amish farmland and the peculiar hex signs on the Pennsylvania Dutch barns. The gash of the mines to the north and west. Vestiges of colonial life (all those narrow stairways, for instance; had they really all been that small?) in the southeast.

Her mother, Addie, was a small woman—only a shade over five feet tall and just clearing one hundred pounds that spring when she and Tom Kavanagh fell in love. For Addie, Burnham College and its surroundings were a revelation. There was no other way to describe her discovery of that corner of Bucks County where the college sat neatly atop a ridge between two valleys. These valleys wound their way east until their creeks, the Nisky and the Kleine, emptied into the Delaware River, the dividing line between Pennsylvania and New Jersey. This beautiful spot was only a two-hour drive from Addie's parents' farm, but it could have been an ocean away. She had never set eyes on this part of the Delaware River until she'd learned of her acceptance, with the offer of a scholarship, and visited the campus during her last year of high school.

She loved all the colonial names—Hampstead and Plumville and Easthampton, Milford Crossing and Gallows Hill—with their echoes of England. There were German ones too, of course; the house she would eventually move into, with Tom, and where Scarlet would spend her carefree childhood and portions of her sullen teenaged years, had started out as a ramshackle fishing cottage perched between Haupt Bridge Road and Kleine Creek. Years later, after his first wife had moved to New York and Tom had purchased the cottage, Addie took stubbornly to calling the stream that slurred through the woods outside their windows "Little Creek." People seldom knew what she meant when she called it that, but that never bothered Addie.

Her favorite name, though, was the local Indian one, Nisky, for the bigger, noisier creek, a small river by some standards, that traveled toward the cottage from the west, meeting up with Kleine Creek under the rickety old Haupt Bridge. It was here, along Nisky Creek, a quarter of a mile or so beyond their house, that Tom had built a wedding gift for his young bride, the bird artist, in the summer of 1966: a blind, constructed in the style of the English bird artists' hides that she'd discovered during her semester abroad. Addie's hide was a wooden structure with a bench and a narrow opening at eye level, tucked inconspicuously into the woods, where she sat for hours, waiting for the birds she would draw—Eastern bluebirds, warblers of various stripes, her beloved wood thrush and scarlet tanager (for which her daughter was named). And she drew others too—cardinals, robins, nasty jays and grackles. In those days she wasn't choosy; in fact she was disdainful of so-called birders ("featherheads," she called them) who valued a species only if it was rare.

This Scarlet had always shared with her mother. Scarlet loved even the great blue herons, which became increasingly common in that protected area near the Delaware as she grew into her teens, their harsh, ugly screeches piercing their mornings and evenings on the screened porch where they ate their meals. She would never forget the sight of one rising from the creek each morning, the spring when she was twelve, as she let the screen door slam behind her on her way to catch the bus to school. That rush of wings and then the silent, massive span above her head, darkening the sky—every time, it made her catch her breath. And she tried to find a way to describe its rising each day on the bus, playing with words in her head: "giant, silent feathered airplane," "blue-gray cloud with wings." Tom, to her ongoing embarrassment, kept her spiral-bound notebooks from those years—notebooks full of phrases like these but rather lacking in homework assignments.

"Herons make you reach for words," she told her father at some point, back when she still spoke fondly about birds with her parents. She knew this because it was written, in Tom's barely legible script, at the end of one of those spiral-bound notebooks, where he had given her credit for it and then included his own addendum: "They certainly don't inspire you to sing." He presented Scarlet with this and other notebooks of hers when they'd begun to speak of birds again, arguing happily over whether music or poetry might better capture their boisterous, rapturous, unclassifiable songs and calls.

This was, in a sense, Tom's life's work. His first and only book, *A Prosody of Birds,* was many things—a diatribe for one, as well as a plea for peace and for ecological responsibility. But also an attempt to create a system, akin to the metrical scanning of poems, for transcribing the songs of certain birds: dashes and breves and accent marks climbing and falling over the pages in rhythmic patterns, supplemented here and there by bars of musical notation. The *Prosody* was also illustrated with some of Addie's earliest work, including plates reproducing five paintings—of a scarlet tanager, a purple finch, a Kentucky warbler, a bobolink, and a wood thrush: birds whose songs were some of Tom's favorites.

Of course others have shared his passion for the music of these birds. Here, for instance, is a description of the voice of the bobolink from a later edition of the Peterson *Field Guide to the Birds:* "Song, in hovering flight and quivering descent, ecstatic and bubbling, starting with low, reedy notes and rollicking upward"—another line that appeared in one of Scarlet's adolescent notebooks, and one she has continued to love. This description from Peterson's *Guide* is a poem in itself, proof, she often said to Tom, that it may take language—bulky, uncooperative, but also perfectly tuned and incisive *words*—to get at just what it is about these creatures that haunts people so. "After reading language like this, do you even really need to hear the song itself?" she asked her father. "And when you do, isn't it bound to disappoint you just a bit?"

But Tom's argument was that no one—no poet, no ornithologist, no field guide author or contributor—had managed to capture the majesty of birdsongs. F. Schuyler Matthews may have come close in his 1904 *Field Guide of Wild Birds and Their Music*, one of Tom's most treasured books. But even Matthews, who wrote of the purple finch that "its persuasiveness is truly loverlike and irresistible," didn't quite pull it off. "Play those musical phrases he's created all you like," Tom once said. "You still won't recognize the song when you step into the woods."

Of course one could say the same about Tom's complex, nearly impenetrable scansions. But it seemed they worked for Addie, who, even with her tin ear, eventually became as adept at hearing, and recognizing, birds in the field as Tom. But then Addie had a bit more invested in the process than the average weekend bird-watcher, as well as a bit more reverence for Tom and his method, at least in those early years.

Ultimately both Addie and Scarlet agreed with Tom that not even live recordings manage to re-create the magic of the singing of birds in the wild—or, for that matter, outside one's bedroom window at the edge of dawn in the early spring. Scarlet once recounted for Tom and Addie a story she'd heard about the composer John Cage (master recorder and transcriber of, among other things, the music of urban cacophony) and his partner, Merce Cunningham, racing back to their New York City apartment after a disastrous weekend in the country, where they had been driven nearly mad by the noisy singing of the birds in the morning.

What's remarkable is that so many people become skilled at tuning them out. Air conditioners help, of course. Scarlet has never been able to sleep with one whirring away in her room; she has Tom and Addie, mostly Addie, to thank for her discomfort with that kind of mechanical hush. Addie, who from time to time, at the dinner table perhaps, or while Tom and Scarlet cleared the dishes, liked to recite from memory the opening lines of Rachel Carson's "Fable for Tomorrow," her opening chapter of *Silent Spring.* "No witchcraft, no enemy action had silenced the rebirth of new life in this stricken world. The people had done it themselves," she intoned hauntingly, while Tom and Scarlet gathered the forks and knives and plates as noisily as they could, humming folk songs under their breath.

A Prosody of Birds was an idiosyncratic hodgepodge, wildly disorganized and provocative to just about every reader. Still, in the end, a pure joy to read, even with all the scansions and bars of music and impossible diagrams: Tom Kavanagh in a nutshell. It enjoyed some success when it was first published, soon after Scarlet's birth, in 1969. Certainly its warning of impending environmental collapse and loss of habitat resonated with audiences of that time, prescient as it was. Out of print for twenty-five years, it was reissued in the late 1990s by a press in Berkeley, in a "millennial edition" that became, to Tom and Addie's surprise, a kind of cult classic, popular with birders, environmentalists, alternative-health advocates, poets, and musicians. Scarlet, however, wasn't surprised. By then she too had come to see it as a brilliant, beautiful book.

Of course Addie's notoriety fueled much of the more recent interest in the book. But it wasn't only her status among young artists and activists; that alone could not explain the book's popularity. If Tom too failed, in the end, to re-create the experience of hearing the birds in the language of either poetry or music, what most admirers of *A Prosody of Birds* seemed to agree on was that Addie's paintings and drawings did, in their airy, almost unfinished way, capture the experience of *watching* birds.

Though the birds in the illustrations were still, it was as if the viewer had just witnessed them in vigorous flight, or pecking at grass or tree bark for insects, or feeding their young. They were, in effect, soulful illustrations of creatures with souls.

There was a strange, ethereal quality to Addie's work in the *Prosody,* something in those early drawings and plates that made it abundantly clear that their creator was in love with these birds, with their surroundings, and, unmistakably, with the author of the book.

But perhaps Scarlet saw a love of the landscape in the book because she loved those woods and creeks and valleys of eastern Pennsylvania as much as her parents did. It was not a breathtaking landscape really. There was none of the salt- and taffy-tinged hominess of the Jersey shore, none of the sheltered feeling she always had in the valleys of Vermont and northern Massachusetts, certainly none of the expansiveness of the coasts of New England or Long Island.

The valleys that encircled the little hamlet of Burnham did not feel sheltering to Scarlet. No doubt there were psychological reasons for this. But maybe too it was the presence of the Delaware—a wide brown river with its own complex history, dividing one world from another somehow, obviously not a true barrier between East and West, not since colonial times at least—though at times it felt like one. And the river itself seemed strangely hemmed in, domesticated—skirted along its course through the northern end of Bucks County by the Delaware Canal. There was a kind of claustrophobia connected with that too; it was as if, following the course of a creek from the Burnham hills down to its end at the treacherous curves of the river road and then the footpath between river and canal, you found, instead of the freedom and openness you were hoping for, a kind of stage set.

Yet the whole area *was* beautiful, in a quiet way. There were remarkable stone farmhouses, peaceful farms nestled in the arms of valleys, curving roads that offered occasional glimpses of the river—brief, fleeting, breathtaking views. And then just as suddenly those roads would drop back down into a dark valley that was cloaked in shadow, no matter how brightly the sun was shining. No truly open vistas. And yet no shelter either.

When Scarlet returned to Burnham as an adult, she always felt a lump in her throat, a longing for the connection she'd felt as a child with the trees and the hills, the rushing creeks and the paths winding all around the woods between her house and the campus on one side, the river on the other. And also a powerful dissatisfaction that she'd never been able to write about this little corner of southeastern Pennsylvania. She was at home there, but also trapped. And she wondered: Did other people feel this way about their childhood homes?

Of course it was Addie who taught her to see it all this way. From the earliest days of her life Scarlet accompanied her mother on her excursions to the Nisky Creek blind. By the time Scarlet was four or five, Tom had built a second one, this time high in an old maple. For Scarlet this was a thrilling tree house, and she would spend the morning happily drawing and reading books while her mother drew. By then, with funds from the sale of the book and a few of her paintings, Addie had acquired a sophisticated scope, one that curved up and out of a small window in the blind, allowing her to train it on a distant bird and, at the same time, draw it comfortably.

Tom had cut a separate, larger window above a little bench at the back of the blind for Scarlet, and sometimes Addie would abandon her scope and come watch with her. Their favorite birds in those days were the black-capped chickadees, playful little performers who pecked at the dollops of peanut butter Addie and Scarlet left along the edge of Scarlet's window when they arrived at the blind each morning. The chickadees would eat and frolic right in front of their noses, staring back at them, as curious as they were. So fearless and trusting.

"You have to admire them for that, don't you think? Why in the world would they trust a human being?" Addie asked one day, and Scarlet never forgot that. She still sometimes dreamed about chickadees. The night before Addie died there was a beachball-sized one in Scarlet's dream, hovering above her head and peering down at her; it seemed to be checking in, saying, "Are you doing okay?" And so she said, "I'm fine, now that you're here," and then she woke up.

Eventually the chickadees would finish their peanut butter and move on, and Addie would go back to drawing at her own window. Scarlet would entertain herself quietly for as long as she could. Then, when she could wait no longer, she would tap Addie on the shoulder and ask for lunch. They would spread their blanket—sometimes below, at the edge of the creek, or, on rainy days, on the floor of the blind itself—and start on their sandwiches. And Addie would tell her stories.

Sometimes, earlier on, they were stories about Addie herself—about her childhood on the farm, chasing their few cows through the pasture with her brother, John; about Scarlet's grandparents, whom she saw only on holidays and for a week or so each summer; about Addie's trip to England at the age of twenty. As Scarlet grew older and hungered for more of these kinds of personal reminiscences (Did you have friends? What were they like? Were there boyfriends? Did you go to parties? Tell me more about Cora and Lou), it seemed that Addie grew more and more bored with accounts of her own life.

What she wanted to tell Scarlet, instead, were stories about birds. About the land and its history. About famous figures in her world—Audubon, Peterson, Rosalie Edge and others connected with the Hawk Mountain Sanctuary to the west of them—people who were heroes to her. But Scarlet was disappointed when Addie's stories took this turn; eventually she began declining her mother's invitations to join her at the blind, opting instead to play with neighborhood friends, or stay at home reading on her own.

At the time, it felt to Scarlet as if Addie was constantly trying to teach her something; she got enough of that at school, she thought. Years later she could see that Addie was, in fact, trying to give a kind of shape to her *own* life in telling her daughter those stories—to place herself in the land-scape, in the footsteps of these people she admired. And many of the stories were ones that Tom had told Addie first, when they'd met and fallen in love, there in that beautiful corner of upper Bucks County, in the woods above and below Burnham Ridge, during a spring spent observing birds, and, when they finally lowered their field glasses, one another.

II

k-selected species

six

THIS MORNING'S SCENE IS a familiar one: Cora at the small table on the screened porch in back, glasses perched on her nose and paper spread in front of her, distractedly petting Lucy, her old collie, who's flopped down at her feet. For as long as Scarlet can remember, Cora has been gray, her hair cut sensibly short. She's also always been pretty. The sweetness and openness in her face and in her wide blue eyes have always somehow invited Scarlet to bare her soul, to share her deepest hurts and most ridiculous longings with Cora—though Cora will never, under any circumstances, do the same. If Cora has ridiculous longings, Scarlet hasn't heard about them; she knows for certain about the depth of Cora's particular pain—but she never hears about this from Cora either.

The two women are bundled in sweaters because it's cool on the porch in the early morning. Sunlight streams in, the early fog burned off by now, and the long, grassy slope down to the beach is wet with dew. A rope clangs against a flagpole several houses down. Tom has been at his scope for an hour or more; Scarlet has been watching him. She knows he'd rather be elsewhere—in the marsh near the lighthouse, for instance—but everyplace screams with Addie's presence now, and there is so much to be decided today. But for now no one can bear to begin that process, and Scarlet sits with Cora, as if it were a year or two ago and she'd just arrived, sleepless and distraught over her love life, whimpering over the mess she'd made of everything. Worlds away from everything she is feeling today.

At the sound of her oven timer, Cora disappears into the kitchen. Minutes later she returns with a tray and sits down across from Scarlet. "Coffee?" she asks, as always. When Scarlet declines, she cocks a surprised eyebrow, then pours juice into a smoothly glazed mug—one of her own—and waits for Scarlet to speak first.

"Lucy's looking tired," Scarlet finally says. She longs for a sip of Cora's marvelously strong coffee but tries to act like she hasn't noticed its intoxicating smell.

"She's an old girl, like me," Cora says as she pats the dog again. "Like all of us, your mother and Lou and I were saying, just a few nights ago. We had the strangest conversation, about all the pets we've had fixed over the years. Wondering if an animal feels something about that, what that means to these poor girls, never to bear young. If it means anything at all."

As Cora bends over Lucy, Scarlet watches the play of morning light and shadows on her face, on the lines at the corners of her eyes and mouth. She knows this face nearly as well as she knew her mother's, before Addie grew so gaunt, if still achingly beautiful, over the past few months, and she knows this comfortable old house nearly as well as she knows the cottage on Haupt Bridge Road. No wonder Addie wanted to die here, she thinks now, with Cora's soothing presence filling every room—the smells of her baking, the fresh salt air blowing through her windows, the dark glazed surfaces of her pots and vases and mugs, beckoning one to grasp and stroke.

And for a moment she is ashamed of her peevish reaction to Addie's asking to be brought here, six weeks ago. "Why not at home?" she'd whined to Tom. At the time she'd felt strangely jealous, reluctant to share both her dying mother and Cora in this way.

"So somehow we got going on animal reproduction," Cora says, "and suddenly we were back in Tom's class, learning about k-selected and r-selected species. Do you remember when we used to talk about that? We would tease Addie when you were four or five, and she would say she couldn't imagine sharing her love with any more children. 'You're the ultimate k-selected mom,' Lou would say, missing the point about species of birds altogether, of course. But Addie loved that. 'Yes!' she'd say, 'I'm a wood warbler! Sharing the planet, taking less space, only taking what my child and I need. No competitive exclusion principle, no intraspecific competition for me!'"

Cora seems lost in the memory. "Then Lou would say, 'But watch out for that Tom, he's a strutting blue jay, don't you think? Don't blue jays have babies everywhere and then leave them to fend for themselves? Or is that grackles? Cowbirds?'" Cora isn't a particularly good mimic, yet Scarlet can hear Lou saying this, the edginess, the whiff of sarcasm always there in her voice.

"Addie'd correct her," Cora goes on. "'No, no,' she'd say. 'Cowbirds are brood parasites. Which just means they don't build their own nests. They leave them for someone else to raise.'

"And then one of us would make that silly joke about phoebes. 'For phoebes! They leave them for the phoebes!'" Cora's eyes are dancing now, glittering. "'Phoebes are acceptors!' And we'd all cackle then because of course at Burnham there was a girl named Phoebe we didn't like, and so we all scribbled that down in our notes right away the day Tom said it in a lecture, and then after that, every time we saw that poor girl— well, I say 'poor girl,' but really she was a horrible snob, truly a nasty person, it was more her nastiness that bothered us than her reputation for sleeping with everyone on the football team—every time we saw her, we'd whisper, 'Phoebes are acceptors—*oh* yes, phoebes are *acceptors!*'

"And then we'd howl. Just like a pack of twelve-year-olds or something. Good Lord." She laughs a little sadly and wipes her eyes.

Scarlet smiles; she has heard this story many times, and she's always loved it—this image of Addie and her friends being trivial and petty, human. A side of Addie she rarely saw. The whole idea of Tom as a strutting jay is mysterious to her, though. Scarlet has always been puzzled by this view of her father, the notion that he was the restless one, the one prone to wander. An Irish rover. That seems to have been his image, in lots of people's eyes, but it's always seemed to her that it was Addie who grew restless, not Tom.

Cora is staring at the table, still picturing the past. "Of course at this point Lou would be off and running, making some off-color joke of some kind, something about cowbirds and deadbeat dads. Something racist or something, you know, faking a Southern drawl. 'Down where ah come from they like to say the cowbirds live over there, over on that side of the tracks.' As if she lived in the heart of Alabama or something, instead of the suburbs of Washington.

"She'd do it to get your mother started, of course. And it always worked. 'See?' Addie would say. 'That's what scientists do. Make so-called impartial observations and then let the rest of the world go to hell with them, segregating schools, dropping bombs, dumping chemicals all over rice paddies.' "

Scarlet shimmies out of the sleeping bag she'd kept wrapped around her legs; the sun is growing brighter, reaching in to warm the porch. "She'd say things like that even back then, even that early on?" she asks.

"Oh, sure. I was always glad Karl wasn't around to hear her, working up steam and maligning everybody from Einstein to Oppenheimer. Never mind that the whole thing started with our completely distorting scientific terms to suit our own ends. K-selected species are just animals that mature later and care more intensely for their young because they have to compete more for resources. 'K' and 'r' are just mathematical symbols that zoologists use to talk about animal populations. As far as I know, they've got nothing to do with how many children a human mother decides to have."

Cora smiles, a little sheepishly. "I'm amazed I still remember that," she says. "See how well your father taught me? Anyway, understand that we were just joking around back then. We'd all be laughing the whole time—even Addie. Back then."

"Right," Scarlet says. "That was the difference, wasn't it?"

Eventually Addie didn't find it funny anymore. Scarlet too can remember her mother's raging against what she called k-selected humans acting like r-selected beasts, squandering resources, sending their young off to die in wars. Tom had always hated it when she'd used scientific theory like that. Turning science into sociology, he called it.

"Tom has always said that scientists are far more optimistic than artists," she says, remembering her parents' endless debates. "He's certainly more of an optimist than Addie was, which I guess isn't saying that much. More optimistic than I am too—as he's always reminding me. 'Poets, painters, musicians, all of them—artists are horrible cynics beneath that pretty facade,' he says."

"And what do you say when he says things like that?" Cora asks. She is staring pointedly at Scarlet.

"Oh, I usually just agree with him." Scarlet feels tired of this conversation suddenly, unnerved by Cora's curiosity. *Actually, I think I may be more of a cynic than even Addie was,* she considers saying, but doesn't. *And that frightens me, now.*

"You know," she says instead, maybe just to change the subject, maybe because of all the questions she herself has now, "all those conversations and jokes about k-selected species always kind of puzzled me. Maybe this was just a kid's egotism, but it always seemed like those remarks were somehow about me. About the fact that Addie and Tom didn't have more children, about how everyone assumed I was dying for a brother or sister. And I didn't really see why. Or was I missing something?"

Cora looks puzzled. Understandably, Scarlet thinks; she knows she's being vague. She takes a breath and tries again. "I guess I'm asking if there was more going on there. More than Addie's personal quest to save the planet, I mean—you know, doing her part to stem the tide of overpopulation." She pauses again, but still there is no response from Cora.

"Okay. Here's what I'm asking. Did Addie want another child, maybe? Or, maybe I'm asking this: Did having me make her decide she really *didn't* want more children? Was it all too much somehow? Was there some kind of secret I never got to hear about?" Scarlet stares at Cora now, forcing herself to stop, to hold back from revealing more than she's ready to reveal. She tries to decipher the look on Cora's face. Is it changing subtly? Is there some hint of realization there behind her furrowed brow?

After a moment Cora shakes her head slowly. "No, no," she says. "No secrets that I know of." She continues to stare at Scarlet, her eyes full of other unasked questions. "You know, everyone just always thought you were supposed to have at least two, so I suppose we always talked about it because we were just curious or something. And Addie had her blue days, just like all of us did—home all day with a cranky baby, no adult conversations for weeks at a time, that kind of thing. But she never showed any signs of regret, Scarlet." Her voice is tender now, and Scarlet feels, suddenly, embarrassed by her questions, by the silly self-involvement Cora must be hearing there.

"No, no. I didn't really mean regret," she says. "I'm not exactly sure what I mean. It's just, well, all that k-selected species stuff, all the 'singleton' jokes and whatnot. I just was curious about it, I guess. I know I'm not being clear. . . ."

"Well, who *is* right now, right? What's being clear got to do with Addie's dying? Was *she* being clear, giving up on treatment like that and—" Cora stops herself, takes a sip of coffee and looks out the window for a moment. She turns back to Scarlet and tries to smile. "Anyway, you didn't seem to suffer for being an only child. There was your friend Peter, and then our boys . . ."

Her voice catches, and suddenly Scarlet wonders why she's doing this to Cora, insisting on this topic of mothers and children. "Yes, right," she says, then tries to steer things to safer ground. "Just thinking about the only-child thing to avoid other thoughts, I suppose. Or, well, I don't know why. It's funny what these last days with Addie have brought up. Apart from all the big stuff, I mean."

"Yes, it is funny. It's funny what we found ourselves talking about. I mean really, under normal conditions when do we ever wonder about what female dogs think about their own reproduction, or lack of it?" Cora looks down at Lucy, trailing her fingers along the dog's soft white belly. "But that's what you talk about. Things like that, things that seem so silly and irrelevant—and then you realize they really aren't." She folds her paper then and starts to tidy the table, a brisk habit Scarlet recognizes. She braces herself for what will come next.

"Addie worried, you know, that she might have somehow turned you away from marrying, or from having children," Cora says when she's wiped away a tiny trail of milk. "She ended up in tears that night we talked—well, of course we all did. Lou kind of fell apart . . . you know how she feels about her girls now, so convinced they blame her for everything."

How, Scarlet is wondering, does Cora always know what she's really thinking? She has done this for years now, greeting Scarlet at the breakfast table, after those long drives and a few hours' sleep, with a fresh pot of coffee and, before long, a seemingly innocent and indirect observation that was meant really as a pointed question.

But Addie has been dead for only seven hours, and Scarlet has slept for maybe three. Though she was sidling up to the topic herself only moments before, she's just not ready, she thinks now, to launch into things like Addie's fears for her. Or what Addie's life might have taught her about love or marriage or having a child. She can't ask the questions she needs to ask, and she can't answer Cora's questions either. Not now.

So instead she asks Cora something else, though here too she's afraid of where her answer could take them. "And what did *you* cry about, Cora, that night with Lou and Addie?"

Cora looks at Scarlet intently for another long moment. Then she waves her hand in front of her face and shifts her gaze to the window. "Not what you'd think, Scarlet," she says. "I cried because beautiful young girls grow up, and grow old. Isn't that silly? I look at my grand-daughters now, and they take my breath away. Bobby's girls are eight and five now. Can you believe that?"

Scarlet raises her eyebrows, feigning surprise, though in fact she's well aware of Cora's granddaughters' ages.

"They remind me of you," Cora goes on. "Of course they're younger than you were when you started coming here with Addie and Tom, but already Lindsey, at least, makes me think of you. She's long and lean like you were, with that same wild, long hair. I love just watching her *walk*, just like I used to love watching you. Young girls are like colts really. Silent and watchful, and restless, under that calm on the surface. Restless and ready to break free.

"And that night I thought, for the first time—can you believe this?— I thought, My Lord, we were like that too, and it seems like it was just yesterday, and now Addie is here in my house, on this huge hospital bed in the middle of my studio, and she's *dying*. And I thought, How can this *be?* We were so young, so happy, tramping through the woods and riding horses and kissing our boyfriends in the moonlight. And then suddenly Addie seemed to leap ahead of us—well, I mean she was always so passionate and intense, but then boom, she was doing this very, very grown-up thing, falling in love with Tom and moving in with him. And then before we knew it we were all doing it—getting married, having families, buying homes, all of it—buried in work, and debt, and caring for children. . . ."

Her voice breaks ever so slightly, and she pauses. Scarlet reaches for her hand, but Cora only lets her hold it for a moment before she pulls it away and goes on. "And through all of that, all those things that seemed to wear the rest of us out, Addie stayed as passionate as ever. Oh, I know she had her low periods. But she never lost all that hellfire and fury that seemed to be burning inside her, keeping her going."

"Remember when Lou told her she should have been a Southern Baptist preacher?" Scarlet says, and they laugh at the memory, briefly, before Cora grows serious. She is quiet, looking out the window again. Morning light like this isn't kind to anyone, but Cora's face has grown lovelier with age; its lines reveal depth, resolve, but there's a softness there too, and it never goes away. Addie had the same softness, Scarlet realizes suddenly, and it hits her like a stabbing pain. It was just hard to see it sometimes.

"You know," Cora says, "it stunned me to look at Addie over these last few weeks, to see all that passion drained from her face. It seemed like she finally wasn't interested in fighting anymore. I still can't decide whether to call that peace, whatever it was she felt at the end. I can't bear to think that she felt resigned, or defeated somehow. Not Addie."

When she says this, both women begin to cry quietly. "I think it was peace," Scarlet says, her voice a hoarse whisper that she can barely hear herself. She isn't sure of this at all. But if it wasn't peace, she thinks, maybe it was still something good, something close to peace, something as close to peace as was possible for Addie. And far, very far from resignation—of that Scarlet is certain, based on Addie's last request. But she promised Addie, when she made that request two weeks ago, not to burden Cora or Lou with this information.

And so she clears her throat to say it again, without necessarily believing it, because she wants *Cora* to believe it: "I think she'd found a kind of peace, Cora. Resignation wasn't really in her repertoire, you know?"

There's a pause then, a heavy one—a quiet between them that, Scarlet knows, Cora would like her to fill with news of what was said, late last night, when Cora and Lou left Tom and Scarlet with Addie. But she isn't ready to relive those last hours that feel, now, like she must have dreamed them. She would like, for just a little while, to pretend that Addie's just asleep—that it wasn't her body they wrapped up and carried down the street a few hours ago, then fussed over ridiculously, as if about her comfort, as they laid her out on the cot.

When they'd gotten her to the restaurant cooler, there, inexplicably, had been Dustin, ready with a plastic sheet and bags filled with dry ice—an "extra precaution," he'd said, in case they needed extra time. He helped Tom and Scarlet position the bags below Addie's head and back, at the sides of her legs, her feet. Scarlet shakes her head at the memory: *Could* she have dreamed it? Had they really laid out her mother's dead body in a walk-in cooler just hours ago? And were they really going to move that body, and somehow bury it on their own, a few short hours from now?

She is not ready for this, not ready for what will come next, not ready for all the questions, not ready for the full wave of Cora's sadness, much less her own. So Scarlet is relieved and surprisingly grateful when—conveniently, miraculously—the sound of an old handsaw grinding through wood rises from the lawn below the screened porch, and she and Cora both turn to look out the window at Dustin, back at work on the coffin he is making for Addie.

"Who *is* that guy?" Scarlet blurts out, her voice rising above the saw's steady hum, and they both laugh, silly with relief. But Scarlet also hears the petulance in her voice. She hears it because she's felt it—petulant, overlooked, hurt—for a good part of the last twenty years.

Who is *that guy?* It's a rhetorical question really. Earnest, idealistic young people like Dustin have been trailing in her mother's wake for years, ever since she started staging her own forms of protest in the face of over-development and loss of habitat—camping out on the sites of planned subdivisions and shopping malls, erecting angry art installations in response to things like pesticide use and declining populations of birds.

Addie has been a darling of radical environmentalist types since she hid out to avoid arrest in connection with a supposed act of ecoterrorism sixteen years ago. She caught on with the art world too, after her run-in with a conservative senator eight years ago. Then, when her cancer returned last year, the news quickly found its way into the publications and listservs and chat rooms favored by both those groups.

She would have nothing to do with traditional treatment this time, she said. No chemotherapy, nothing. Despite the time it might buy her. No more battling the cells exploding everywhere inside her, growing fast and furious—her own internal suburban sprawl.

"There are too many toxins inside me already," she said, her voice clear and steady as a bell, that day in her oncologist's office eight months ago. "I'm finished." And with that she stood and walked out the door, leaving Tom and Scarlet to thank the good doctor for his suggestion of another round of full-scale chemotherapy and shake their heads no. No, no—they wouldn't be trying to persuade her. Not this time. No.

Thirteen years before, they'd sat together in the same office, between the rounds of chemotherapy and the radiation. Addie—pale and slim and bald, looking younger than her forty-five years—was a striking presence; it shocked Scarlet to realize that the oncologist seemed almost afraid of her.

Addie's dark eyes flashed, but that time she said nothing as the doctor urged her to "cover all the bases"—radiation next, followed by hormone therapy: a daily tamoxifen pill for the next five years.

Tom took her hand and kissed both her cheeks. "I know you hate this, Addie. But please, love, let's try it. Please."

"*Let's*?" she snapped. "'Let *us* try it'? Who exactly is *us*?"

And then, Scarlet couldn't help herself: She started to cry. No, to sob. The chemotherapy had already made Addie so sick. Scarlet and Tom had insisted on that, refusing to listen when Addie had proposed looking into alternative therapies first. But what were they supposed to do, Scarlet had asked herself then. Sit back and watch her *die?*

Addie could never bear to see Scarlet cry. Past the age of four or five, she'd seldom done it in her mother's presence.

"I'm sorry," Scarlet whimpered, reaching into her bag for tissues. "I'm sorry, Addie." She couldn't think of anything else to say.

Addie looked at Scarlet and opened her mouth as if to say something, then closed it again.

"All right," she said, her voice hoarse. Tired. "Yes, all right." She started gathering her things—her bag, the book she was reading, her jacket. "I'll do whatever you say. We'll call to schedule it. Right now I'm tired. I need to go home."

And Scarlet and Tom walked out behind her, after wordless handshakes with the doctor.

And she had the radiation therapy, and took the tamoxifen.

And now they all know that in some cases additional hormones—so-called adjuvant therapy—eventually lead to changes in the uterine wall. The place where Addie's cancer showed up next.

Oh, but Addie, Scarlet imagined saying to her, so many times: We were only doing what we thought was right. Just a few big bombs to blast that overdevelopment in your tissues. Then a pill a day to stanch those strip malls and Wal-Marts and drive-through pharmacies in your lymph nodes. It all seemed so sensible at the time.

And then she imagined Addie's response: Right. Kind of like Hiroshima.

They did talk briefly about the tamoxifen two weeks ago, the last time Scarlet visited before these last few days of gathering again in Cider Cove for Addie's imminent death. "I don't blame you for that," Addie said to Scarlet and Tom then. "I've made my own decisions, all along. I took the damn pill each morning. No one held a gun to my head. I just filled a goddamn glass of water and swallowed the stupid thing. Of course I wanted to fight it then, of course I was going to do what they told me to do. It's all as simple as that, isn't it? You can't think of anything else to do. You assume they know what's best. You follow instructions."

"And then you die," Tom said. And they all laughed.

"Right. No surprises there," Addie said through her laughter. And then she coughed, painfully.

"And now I've made this choice," she went on when the coughing subsided. "And I ask you, please, to honor it. And not out of guilt. Simply out of your love for me." That was when she told them where she wanted to be buried.

But guilt and love aren't so easily separated, Addie. Another thing Scarlet considered saying, but didn't.

Both Cora and Lou knew, early on, that Addie had refused to consider any treatment this time around. Lou fought valiantly, via an endless stream of phone calls, to persuade Addie, then Tom, then Scarlet, to try to change her mind. "Stupid, misguided, namby-pamby environmentalist bullshit," were her exact words, her parting shot at Scarlet at the end of their last phone call. Followed by this: "You're letting her commit suicide, Scarlet. I hope you can live with that." It was clear she'd had quite a lot to drink.

But what could anyone do? This time Scarlet stayed out of the way. This time she didn't want her tears to force her mother back into the multiple agonies, for her, of chemotherapy. For most of the fall she hid out in her apartment in New York, tending to other things there. Eight months ago—even two months ago—she never would have dreamed that she'd be in Cider Cove the morning after Addie's death, longing for her, physically longing for her, as if she were a child again. Eight months ago, before a series of unexpected events, Scarlet had told herself it was Addie's decision, no one else's.

What is it, when someone says no to all her doctors have to offer? Some pinpointable stage in the process of dying? Angry self-destructiveness? Resigned despondency? Peaceful acceptance?

Probably a bit of all those things, Addie had told Scarlet and Tom two weeks ago, clearly uninterested in pursuing the question further. And then she'd laid out her instructions for what she ardently hoped they would do with her body when she died—making it clear, when she'd finished, that she didn't wish to talk about her death any longer.

So now they are left to decide for themselves what to make of it all. For people like Dustin, Scarlet imagines, it's easy: Addie's death was a suicide, yes—a deeply principled one. Martyrdom, actually, in the eyes of Dustin and Addie's other followers. It's easy for them to see her death this way, Scarlet thinks, because, of course, she isn't *their* mother. Which, at this moment, she desperately wishes these scattered children of the art world and the environmental movement would remember.

The sound of Dustin's sawing—now a steady whine—has become grating. Scarlet desperately needs a cup of coffee.

"Doesn't he have a mother of his own?" she asks, her voice cracking.

Cora just looks at her, saying nothing. Waiting. There are more tears, Scarlet can see, at the corners of her eyes.

She has always waited like this for Scarlet.

And as always, in the warm light of Cora's gaze, Scarlet begins—rapidly—to melt.

"I'm pregnant," she says.

"I wondered," Cora answers.

And then Lou opens the screen door and pulls a chair up to join them.

seven

HAD HE EXPECTED HAPPINESS? Success? Both?

Though not given to long bouts of introspection or nostalgia, sometimes Tom would try to answer such questions. Or he would try to conjure the feeling he'd had, that first spring, as he sat in his Burnham office late into the night, avoiding going home, reading his students' field notebooks. He saved Addie's, "the artist's," for last, teasing himself with it, at first simply curious but, by the middle of May, almost unbearably eager for what he would find there.

It was difficult to say which excited him more: her glorious drawings or her forthright prose. When he thought back to those years, it seemed to him that this was the moment, the precise moment when he began to see the possibility of happiness. And to long for it.

Before that he'd felt happy, certainly. But his happiness, as a boy, and then as a student at university, then in an American graduate program, had always been tinged with other feelings. A hunger to know more. A kind of desperate striving.

And when he recalled these feelings of his youth, it wasn't his mother he thought of, or Polly, or anyone else in his family; instead he saw the youthful face of his teacher Sister Catherine. Sister Catherine, who, he realized later, had made him into the teacher he'd become by that spring when he met Addie—a teacher who looked for hungry students like he himself had been, and happily gave them what they needed.

Though he'd let go of much about his childhood in Ireland when he left in 1955, he would never forget the early mornings. The long, quiet walks to school along the rutted lane, more a path than any kind of road really, that led from his family's crumbling old farmhouse into Falcarragh.

He'd leave even earlier than he needed to, purely for the pleasure of hearing the rousing chorus in the trees above his head and then, as the lane wound its way from the sheltered valley to the edge of the hill above the sea, for the view—not just of wisps of morning clouds above a gradually receding tide, not of the quiet waves rolling slowly in from the protected cove. What he watched for, and the thing that left him breathless, every morning, were the seabirds. Soaring and diving, floating regally, perched magnificently alongside the tidepools.

He couldn't have named a single one. Nor could he have named any of the glorious singers above his head in the scattered trees between his home and the sea, or the family of gray-brown and black-spotted ones with the flash of white under their wings whose nest he discovered, one morning when he was ten, in a shrub abutting the stone wall outside his school.

He'd been scaling the wall at a safe distance to watch them furtively each morning for a week when, one day, as he strained to see what the mother bird was dropping into her babies' mouths, he felt something tapping at his leg.

It was a pair of field glasses. In the hands of a nun, whom he recognized immediately as the young and mysterious Sister Catherine—not yet his teacher, though she would be the following year. Instinctively he jumped down from the wall and prepared to apologize, ready for a scolding, and as he did the mother bird flew from the nest as another bird in a nearby tree—the father, Sister Catherine explained later—gave a loud, grating call, not musical in the least, and not designed to be, she explained; it was instead meant to discourage intruders like the two of them.

"What a wonder you've not heard it before," she said to him that morning. "That's a tribute to your stealth! You're a good observer of birds, I know," she added. "I've been watching you these last few days." Again she held out the field glasses to him. "That's why I've brought you these. They'll make the task much easier."

He took them from her then, tentatively, his hands shaking. But he had no idea what to do with them.

She laughed, kindly, and held them to her own eyes to show him. It took a while, but finally he got the nest in focus. And when he did, and he saw the open, crying beaks, the long, awkward necks, he found he wanted to cry.

He pulled the glasses from his eyes and swallowed hard to stop the tears from coming. Sister Catherine had been watching him closely, and now she took his hand and led him to a bench by the gate in the wall, and there she pulled another surprise from the folds of her habit: a small, well-used field guide.

She showed him how to look for the bird he'd been watching. She'd known all along, he realized later, that it was a mistle thrush. But she let him believe he'd made the discovery on his own. And that was his beginning.

"You may keep both the glasses and the guide," she'd said, "as long as you care for them, as I believe you will. And for as long as you remain interested in observing the birds."

He had them both, still. The glasses remained his favorites, and eventually Addie stopped rolling her eyes and laughing at his preferring them to the many lighter, and far more powerful, pairs of binoculars he acquired through the years.

As his teacher for the next two years, and then as his friend after that, it was Sister Catherine who helped to foster his talent in math and science. It was this gift, she helped him see, that could buy his freedom, as a scholarship student at Queen's University, from the lives of his older brothers and sisters—gifted musicians, all of them, but all trapped in the lives of farm laborers and factory workers, in the north of Ireland.

He met Polly while he was at Queen's, when both of them joined a small group of musicians who played regularly at a pub popular with students and young office girls, like Polly. She was a "fiery Irish redhead," in the words of his adviser at Cornell, where, newly married, they arrived in the fall of 1955 for Tom to begin his graduate work.

When he told her this, Polly rolled her eyes at the stereotype, then turned away, flushed, and, he knew, pleased to be seen this way. For she *was* a fiery redhead, a stunning girl, and a beautiful singer. And in no way suited to be the wife of a scientist, particularly an ornithologist, "forever stuck in the woods," as she put it, adding, "I may as well have stayed in Belfast then," when one of her dark moods set in. Though these were less frequent in Ithaca, where she began singing with another group and quickly gathered a local following.

It was for Polly that he made what, in his younger days, he saw as a deciding sacrifice in his career—opting for a job at tiny, nondescript Burnham College in southeastern Pennsylvania, instead of the far more prestigious research position he'd been offered at the University of Illinois. What would there possibly be for her in the middle of the country, in an unknown place called Champaign, Illinois? Polly had asked, incredulous to think that finally, after five years in tiny Ithaca, he would even consider turning down a job in reasonable proximity to cities like Philadelphia and New York.

His adviser only shook his head, mumbling something about Tom's fiery redhead and how at least he'd be happy in the bedroom.

Which he was, for a time. Their first two years in Burnham were, in fact, relatively calm. Polly found a voice teacher in Philadelphia who persuaded her that, with proper training (which meant several sessions per week with him), she had a future as an opera singer. And Tom realized rather quickly (perhaps, he sometimes admitted to himself, he'd always known this) that a job at a small school like Burnham would allow him to do the two things he most loved: teach, and pursue his own idiosyncratic study of the music of birds—work that he knew, from his experience at

Cornell, would never have been considered serious or scholarly enough to earn him a long-term career at a school like Illinois.

And so, slowly but surely, his work—as a teacher and, in the eyes of traditional ornithologists, a renegade researcher—became all-consuming.

And he developed a pronounced distaste for opera, and for New York City, both of which he'd rather enjoyed, when he and Polly were younger and newly arrived in the U.S.

And Polly began to drink more heavily, as the months and then the years passed, and then her first teacher left Philadelphia for New York, and her "career" as a classical singer failed to blossom—stymied, she was sure, by Tom's refusal even to consider renting an apartment in New York, where, she said, she might live during the week and he could join her on weekends. How, he asked repeatedly, could he possibly pursue his research, much less finish his book, without time on the weekends and semester breaks, time away from the demanding work of his teaching, to be in the field?

Her parting shot, after she'd packed a larger bag than usual for the drive down to Philadelphia that day, had stunned him. "You aren't even man enough to give me a child," she hissed at him, eyes flashing, tangled curls tumbling about her face.

He stared at her, at her beautiful body in her skirt and tight red sweater, her perfect skin, flushed now with anger. And for one confused moment he felt a powerful wave of longing for her. "I'd no idea you even wanted a child," he might have said; she had always seemed far too consumed by her singing to consider starting a family.

What he said, instead, was "And you're not fit to be anyone's mother." He said it softly, his voice an angry snarl, to her back as she walked out the door. He never knew whether she'd heard him or not.

And so, ironically, he found himself, by his third year there at little Burnham College, increasingly delighted by his work. And routinely alone in the bedroom.

Until the spring of 1965—a spring ushered in by torrential rains and violent winds, then followed by two and half weeks, in early May, of brisk, crystal-clear mornings and the richest round of songbird migration he had yet witnessed in the northeastern United States. Punctuated, each morning, by the song of wood thrushes high overhead, nesting in at least three of the college's majestic old trees. And by the arrival of Addie Sturmer in his life—rushing in like that spring's near-to-flooding Nisky Creek, or like the dizzying swoop of a tree swallow, bringing with her a future filled with more happiness, and success, and sorrow, than he had ever imagined his life would hold.

Certainly more than he ever expected when, on a cold and damp April morning, he woke early to find that Polly had, once again, failed to return the night before from her so-called lesson with her new teacher in Philadelphia—another young man with his sights set on New York. And when, striking a match to light the stove and boil water for his single cup of tea, he admitted to himself, at last, that his marriage was over.

Addie's innocence, combined with a passion that matched, or maybe even exceeded, his own, took his breath away. She had been invited to work in the studio of Clive Behrend! She had no idea what that meant, asking him, in her field journal, if he'd heard of him, of one of the finest bird artists of their day.

Also the illustrator of the first guidebook he himself had owned, the delicate little book from the '20s that had belonged, originally, to Sister Catherine. Later, in secret, she'd also given him a copy of a zoology text from her days at university in England: his first look at Darwin, his first inkling of a wider world. A world she had left behind, she said, without regrets, for her own very private reasons—but one that he should be aware of, and consider finding for himself.

He'd corresponded with Sister Catherine faithfully through the years, and on that first return trip to Ireland with Addie, the year after they married, he visited her in Falcarragh. She was even approving, he thought he could see it, of his new bride (if so, she was certainly the only one in Ireland who *was* approving of his having one annulled marriage and now a second—and Protestant—wife). If Sister Catherine disapproved, she'd shown no sign of it; instead she was kind and warm, and admiring of Addie's drawings from their weeks in the Lake District, and then along the coast of Donegal.

They made pilgrimages to the homes of both their mentors on that trip. Miss Smallwood still doted on Addie, but her response to him was cooler, to say the least; a tiny, sharp-beaked woman swathed in wool and tweed, she eyed him with obvious mistrust as the three of them tramped through muddy farm fields and scrambled over stiles at the edges of pastures outside Oxford. Once, as they paused for a drink of water alongside a wood, Tom ventured on in search of a warbler he was certain he'd heard, despite Miss Smallwood's protesting that it was "highly unlikely" at that hour. Peering through his glasses, he heard her ask, rather churlishly, he thought, "And what will there be for *you* in this little Pennsylvania town, Adeline?"

A rustle of leaf and wing then, and his warbler was gone. Addie only laughed and said she was lucky to have work she could do anywhere, "anywhere there are birds," which meant pretty much anyplace at all, didn't it? Emerging from the woods, Tom saw the bemused look on her former teacher's face, even though she said nothing, and when he mentioned it to Addie later, she only laughed again.

"Well, I'd sooner be an ornithologist's wife who gets to work at my pictures, whether anyone ever sees them or not," she'd said, trailing off then, too kind and too fond of her former teacher, he assumed, to conclude with what she surely was thinking, "than a lonely old maid like her."

But then, perhaps only *he* was thinking this. Years later he would wonder about it, about the warning tone in Margaret Smallwood's question (and might she have raised other doubts and questions, in later letters and private conversations?). And he would remember one other thing then too: the pang he'd felt—in the midst of the flush of elation, the shaky thrill he'd felt when reading Addie's field notebook that first spring—when she wrote fondly and longingly about New York City, and about drawing in Central Park.

Would every woman in his life feel this tug, this longing for the city, for a life that would pull her away from Burnham, from the work to be done there, from him?

Even his daughter, for Christ's sake, he'd think years later, laughing to himself. Because of course Scarlet wouldn't stay in Burnham. Though he wished, sometimes, that they could have kept her with them there forever, forever a cheerful, busy child of five or eight, even her quieter, more serious self of twelve or thirteen—the three of them still happily ensconced in their warm little cottage in the woods.

Was it his own happiness, or his own success, that he was thinking of, then, back in the early summer of 1965? When—despite the shocked faces and murmured doubts of colleagues and friends—he secured a small grant from a conservation society in Philadelphia and "hired" Addie as his research assistant, for his ongoing project of delineating, and scanning, the songs of migrating warblers.

Everyone at Burnham knew, of course, that Polly had moved out of the little house she and Tom had shared on the campus's "faculty row," a street of small bungalows behind the gymnasium. They knew, as well, that much of Tom's grant had actually gone toward the purchase and restoration of the old fisherman's cottage on Haupt Bridge Road, where his so-called research assistant was staying and where, after she graduated, Tom himself was clearly spending most nights.

So there was a bit of a scandal, in the style of a small liberal arts college that, while filled with as much gossip and envy and mean-spiritedness as any other self-enclosed community, tried hard to present a face of open-minded tolerance. Somehow Tom—who, conveniently, had been awarded tenure the year before—didn't mind; when asked about Polly, he calmly explained that she had left him for her voice teacher, and for the life in New York City that she had craved since they'd both arrived in

America twelve years before. If the precise order of various events—Polly's deep dissatisfaction and her eventual departure, his falling, unmistakably, in love with a student nearly fifteen years younger than he—was blurry in the minds of others in the community, even in his own mind, what did that matter really?

Because clearly, now, everyone was happier. No one more so than he.

And, from all appearances, Addie as well. Addie, who grew glowingly suntanned that summer, her long hair, lightened by the sun, in a long braid down her back by day and, at night, sweeping over her bare shoulders, glowing in the light of a single candle by the mattress they shared on the floor of the fisherman's cottage. Who cheerfully cooked their dinners on the rattling old stove he'd installed in the cottage's rough kitchen. Who eagerly typed his daily notes and tidied up his complex, and nearly unreadable, diagrams of the songs of pine warblers and wood thrushes and vireos. And who had, at last, what seemed to her boundless time and boundless space—and, with that, boundless energy—to watch, and to draw, and to paint.

She seemed impervious to what others might say about her. The stares and snickers of other students (all except her fellow "loons" from Biology of the Birds, who followed the lead of Cora and Lou, and whose unflagging loyalty to their teacher Tom Kavanagh led them to simply take the affair in stride). The shocked indignation of her parents when they learned of her plans for the year following graduation—and who suspected something, immediately, when they met Tom Kavanagh at Addie's graduation. To all these reactions—vexed, jealous, titillated, appalled—Addie only stared back silently, blankly, eyes wide open and unblinking, seeming to feel no particular need to explain, certainly none to apologize.

It was Tom's first view of her flinty resolve—her ability simply to *not see* any objections or disapproval that struck her as ungrounded, even absurd—when she was convinced she was right and others were wrong. As, more often than not, she was. Convinced, that is.

By the beginning of the winter term, in January of 1966, Tom and Polly's marriage was officially annulled, and Addie and Tom had begun, quietly, to plan a small wedding in May and then his official move, following graduation, into the cottage. Then one day in March, he was called to a meeting with his old friend the dean.

This meeting was surprisingly awkward, far more so than those discussions, in Tom's pretenure days, following a student's or parent's complaint, of Tom's impassioned teaching of the theories of evolution. On those occasions they'd been able to close the door and chuckle together over the need to "tone down" scientific fact when, say, a potential future donor to the college had had his or her religious convictions threatened.

"If they're so certain they know the truth, why does it even bother them?" Tom would always ask, genuinely puzzled. Certainly he'd known plenty of people—starting, as a child, with Sister Catherine, and then as a student in Belfast—whose religious beliefs hardly needed such careful coddling.

"I know, I know," his friend the physicist would answer, closing his eyes and nodding. "Only maybe tone it down a bit for a lecture or two, might you? And then it will all blow over, as it always does."

Then they would spend the rest of their meeting discussing their research, or the plight of the college's basketball team.

But this meeting, in the early spring of 1966, was clearly different. Instead of getting right to the point, the dean, who seemed unusually nervous, made idle small talk, which had never been his wont, before closing his door portentously, then sitting at his desk and staring out the window for a moment.

"Well," Tom said at last, uncharacteristically nervous himself by now, "what is it this time, Dan? I'm not even teaching zoology right now— can't be complaints about Darwin, can it?" He laughed hollowly.

The dean looked back at him for a moment, then stared at a letter on his desk.

"No, Tom, no," he said, his voice hoarse. He cleared his throat and looked up. "I've been asked to speak to you about your intentions . . ."

"My intentions?"

"With regard to the Sturmer girl."

"The 'Sturmer girl'?" Hearing her referred to in this way—like a problem student, or like a specimen, he thought—made him bristle. "Her name is Addie Sturmer, Dan. And I assure you, my 'intentions,' as you put it, are decent ones."

It did disgust him, and, truthfully, humiliate him as well, to be asked such a question. And yet part of him felt for his old friend—clearly so ill at ease with the situation, forced into discussing something so private, no doubt by a president and board of trustees who'd gotten wind of certain rumors.

"Dan," he said, "my marriage to Polly was annulled only a month ago. Now that the way's cleared, I do plan to marry Addie, soon."

"How soon?" the dean asked, and Tom was shocked by his curtness.

"Well, presumably later in the spring. She'll need time, of course, to prepare her parents, that sort of thing. Surely you understand?"

But he didn't, Tom realized suddenly. It was the first time he realized how few of his friends and colleagues did, or could, understand. Was it so peculiar to have fallen in love twice? Because yes, he knew he *had* loved Polly, once—though he now knew that to have been a youthful love, immature, more a product of his and Polly's shared desire to leave Ireland and discover something new. Of course he knew that Addie was the age he'd been then, but already, at the tender age of twenty-one, Addie seemed to him to have a maturity, a depth really, that somehow transcended age. Certainly, he felt, she was worlds away from the tender, unformed boy he'd been at twenty-one. How could he have known, when he met Polly at the age of nineteen, fresh from the countryside and as ripe for sexual awakening as any rural altar boy, that so much still lay ahead? First would come his timid, country-boy acceptance of his pairing with a taxonomist as his adviser at Cornell (where he finished his dissertation, a dry-as-dust taxonomy of the birds of New York state, in record time). He'd been unable, back then, to admit that he longed to work with other, younger faculty members at Cornell—early pioneers in the recording of birdsongs. It wasn't until he was at Burnham, holding an academic position of his own, earning a bona fide American salary, that he'd been able, at last, to delve into what would become his life's work, on songbirds and their music, as well as their tenuous survival.

Then, eight years later, would come the unexpected, delirious discovery of this delicate yet steely bird herself, Addie Sturmer the artist, brash and fitful and timid and hesitant and gifted beyond words, a child of ten in the woods of Pennsylvania the year he crossed the Atlantic with his bride, drawing with Clive Behrend in a rustic hide on the outskirts of Oxford as his marriage began its slow dissolve.

How could he have known? What could he possibly have done differently? And how could he possibly change anything now—now that real joy was there, within his reach, the delight of work that he loved and that he knew would last and then, on the heels of this, a kind of romantic passion he'd never even imagined, so different from what he'd felt for Polly? A kind that made him ache, and not only sexually—though his physical longing for Addie had been keen, almost shocking really, after he'd read her first field journal. But also an ache of, what exactly, protectiveness? All right, a kind of fatherly protectiveness, perhaps.

But that wasn't all of it, by any stretch. Because he felt awed by her as well. Genuinely awed. By her raw talent, her true lack of concern for convention, for others' expectations of her.

Over the years he'd had a number of students who shared his deep, almost visceral, love of birds; watching them in the field, he could see it. A few had gone on to do graduate work in zoology—one even landing at Cornell and, to Tom's surprise, *choosing* to do taxonomic work because, she said, she so loved the music of the birds' Latin names.

But Addie was different; accompanying her in the field those first months, his counts were always low—because he couldn't take his eyes off *her*. Perched on a low branch, drawing furiously and silently, with rapt attention, she was so immersed in what she was doing that she wouldn't notice him, standing maybe twenty yards away, with his field glasses poised—and focused on her. Noting her identifying characteristics: the soft curves of her brow and cheekbone. Her full, wet lips, which she licked slowly as she drew. Downy hair on the nape of her neck, a glittering trail of sweat snaking down her breastbone, breasts rising and falling with her steady breath, muscled legs gripping the branch below her.

At times, that first May, he had moments of doubting that her interest had much, if anything, to do with *him;* it was the birds she was after, he feared. *Was* there an openness to him, an interest in him, in those lines of her field narratives, he would ask himself—or was he just a foolish, deluded older man, unhappy in his marriage, mistaking her passion for birds and art for some sort of feeling for him? But then the way she looked at him, that Saturday morning in the field, the two of them alone . . . surely, he thought, he wasn't imagining it.

When they stepped onto the rocks to cross the creek and she slipped, midway across, he stopped breathing as he reached to steady her and felt, he was sure of it, her leaning all her weight there against him. And then she turned and lowered her glasses, and looked at him, and then he knew for sure, and his hands held her waist, and he kissed her, and he could have been a boy again, a hungry boy. Waiting, until the course's end, to make love to her, reading her now completely open field notebook entries—it was all pure agony, and pure bliss. On their first night together, a fresh sheet spread over the mattress he'd carried down to the cottage, she told him she'd never had intercourse, and for a moment he panicked, and nearly fled.

And then she laughed, that silvery wrenlike laugh of hers that never changed. "I was always told I should 'save myself,'" she said, "and I could never understand why." She reached for his face with both her hands. "Now I see what I was saving myself for." After that night he'd never stopped thinking of her beautiful, small body—open to him, reaching for him—as the most miraculous of gifts. Later, in the heat of summer, sweating already in the early-morning hours, he would train his field glasses on her again. When she put her pencil down and turned to see him watching her, she smiled, then lifted her T-shirt over her head, unfastened and lowered her bra, and turned to face him, beckoning him to join her as she continued, unzipping her cut-off blue jeans.

They rarely left the woods, that first summer and on into the fall, without making love. In the grass or the leaves, in whatever spot they could find that was free of nettles and poison ivy. They didn't want or need a blanket; it felt to Tom, every time, as if they were flying, floating above the earth, their bones as light as air. After, he would find himself humming. Adeline, sweet Adeline. His wood thrush, his airborne beauty.

She was a bird, to him. There was no other way to describe it. But imagine trying that metaphor on the dean. She is a bird, Dan. A delicate, dewy warbler on its first trip down from the wilds of Canada. And my love for her? It is my own soaring, alongside her, weaving wildly with her in tireless flight.

Does this make things any clearer?

Of course he couldn't, and wouldn't, reach for such lyricism with Dan. Though they had, on several occasions, discussed the poems of William Carlos Williams and Wallace Stevens. And though, Tom was convinced, scientists could grasp metaphor far more readily than many a nonscientist. It was scientists, in Tom's estimation, who were the last great Romantics, the only real optimists left in a world driven increasingly by fear and doubt and cynicism, all of which had been laid, astoundingly, at the feet of the likes of Charles Darwin.

"These are troubled times, Tom," he heard the dean say then. "We're a nation at war, and our students are facing so many uncertainties. . . ."

Yes! he wanted to scream. Yes—precisely. That's precisely it, and now I can tell them, and tell them honestly, there are things of value, even here, even in a world crazed with fear and driven by greed and staring at the possibility of ecological disaster. . . .

"The president is worried, and he's getting all kinds of pressure, from all sides, you can imagine, worries about student unrest, that sort of thing. There are concerns about what some members of the faculty—and you in particular, Tom—are doing, in and out of the classroom, to stir the students up."

Here the dean cleared his throat yet again—a sign, Tom had always believed, of the dean's discomfort with this aspect of his job. "There are concerns too," he continued, "about collapsing moral standards. . . . Maybe you can see where I'm leading here. . . ."

But where in God's name *was* he leading? "Collapsing moral standards"? All these disembodied "There are concerns.". . . Tom hated language like this, the blank, faceless double-talk of bureaucracies, academic or governmental or otherwise. The sad thing was, he felt that despite his dutiful mouthing of the words, his old friend Dan could surely see as well as he could the dangers of keeping silent, of *not* "stirring the students up."

He knew what he wanted to say; it was quite simple really. It was the same thing he'd been trying, each semester in recent years, to convey to his students. Even here—even in the midst of all these terrors—there can be this: the opportunity to teach and learn. To do work that you love. And there can be true passion—true, unadorned love and passion between two people.

Surely he could say this to Dan, he thought, to his friend of seven years now, someone who understood him, who valued his work and shared, in so many ways, his view of the world.

Before he could begin, Dan spoke again. "And so what we'd like to propose is that you take a sabbatical next year—a year's leave, partially paid, of course, even though you haven't yet gone through the official channels. You know, get away from Burnham for a year, let things blow over a bit. Why don't you set something up at Cornell, take Addie to Ithaca with you—after you're safely married?"

Tom was stunned. He struggled to put a brake on his thoughts—still wrangling with the task of describing his love for Addie, his conviction about his work—and to absorb, fully, what the dean had just told him.

Slowly the last words took hold. A year's leave. Time away from Burnham. He knew what this was: a quiet reprimand disguised as a gift, maybe even a kind of bribe, with the built-in assumption that he would return, the following year, "rested," revived by a year of research. And quieter.

Most people in his position would, Tom knew, seize this opportunity eagerly. Most people would be grateful. Perhaps he should have been too. But that wasn't how he felt. Cheated was more like it. Robbed. Robbed of an opportunity, yes, an opportunity, in a world growing madder by the day, to show his students another way to live. A way of following one's passions, not suppressing them.

Addie, on the other hand, was ecstatic when she heard the news.

"We can go to England!" she said. "You can take me to Ireland to meet your family!"

But, Tom said, his work was on *American* songbirds—specifically songbirds that migrated through their own region of southeastern Pennsylvania. And even supposing he eventually hoped to expand that work to include other regions of the United States, what, for God's sake, would he do in England and Ireland?

"Write," was Addie's answer. "Finish the thing." Indeed, as Addie reminded him, he did have far more notes than he needed, already, for a book. But he'd been hesitant to start, fearing he lacked the one thing— the one perfect example, the one perfect moment in the field—that could somehow bring all his ideas together.

It was Addie, in fact, who made Tom Kavanagh's one and only book happen at all. "It's time to take the next step, don't you think?" she asked him gently that afternoon after his meeting with the dean. He'd stepped quietly into the front room of the cottage and found her sitting by the woodstove, painting, her back to him. She hadn't heard him come in, and for a while he stood and watched her, the way she stood suddenly, peering at the canvas, her face inches from the image, then sat back down on her stool and made the slightest adjustment with the tiny brush she held. She was painting a trio of black-capped chickadees, playfully swinging from several branches of a crab-apple tree. They were so lifelike he felt he could hear them—*dee-dee-dee-dee*—and he thought, then, What matters is this, this quiet, invaluable work. Though he hated to do it, he cleared his throat, to interrupt her, and tell her his news.

"We'll work on it together," she said. "It will be easier to do it somewhere else, don't you think? Without all the distractions you have here? And in the meantime I can work on new species—birds I'll never get the chance to draw here."

At that moment he knew that whatever happened in the following year, or the years after that, he had made one perfectly right decision: to be with her. And like Tom's other certainties—the importance of work that one loves, the redemptive powers of music and poetry, the unquestionable clarity of evolutionary theory—he remained unflagging in this as well, in his love for Addie Kavanagh, "the Sturmer girl," despite countless trials, for the rest of her life.

They spent the early fall in the house known as Schaumboch's, at Hawk Mountain, the well-known preserve fifty miles west of Burnham. Tom had visited Hawk Mountain as soon as he'd arrived in Pennsylvania to begin his job at Burnham, armed with a letter of introduction from his adviser. Since then he'd been taking some of his better students there every fall, spending hours perched on the Kitattiny Ridge, glasses poised, counting the migrating red-tailed, sharp-shinned, and Cooper's hawks, and the occasional, thrilling peregrine falcon.

Later that fall, Tom and Addie lived for two months in a cottage at

Cape May, at the very tip of New Jersey, where Addie drew her first osprey and pelicans, and tried her hand at the double-crested cormorant. Then, in early 1967, they sailed to England, where they revisited Addie's old haunts, then made their way to Donegal to see Tom's ailing mother.

Wherever they went, they spent mornings in the outdoors, looking for birds. Gradually, as they both became more absorbed in the work they were doing—watching birds, drawing and writing, refining and revising, and, increasingly that year, reading harrowing research about the decline of more and more species—they found themselves able to be together in the field without tearing off their clothes and searching for a soft, hidden, nettle-free spot.

"Probably a good thing," Tom laughed one evening as they drank their pints beside the fire in a pub in Ambleside, "considering how cold and wet these boggy English trails are."

"And how crowded with sturdy English walkers," Addie agreed, taking a long, thirsty sip from her glass.

And so they settled into a routine of working together: mornings in the field, observing and drawing; afternoons at desk and easel; occasional evenings spent looking over each other's work, making pointed but gentle suggestions. They eased comfortably into a collaboration that, Tom blithely assumed, would continue for the rest of their lives.

By August, when they returned to Burnham, Tom had mailed the manuscript that would become *A Prosody of Birds* to an editor recommended by a colleague, and Addie was refining the paintings for the plates that would accompany it. A month later, they received three significant phone calls in the space of a week. The first was from Tom's brother, telling him that their mother had died. The second was from the university press that wished to publish Tom's book. And the third was from the college physician, informing them that yes, Addie was indeed pregnant.

Journal—Field Entry

16 May 1965
Sunday

Rising Valley, Burnham, Bucks Co., PA (convergence of Kleine/Little
and Nisky Creeks, site of an abandoned fishing cottage, 1 mi. from the
Burnham College campus)

Time: 5–8 P.M. (I can't be military about this anymore.)
Observers: Addie Sturmer, and everywhere, the scent, the sound—the
    ghost of Tom Kavanagh
Habitat: Creek bank. Smooth rocks and rich green moss that is delight-
    fully slippery. Ice-cold water. Something in the air that's making me
    feel drunk.
Weather: Temp. 75 degrees F, or so; a red sunset back there, behind the
    ridge
23% cloud cover, I'd say; a bit more than yesterday, when the valley was
    awash in something golden that I find I can't describe, or paint
Remarks: I keep thinking about the fact that you *are* married. It's diffi-
    cult to concentrate on this drawing, which isn't going anywhere.

SPECIES LIST
Wood Thrush, *Hylocichla mustelina* (which is like music too) 1. Ours.
    He was here again; I heard him and found him the moment I
    arrived.

Number of species: 1; *Number of Individuals:* 1; *Time:* 3 hrs.
Comments: All the same, married or not, I would kiss you again. And
    again. Water splashing at our feet, smell of someone's wood fire
    burning. Wood thrush trilling overhead. Your hand at my back,

steadying me on the slick rocks, then at my waist, turning me to face you.

16 May—I can't give you the owl caricature because I need what's on the back of it. It's a sketch I did, immediately after class that day, of your face. It's only for me, and I'll keep it forever. I never want to forget the way you looked to me that day.

I haven't yet told you that I draw you almost as obsessively as I draw the sandpiper, and now the wood thrush.

Now I've told you.

Now I have to find a way to draw your *mouth*—now that I know its taste. And also the feeling of your smooth jaw below my hand.

Will I kiss you again? I can still hear the wood thrush, now. But already I'm afraid of forgetting how it felt when I nearly fell and you reached for me and I lowered my field glasses and there was your face, your mouth, reaching for mine—the thing I've longed for since the day you walked into the classroom with that ridiculous stuffed owl.

eight

THE BURR OF CERTAIN birds' songs—as in blurred, as in a kind of simultaneous whistle and hum: Addie heard it, truly heard it, for the first time when she was pregnant. Especially in the early and then the late months, in the fall and then the spring, during the blurry—burry—bookends of her pregnancy. And never more so than in the song of the scarlet tanager—"robinlike but hoarse," in Peterson's words, "like a robin with a sore throat."

Or, in the words of F. Schuyler Matthews, "a lazy drowsy, dozy buzz," depicted on his musical staffs as a series of trilled notes—as if a trill could in any way capture it, said Tom, who wrote of the guttural something or other one hears, or imagines hearing, in an Anglo-Saxon poem.

Eight months pregnant and checking proofs for *A Prosody of Birds,* Addie said nothing, though she found this inaccurate; "lazy drowsy, dozy" came closer, but still failed to capture how she felt, which was how the scarlet tanager sounded: woozy yet alert, all soft and full and rounded at the edges, all readiness and peace.

And at home with inaccuracy, for a change. After all, she knew her accompanying plate was not quite right either—the particular orange-red of the breeding male still so elusive to her, still not quite there.

"Learn not to fear contrasts in the same field of color. They are hard, *but they occur,* and are consequently to be reckoned with." So wrote Louis Agassiz Fuertes to his protégé George Miksch Sutton, in a letter included in a book by Fuertes's daughter that Addie would read years later. She'd struggled mightily, day in and day out, through the year of her "research assistantship," to hone that kind of precision, that accuracy in degrees of color, in nuance. She'd longed for someone to guide her toward it, a mentor or teacher who could show her the way. But she was too timid to send anything to Clive Behrend, and Tom seemed, genuinely, to adore anything she painted or drew.

But now, back from their six months abroad, filled again with the English, and now too the Irish, countryside, so pleasantly full, blurry and full, with the birds and their songs and her love for Tom and, now, the baby that she carried, precision and accuracy seemed, somehow, beside the point. It was the burring she was after.

Which was there, too, in the brown mud, the richly rotting leaves along the creek's edge and the loose, fragrant trails through the woods. And also in a kind of smudged quality to the air and sky—gray and filmy and dreamy—throughout the fall and again in the spring, the seasons before and after the crisp clarity of winter. Winter, when she got practical and filled the larder and shaped a cozy nursery in the alcove of the bedroom she shared with Tom. Winter, when the cold and bright and cloudless days—a hawk's view of branch and sky—took her away from painting and into obsessive reading of books that Tom, her emergent ecologist of a husband, was recommending: Aldo Leopold's *Sand County Almanac* and, most importantly, Rachel Carson's *Silent Spring*.

But in the fall and spring, when the songbirds did in fact return (she'd begun, genuinely, to fear they wouldn't, so powerfully had her January reading of *Silent Spring* affected her), she settled into the burring, the gentleness of the smudged edges, and produced what certain devotees of her work (her daughter among this opinionated group) would eventually consider her finest work. Those paintings of the gentle, softened strokes, the strange sense of an echo of flight still there in the bird's wing. The paintings that came well before the later, harsher work, but were also worlds away from her earlier concerns with accuracy, with precise contrasts in the same field of color.

Still, though, the seeds of her later, angrier work could be found in the sharp-eyed reading she was doing that winter, during her busily focused middle trimester. What, for instance, might have caused that recurring haziness, that poetic, but probably somehow faintly poisoned, smudging of the air? In the crispness of January, February, early March, she wondered and worried. But by May, as the birds sang, as she grew big as a mountain herself, paintbrush poised on the ridge of her belly, she forgot her worries for a while.

Of course by the time her labor commenced Addie had known, for quite some time, that her child would be named for a bird—specifically for the bird that somehow embodied her feelings during the fall of 1967 and the spring of 1968: Scarlet if she was a girl, Tanager if a boy.

"Surely lucky you were a girl," Tom would say years later—though in fact Scarlet had always fancied the name Tanager Kavanagh. Unlike the more practical Tom, who, after the chaos of his own large, mostly unhappy family, had never really imagined himself with a child of his own. Who, like most fathers of his generation, left most decisions having to do with childbearing and raising to his young wife, and who swallowed his fears and worries when, on the heels of her wintertime reading, Addie announced that she would have her child at home, assisted by an illegal midwife.

Her confidence was deceiving. Because she had her fears and worries too, and, like Tom, struggled to imagine herself as an actual parent. She was, after all, still so young, and she felt, in many ways, like a child herself. But things happened, and she was aware of a funny kind of longing that she hadn't felt before. There was Cora, for instance.

The fall before their travels to Cape May and then to Britain, on their way back to Burnham from Hawk Mountain, Addie and Tom had stopped to visit Cora and Karl and their placid, three-month-old baby boy in Bethlehem. Never before had a baby had such an effect on Addie. She'd held him through the entire visit, and there had been something about his wide, trusting eyes that overwhelmed her. She'd cried during the whole hour's drive back to Burnham, and she'd been completely incapable of explaining why.

And then, the following May, was the strange exchange she'd had with Miss Smallwood. "Have children," she said to Addie, unaccountably and out of nowhere, there in the vestibule of her row house where they stood, pulling off Wellingtons and layers of sweaters, scarves, jackets. Tom was still outside, looking for a place to park the car.

"I should have, I might have—but I didn't. And then, you see, you're left with nothing." She waved her hand toward the warm interior of the front parlor—which, with its book-lined walls and Persian rugs and marble-edged fireplace, hardly looked like nothing to Addie.

She was so taken aback by this unexpected, offhand advice (they'd just been talking, as best she could recall, about the struggles of John James Audubon's wife, Lucy, left behind in Louisiana with their two sons while Audubon journeyed abroad for three years) that she could think of nothing to say. And she stood there, speechless, boot dangling from her hand, as Miss Smallwood gave her a sad smile, then threw her coat at a hook and darted toward the kitchen, calling, "I'll start the tea, then."

She said nothing about it to Tom. But a month later, on the beach near Falcarragh, where he stood silent, tears filling his eyes, after their visit with his ill and senile mother, she took his hand and said, "Maybe we could have a baby." How she knew this was the right time to say such a thing was a mystery to her. But there the words were. "Maybe . . . a baby." He looked at her then, for a very long time, and then nodded. A month later he finished his manuscript, sitting at a desk in the British Museum. And the next day, as they set sail for home, Addie suspected, rightly, that her misery was not due to seasickness alone.

And so by the summer of 1968, everything was different. Tom was back to teaching, with more passion than ever—buoyed by his new book, his new role as a father, an ecological awareness refined by his months in Britain, his fury over the ongoing agony of the war in Southeast Asia. And Addie—the brazen young woman of two years before, the one who'd stared blankly back into the many disapproving faces on the Burnham campus—suddenly Addie, the new mother, was beloved and respected in all quarters. It started with being noticeably pregnant. When she walked on the Burnham campus that spring semester, to return books to the library or, on sunny days, to meet Tom for lunch in the garden outside the Hall of Science, everyone—even sour old Mrs. Hodges from the college bookstore, who, Addie was convinced, had hated her since her days as a student, counting out her last bit of change for a new paintbrush or sketchbook—smiled and greeted her warmly.

It would never cease to amaze her, the power of motherhood to transform a woman in the eyes of others. Later she would learn how tenuous a mother's hold on that brittle respect could be. For now, though, she was the darling not only of the Burnham College administration, but also of her own parents, who would eventually settle into the role of in-laws to a college professor only fifteen years younger than they were, as well as grandparents to a brown-eyed girl with perpetually tangled reddish-brown hair, a wild little thing who was, in their opinion, allowed to roam far too freely along the banks of that menacing creek but whom, nonetheless, they doted on.

Back from England and settled comfortably into the cottage with Tom, Addie was drawing and painting better than ever, and with the publication of *A Prosody of Birds* had come additional—paying—work as an illustrator. Suddenly she was a working artist, a professional in her own right. Though of course she was distracted from that work, for a time, when Scarlet was born. Sitting in the morning sunlight, nursing the weeks-old Scarlet, she could lose herself for hours, alternately dozing and slipping in and out of a reverie triggered by, of all things, her infant daughter's smell.

She knew Tom's smell—the mix of soap, sweat, and wood smoke—and loved it, on his clothing, on her own skin. But the smell of her child was more powerful than that, more real to her than the scent or the feel of her own skin. What, exactly, does one's own newborn child smell like, there at the level of her still forming flesh, below the creams and powder, below the fresh, wind-dried diaper smell? Bread, maybe—warm bread. The yeasty scent of breast milk on her tongue. The fur at the nape of a kitten's neck. Adam or Eve before the fall.

If ever she'd needed proof confirming her husband's preoccupations as a teacher ("We ourselves are mammals, after all; never forget this when someone tries to persuade you that you were magically 'created' out of dust," she could still hear him intoning)—which she hadn't—here, in the form of this screaming little mammal tugging at her breast, it was.

She was exhilarated by the flood of her love for Scarlet. Exhilarated by it, and exhausted by it too; she spent the first weeks at home with her new baby—assisted first by her mother and then, off and on, by Lou and by Cora—in a fog of happy exhaustion, nursing her baby, staring at her with the eyes of a lover, laughing with her friends and even with her mother.

Her favorite days were those when Lou and Cora arrived to visit, Lou driving over from her mother's home in Philadelphia, Cora from the graduate school apartment she, Karl, and year-old Richard were living in in Bethlehem. Lou filled the hours with outrageous stories about her increasingly odd and reclusive parents and the usual sagas of her various love affairs, stepping outside every hour or so to walk along the creek and smoke a cigarette; there was something sadder about Lou, Addie thought, watching her from the window while Scarlet slept and Cora tried to interest silent, staring Richard in playing with a set of giant blocks.

After graduating from Burnham, Lou had gone to California with Mr. Premed—or Ted, as they all knew him now—who was, in fact, trying out medical school at that point and who was, to everyone's continued amazement, still her boyfriend. Each of them continued to have other lovers—a feature of their relationship that, unfortunately, Lou would tire of well before Ted did. Specifically in 1979, when their first child, Elizabeth, was born, and Ted was now Mr. Political Science and in his third year of "polishing" his dissertation, still supported by his not-so-happily long-suffering wife, who thought perhaps a baby might speed him along toward the job market. Which, happily, Elizabeth did, and Mr. Political Science became, in the next several years, Mr. Aggressive Academic Climber, and, before long, an assistant dean at Georgetown.

Addie and Cora would have predicted none of that during those late-spring days in 1968, there along Nisky Creek, tending to the two babies, reminiscing about their rambles through the hills surrounding them only three years before, when they had been giddy girls in Tom's Biology of the Birds class. The quiet now, while Lou walked along the creek, was nice. But—and this had always been true, Addie realized, watching her friend from the window—as soon as Lou left a room, she missed her.

"Lou seems more thoughtful somehow," Addie said to Cora. But Cora only laughed when Addie wondered, aloud, whether Lou might not want to have a baby too.

Cora seemed happy, caring for Richard while Karl struggled to complete his graduate degree in electrical engineering and worked two jobs to support his new family. What she didn't tell Addie was that sometimes, in the first years after Richard's birth, she lay awake at night, worrying about her young son's peculiar placidity, his lack of responsiveness. But in the morning she busied herself with washing diapers and cooking a hot lunch for Karl to eat on the run, and so her days went, and before long Karl had finished his degree and landed a job in southern New Jersey, and then she was pregnant again. Not until Robert's birth, the following spring, when they were settled into their first little house, in Toms River, when the differences between their two sons, along with Richard's hab-its—the rocking and humming, the strange periods of withdrawal, and, most disturbing, the banging of his fists against doors, walls, his own head—became impossible to ignore did they decide to seek advice from a specialist in Philadelphia. Who said it was clearly autism and that, un-fortunately, there was little they could do.

But now, on this warm and lovely June day in 1968, what Addie knew was that her baby was healthy, she loved her husband and her life with him, and her dearest friends were with her. There was also a war to worry about, of course, and a draft; there were reckless uses of pesticides, industrial toxins filling the air, and careless destruction of animal habitats right in their own backyard; there were brutal seizures of land and homes and plans to build a useless, and environmentally devastating, dam less than a hundred miles upriver from them. But somehow, during those first weeks of Scarlet's life, all that knowledge, all that painful awareness, faded away each time Addie looked into her newborn daughter's eyes, or watched as Tom held her and sang to her, or sat down to reminisce, and laugh, with her old friends.

But then Lou went back to California, and Cora came less frequently, busy, by the summer's end, with caring for her own ailing mother. And Tom went back to regular hours in his office and to teaching summer courses, because of course they'd need the extra money now. And for several weeks, every time Addie got Scarlet dressed to take her out to the blind, hoping to do even an hour of drawing in the morning, something would happen. An explosion in the diaper and only one clean one left, which meant she'd have to wash more immediately. Gas pains or a prickly rash or a bad dream or something—who knew what went on in that tiny head?—that roused Scarlet from sleep inside the sling Addie had so carefully nestled her in to carry her out to the blind. Then she'd wail, inconsolably, refusing to be comforted until Addie finally extracted her from the sling and sat down, yet again, in the rocking chair by the south-facing window to nurse her.

The rocking chair by the window where the sun streaked in every morning, white-gold and gleaming. The sunlight that, only a week or so before, had made her weep with happiness, remembering that same gold light shining on her and Tom in the morning, waking on their mattress on the floor, feeling drugged with the happy ache of a night of lovemaking. And then to sit in that same light, in her beautiful oak rocking chair, the one that had been her mother's and her grandmother's before that, baby suckling contentedly at her breast. It felt like it was almost too much, more happiness than she could bear, she'd written in her field notebook.

Only a month ago that had been, she realized one steaming day in August. But that day she was sick of the rocking chair—that and her bed the only places she'd been for a week, it seemed. Sick of the chair and sick of the sunlight, that same summer light, still yellow-white, but now it seemed a sickly yellow to her. Hot and cloying. How she wished it would rain.

Because it would be an awful day for birds now anyway, she knew. Too hazy, too still. And by then it was after ten; no birds, if there were any near the creek at all, would be stirring by then.

So she would put Scarlet, sated and sleeping soundly, in the bassinet. And she would sit down to type some more of Tom's notes. And she would fight the urge to cry. Because she was so terribly, miserably, indescribably bored—bored with washing diapers, bored with sitting and nursing, barely able even to read because she couldn't turn the pages without rousing, and angering, her demanding baby. Bored too with typing Tom's words about the songs of birds, instead of hearing—and more importantly, for her, *seeing*—the things themselves.

That kind of boredom, boredom and exhaustion with the whole enterprise of being a wife and a mother and "making a home," was a hard thing for someone like Addie Kavanagh to admit, in Burnham, Pennsylvania, in the summer of 1968. Even harder to admit than the boredom was this simple fact: She didn't entirely love motherhood. She wasn't even sure she loved her husband, at least not in the way that she had only a year before.

Tom saw the change and tried, as best he could, to help. It's perfectly ordinary, happens to every woman with at least one of her children, typically the first—so his married colleagues in the Hall of Science assured him at their morning coffee break.

"Just the baby blues," Jack Gaines, a jovial chemist and father of four, told him. "Get her out of the house, take her to dinner. Give the baby her bottle and change a diaper from time to time. She'll snap out of it soon enough."

Tom didn't have the heart to tell him that he and Addie both hated going out to dinner, preferring food they'd cooked themselves. And he'd changed many diapers. And Scarlet had never had a single bottle; what would be the point of that, Addie had said, when her breasts were perfectly adequate, and far better for Scarlet?

But the getting her out of the house part—that made sense to him. And so when he returned home from campus in the late afternoons, Scarlet's fussiest times, he pulled both mother and baby out of the house for a walk along the creek. He held Scarlet, bouncing her and cooing to her, trying to stop her crying. Addie looked better after these walks, he told himself, as evening came on and she nursed Scarlet on the porch before they went inside for dinner. A bit more color in her cheeks, less sluggishness in her steps.

But, Tom knew, it wasn't just the "baby blues" for Addie. For Addie it had something to do with the birds, and her work. As the fall deepened, he would urge her to go to her blind early on the weekend mornings. He learned quickly not to ask her how things had gone, what she'd seen or drawn. She refused to show him the few sketches she came back with. More often than not, she came back empty-handed.

Still she persisted in going to the blind, often, in those early years, taking the increasingly independent Scarlet along with her. Eventually she started producing again—workmanlike illustrations, adequate for most of her paying work. But (and of course Tom could see this, though he said nothing; they never spoke of it) completely lacking the energy and focus, the bright life of the plates in the *Prosody*, say, as well as of her work from the months of her pregnancy.

Meanwhile, his own work had never felt more absorbing. Since publication of the book he was called, from time to time, to provide commentary on issues like habitat loss, waste disposal and the water supply, any noticeable decline in migrating species. And the teaching! It had never been better. In part it was the students, who, he was delighted to find on his return from the sabbatical, had suddenly become angry, committed, vocal; the cultural revolution had, it seemed, reached even the tiny Burn-ham campus.

Suddenly they were *all* hungry for his courses, hungry for his recitations from Yeats and the English Romantics, but also for his lectures on Darwin and Haeckel. As the months, then the years, passed and the war dragged on, it delighted him to drive Addie, Scarlet, and a van full of students to antiwar rallies and marches in Philadelphia and, on occasion, Washington.

Suddenly, it seemed, even the Burnham administrators, including the new president, had come to share the views of Tom and many of his colleagues on the misguided war, even to tolerate the students' angry voices. It was the dawn of a new decade, and the concerns for the planet that he and Addie had voiced in the *Prosody* seemed to be catching on with the public at large. (Who knew, in the giddy spring of 1971, that even Earth Day would eventually become an occasion for corporate sloganeering?)

It was at one of the Philadelphia marches, when Scarlet was three, that Addie discovered the Bucks County Mothers for the Earth (or "Bucks Mamas," as they called themselves). And for a number of years, busy as she was, first with petitions and letter-writing, then with teach-ins and sit-ins and more, Addie seemed barely to notice, and certainly not to mind, how seldom she made it into the field to observe and sketch. An hour or two of work in the mornings, mainly just revisiting older pieces or working from one of the countless sketches in the notebooks piled below her work table—this was enough to generate some income. And then the rest of her day was free for more pressing tasks.

First was the shopping mall slated to be built on a swath of woods and uncultivated farmland outside Doylestown, an area that was a known breeding ground for an increasingly rare butterfly called the regal fritillary. Later it seemed almost quaint to think of Addie and her fellow Bucks Mamas, gathered around someone's kitchen table to write their indignant letters, or squeezed into some state legislator's tiny local office to present their list of concerns. Many, like Addie, would be dressed in cotton skirts and hand-knit sweaters, long braids down their backs—some with nursing babies tucked in slings, others with grubby, ragamuffin kids like Scarlet trailing in their wake. Others were tidily dressed suburban homemakers with equally tidy children, carting everyone in their boat-sized station wagons. All of them, it seemed, had read *Silent Spring;* all were worried about contaminated water, about cancer, about their children's futures.

They lost the battle over the shopping mall, of course. But by then Addie's appetite was whetted. And she'd learned some lessons from that sad failure. Forget the letters and the polite visits to legislators' offices was one; she'd seen the patronizing contempt behind the fat, self-satisfied state senator's fake smile, his smug "You ladies are doing the most important work of all, after all." Eventually Addie and a few of the other Bucks Mamas broke away from the larger group and joined up with another loosely affiliated group of local activists—a few graduate students from Penn, a handful of back-to-the-landers who were living on a minicommune near New Hope, a disgruntled former engineer at Bethlehem Steel. And eventually a quiet, secretive, and disturbed high school student from Riegelsville named Brian Kent.

It was better, Tom told himself, to see Addie passionately engaged in something once again. No question about it. Of course he missed the days when she'd seemed just as enthusiastic about the work that, for a while at least, they'd shared. The trips they'd taken together, their time in the field, with Scarlet riding along in her backpack.

Still, better to see her busy and happy again, though the group she was now involved with grew daily more provocative in its actions. Setting up camp and squatting on land that was slated for development. Seeking arrest. By this time, Scarlet was eight, nine, ten—old enough to be bothered by a mother who routinely went to jail. At times Tom felt he could barely remember the younger Addie, the eager artist, there at her easel by the woodstove.

Journal—Field Entry

24 May 1965
Monday

Sunday Woods—back to where we started

Time: 5:30–8 A.M.
Observers: The Surviving Loons + Tom Kavanagh first; then Addie S.
off on her own, in her makeshift blind at the convergence of Little
and Nisky Creeks
Habitat: Trees
Weather: Beautiful; there is no time like mid-May—nothing compares.
Oh—and 16.65% cloud cover.
Remarks: Species lists are, as I've told you, for madmen—as silly as a
stuffed great horned owl. (As I mentioned early on, I only need to
pass!) But I do hope you like my drawings. The wood thrush is getting closer, don't you think? Others less so, I know.
Comments: I drew a scarlet tanager for an hour and a half. There is
something I can't quite *get* about this bird—and it's so much more
than the color. "Some mysteries remain."

24 May—Of course there have been important women. Thank you for
making me aware of this. I went to Hawk Mountain on field trips as a
child. How is it that no one told me about Rosalie Edge or Irma Broun?

Yes, I'd enjoy visiting either Hawk Mountain or Audubon's home at
Mill Grove. But to be honest, I'd rather you joined me at the cottage this
weekend, if you're sure you now feel free to do so.

I'm sorry I can't seem to say I'm sorry that Polly has decided to move
to New York with her voice teacher.

No, I'm not. I'm not sorry at all.

I have a camp stove. We could have franks and beans and wine. Why not?

And yes, both Cora and Lou know. But they're sworn to secrecy, and they are completely trustworthy. Maybe you noticed, early on, that Lou abandoned the challenge of you to turn her sights on Mr. Premed? I'd said nothing to her, but as I told you, she's a sharp observer; she watches more closely than anyone realizes. Too bad Princess I Hate These Bugs was so slow on the uptake. But I can't say I miss her much.

Though I haven't spent much time with the Surviving Loons for the past week or so, I'll miss this class when it ends (for more than the obvious reasons), as I know you will. Who'd have guessed that Mr. Premed would show so much skill and enthusiasm—or that Lou would have stuck with him for these three weeks?

Whatever you decide about the weekend is fine. I'll be happy to listen for owls or watch for hawks or work further on my sweet wood thrush—whatever we do. Knowing that I'll be with you, that things are quiet for you at home now, imagining a summer in the field and at work on the cottage—it's all made me more content than I've felt in months. Since England really.

And I'm painting better than ever, I think. I have lots to show you when you come by the studio tomorrow.

nine

AT SOME POINT, ADDIE'S attention shifted to dead birds.

There were lots of them. More than most people realized. Some slammed into windows. Others, their bodies wrecked by pesticides, by contaminated water, by insect-borne disease, simply fell from the sky one day, dead.

Eventually she couldn't stop seeing them, everywhere. They populated her dreams, the way living birds—soaring, singing, mating, migrating—had fluttered there behind her eyelids, waking or sleeping, when she was younger.

But not for a while. For a while, she remained happy—focused and happy. Scarlet had not one but two happy, contented parents: happily and contentedly doing their work each day. Rising readily, eager to get to it all. And at the end of the day, sleeping the sleep of those who've earned their rest.

Were they distracted by their young child, by worries about money, by the demands of distant family members, by their friends' joys and sorrows? Of course. But consider the difference between happy parents who have distractions, and some of the other kinds. Then perhaps Scarlet's reluctance to write a memoir will make more sense. Yes, her parents were colorful. But maybe, she thought, she wasn't angry enough, at least not now. Shouldn't a young writer recalling colorful parents like Addie and Tom be angry?

It was true that Scarlet wished Addie had been willing to try the traditional treatments again. It was true that she found her mother's choosing to fight a local developer (even from the grave) instead of her own disease a bit ridiculous, and also selfish, in Addie's peculiar way. It was true that Scarlet had had her doubts, as she grew older, about the strength of her parents' bond. It was true that, as her mother's work changed dramatically, Scarlet began to question its value—troubled, as she was, by the rage that seemed to fuel it and by what seemed to her its too unsubtle agenda, longing instead for the gentler strokes, the comforting realism of the paintings from her childhood. And it was true that she'd felt lonely at times, baffled by her mother's anger.

On the other hand, Scarlet couldn't think of a single time when Addie had directed any of that anger at her. Instead she had learned, from both Addie and Tom, that when you're angry, or despairing, or lonely, what you really need to do is keep working, always working—whatever your work might be: painting, scanning birdsongs, camping out and getting arrested and lying to the police to protect someone who can't protect himself. When Scarlet declared to her parents that she had decided her work would be the writing of poems, Tom and Addie, unlike the parents of a number of her friends, were pleased. She hadn't expected this from Addie.

"I know no poet is ever going to save the world," she said to Addie, shyly, after reading them a few of her poems on a visit to Burnham when she was a graduate student. She was sitting on the floor, leaning her head back and onto Addie's lap, where she sat on the sofa behind her. Tom had risen to add a log to the fire in the woodstove.

"Well, no one's going to manage to do that, I'm afraid," Addie said as she fiddled with her daughter's newly shorn hair. Scarlet could see Tom's shoulders slump when she said it; it wasn't the answer he'd hoped Addie would give her, Scarlet knew, and yet it didn't upset her at all. She doesn't mind, was all Scarlet thought; I said I couldn't save the world, and Addie doesn't mind.

"You've got as good a chance of saving it as some lunatic painter like your mother," Addie went on, then tugged playfully on Scarlet's hair. Tom's smile, when he sat down next to Addie and reached to pull her toward him, looked worn. But something about that moment made Scarlet feel irrationally happy. As happy as she'd been as a child.

Because in truth Scarlet's childhood had been quite happy. A comfortable home—a cottage still, really, even with Tom and Addie's many improvements and additions through the years—filled with books and art (Addie's right alongside Scarlet's own childish efforts), warm rugs and quilts, the smells of wood smoke and the bread Tom baked on Sundays and various and sundry happy, muddy dogs they took in over the years. And at night, the sounds of Nisky Creek, of crickets, frogs, owls, and lullabies—Addie, despite her so-called tin ear, singing in a breathy, reedy voice while she washed the dinner dishes, Tom playing his fiddle, pausing now and then for sips from a glass of scotch, his one indulgence.

Scarlet would doze on the rug by the woodstove, a book open before her, half dreaming along to "The Seal's Lullaby"—Kipling's words set to a tune of Tom's own devising. "Now hush thee my baby, the night is behind us / And black are the waters that sparkled so green. . . ." Tom and Addie sang it together, and as Scarlet drifted in and out of sleep the creek outside their door turned into the sea, black and sheltering, and she into not a seal but a cormorant, warm in the nest of her mother's arms, floating there, flushed with warmth despite the cold surrounding them. Smelling smoke and yeast and her mother's own smell—dusting of talc, faint trace of sweat on her pullover, turpentine on her fingers—buoyed by her parents' apparent happiness, by the sad, sweet tunes her father played, everything as safe and sure as Eden.

The creek was always there, clear and full in spring, often just a trickle by fall. Banked, at spots, with cool, soft sand, full of smoothly rounded stones and endless tadpoles and minnows and crawfish for catching, lazy catfish in shaded pools and belching frogs on the low branches of a giant elm on the bank.

During the day, when Tom went off to teach, Addie was distracted by her own work. And so Scarlet quickly learned to rely on her own imagination, creating elaborate stories that featured her. Addie let her loose with crayons she could use anywhere, including the walls and floor of her blind and, on occasion, the house.

Scarlet felt wrapped in a safe cocoon of k-selected nurturing; she ate well, she slept well, and eventually she discovered playmates there along the creek—the children of her father's colleagues, her fellow tree climbers, bike riders, waders and stone skippers and crawfish catchers. Words and music and pictures and a boundless out-of-doors. And, when she was eight, the arrival of Peter Gleason, an only child like Scarlet and her soulmate-to-be, son of Tom's colleague Richard, from the Burnham English Department.

If Addie and Tom, together, were Scarlet's first great love, Peter was her second. His imagination matched—actually probably surpassed— her own, and when Addie abandoned her second Nisky Creek blind for a better, more secluded one a half mile from their cluster of ramshackle houses, that crayon-bedecked tree house became Peter and Scarlet's stage. A turreted castle on some occasions, a cave of secrets on others. And, some years later, when both were immersed in Tolkien, Middle Earth.

Earlier, though, it was often simply their "house"—complete with doll/child (always only one), stove and cookery, desk and easel: their own households in miniature. Once, when they were nine, they kissed, as they'd seen their parents do often enough, then decided rather quickly that it wasn't worth the sticky discomfort. Actually, Scarlet had liked it more than Peter had. But she would never have admitted this to him.

When Scarlet was twelve, and preparing to enter junior high school, Peter left for boarding school in New England. There he eventually discovered, or perhaps admitted, that he was gay. In those junior high years, distracted and busy with schoolwork, the volleyball team, the school chorus, Scarlet felt privileged, and cool beyond words, when Peter came home on long breaks from boarding school and regaled her with stories about his various boyfriends, his fling with his drama teacher. She smoked her first clove cigarette (and very nearly threw up that morning's buckwheat pancakes) on a frigid walk along the towpath between the river and canal, one Christmas vacation when she and Peter were thirteen.

But she also knew by then that Peter was lost to her. And the following summer, Scarlet would move on to her next great loves—Cora and her family, and the Jersey shore. She and her parents spent a week with Cora,

Karl, and their sons Richard and Bobby at the end of that summer, in 1982. The next summer they spent another two weeks in Cider Cove, theoretically to help Cora and Karl work on their drafty old house. Though in truth Scarlet spent most of her time biking or at the beach with the boys, and each morning and evening Tom and Addie disappeared, spending hours watching birds from various vantage points along the Delaware Bay. They traveled back regularly, for weekend visits, through the rest of that summer.

Because Addie had rediscovered cormorants and ospreys, common eiders and American bitterns, the birds she'd begun drawing sixteen years earlier, when she and Tom had spent a part of that year's leave in Cape May. Coastal birds, and a new style of painting, and too her dear friend Cora, who was struggling with her son's growing isolation and sadness. All of these were important discoveries for Addie, considering that her work had begun to grow stale in recent years, and she was bored and searching and, increasingly, unhappy—hints of a kind of restlessness that, Tom thought, he recognized, and dreaded.

Add to that their fifteen-year-old daughter (yes, childhood is easy; it's adolescence that leads to bitter, raging memoirs)—who had hated the first year of high school with a passion. By that age Scarlet had begun to show signs of becoming a darkly sullen teenager of a kind that was common enough in Delaware Valley High, the regional high school to which Burnham youth were bused, along with an odd conglomeration of farm kids, transient youths living in the river towns, and the children of owners of gleaming new homes in the earliest of those Bucks County housing developments Addie hated so much. Delaware Valley High was known, in those days, for its high number of teenaged suicide attempts. Hence Peter's parents' decision to accept his grandmother's offer to pay for boarding school. Something Tom and Addie never could have afforded, and something they would have scoffed at (in fact did scoff at, behind closed doors at night) even if they could have.

"School is school, wherever you are," Addie would say. "You don't really learn anything of substance until college anyway. Before that it's all just navigating the social maelstrom, wherever you are." A sentiment that, even if he didn't share it (certainly his own experience in Sister Catherine's classroom gave such an idea the lie), seemed to please Tom.

And so Scarlet was fifteen, and angry. At her parents, at her peers, at the narrow world she found herself in—made more narrow, and more confined, by that ribbon of unused canal, hemming in the last remaining wild river in the United States. Despite the books and artwork, the rugs and quilts and homey smells, the fire in the woodstove, the music at night—itself less frequent now, as Addie, and therefore Tom, rarely seemed interested in it anymore. Despite those things, or maybe because of them. Who can possibly understand the mind of an adolescent?

By age fifteen Scarlet had begun to feel, and high school had certainly served to magnify the feeling, that in fact there was something *pretty weird* about her parents. Her parents, who never went to church. Who both had work that so engrossed them that they did it all the time, even on weekends. Who drove a rusted, thirdhand station wagon when they had to, but preferred getting around on their old, equally rusty bicycles. Who showed no signs of planning to move to a split-level in one of the new developments (as many of their peers at Burnham had begun to do), one with modern conveniences like, say, a television, anytime soon. Who—at least in Addie's case—would, from all appearances, eventually prefer seeing a house like that burn to the ground to living in one.

By 1983, Ronald Reagan was president, and Scarlet was fifteen and living with parents like Addie and Tom while attending high school with a lot of kids who lived in those split-levels with televisions (and dishwashers and manicured lawns and at least two—new—cars per family). And while, deep down, she was contemptuous of all that excess, all that "bilge and ruin" (to quote from a poem she wrote later) even then, still she was young. Young and lonely now that Peter was gone, and increasingly embarrassed by a mother who was growing ever more restless, whose despair over rampant development and environmental losses— from the fritillary butterfly of Scarlet's early childhood to the pesticide-laden groundwater and the lost woodlands of recent years—was leading her to keep company with an odd assortment of punks, aging hippies, and other outcasts. For a while Scarlet clung to Tom, her laughing, singing father, who, at least on the surface that she saw, seemed mind-bogglingly oblivious to everything save his work, and his family.

Though perhaps he wasn't so oblivious. Because it was his idea to keep returning to Cider Cove, renting the little house before the official summer season began, and then staying for long weekends with Cora and Karl and their sons. Cider Cove, where, it seemed, they could all breathe again, after those particularly cold and gray Burnham winters. Cider Cove, and the shore, and bike rides and swimming and long, noisy dinners with Cora and Karl, Bobby and Richard.

At first they'd had to work a bit to adjust to Richard's peculiar habits, the way he'd suddenly shift from avid talk and voluble laughter to a brooding, distracted silence. Or at least Addie and Scarlet had to work at it; Tom had a natural way of being with Richard from the beginning—listening, with what seemed to be genuine pleasure, to Richard's obsessive prattling about baseball scores and batting averages, the guitarist Django Reinhardt, the possible evolutionary link between dinosaurs and contemporary birds. At other times he and Richard worked together in silence for hours, constructing surprisingly realistic, and often quite beautiful, models of birds' nests.

Tom kept a number of these in his office at Burnham, where they were less likely to upset Addie. The oriole's nest, that delicate, swinging pendulum woven from plant fiber and hair, made Scarlet cry every time she saw it. She could still see Richard's face as he held it up for everyone to view one evening at dinner, swinging it slowly back and forth and following it with his eyes, a look of rapture on his face.

"They must build it this way so the wind can rock it back and forth like this, to soothe the babies," he said as he watched the nest. "Like the cradle in the treetop."

Everyone smiled, enjoying that thought, and also Richard's obvious pleasure. No one said anything about how "Rock-a-Bye Baby" ends.

Bobby had the same natural ease with his brother. They were like all young teenaged brothers everywhere, Scarlet supposed—wrestling playfully in the sand, arguing over possible interpretations of Pink Floyd lyrics, jabbing each other at sighting a pretty girl in a bikini on the beach. After years of steering his brother away from other children's taunts, Bobby had developed a steely, protective edge that almost seemed to dare kids who didn't know Richard—the local kids at first, then tourists on the beach or at the arcade—to taunt his brother now. Maybe because of that protective edge, in Cider Cove it seemed that no one ever did.

Cora was calm and natural with Richard too, a loving mother with her teenaged son; both she and Karl worked tirelessly to make Richard's life as normal as possible. But maybe because Scarlet learned to watch Cora and Richard through Addie's eyes, she always felt she could see the pain and fear around the edges of Cora's playful hugs and jokes, her exasperated reminders to both her sons about hanging their wet towels outside or putting their bikes away in the garage.

Once Scarlet walked into the kitchen just as Richard was extracting himself from his mother's embrace. "Mom, I'm all right," he said softly, then hurried out of the room. Before Scarlet could hurry out of the kitchen as well, Cora turned to face her. In the split second before she put on her well-tuned smile, Scarlet was certain she saw her swallow a sob.

Soon, though Addie and Scarlet might not have been as comfortable with Richard as Tom and Bobby seemed to be, they were all used to his mood swings and his various obsessions, and the majority of their time spent with Cora and her family in those early years was sun-filled and happy and raucous. Those times at Cider Cove saved Addie and Tom and Scarlet, at least for a while. From one of several serious crises Addie experienced as an artist. From Scarlet's adolescent purgatory.

That first visit late in the summer of 1982 stayed with them into the beginning of the cold months that followed; they had their suntans and sun-streaked hair to remind them, memories of evening picnics on the beach, Addie's new paintings in the works, Tom's revived interest in shorebirds and the coastal migration. And during the next two summers they would return as often as they could—spending weeks at a time in Cider Cove, practically living at Cora and Karl's.

But by the summer of 1983, when he was seventeen, Richard had already begun to show signs of the trouble ahead. His periods of silence and withdrawal grew longer, and only Tom and Bobby were able, occasionally, to pull him out of the house, for a bike ride or a look at some of the feeding birds in the nearby marsh at dusk. And in the year that followed, Addie grew restless again. Tom seemed less oblivious now, but also uncertain. What could anyone do?

By the next summer, when the kids Richard had known in high school were busily preparing for college and he was working in the copy room at his father's office, with no clear prospects for going elsewhere, he rarely joined the two families for meals. Scarlet's clearest memory of him, that summer, was of passing him in the upstairs hallway in the evening—this sullen, unshaven young man who, only two years before, had been laughingly riding the waves or careening on the old bicycle in front of hers—trying to at least say hello, while he slouched along, hugging the wall and staring at his feet, refusing to meet her eyes.

Years later, Cora sometimes wondered whether Richard's diagnosis should have been Asperger Syndrome; he was clearly intelligent, and self-sufficient in many ways, a talented artist and guitarist and, for a time and under Tom's influence, obsessively interested in birds. But surely Asperger's along with significant depression, Cora's friends thought, or maybe bipolar disorder. He was always an isolated child, a loner whose family did everything they could to include him, in games, bike rides, romps on the beach, trips. But as he grew older it became harder and harder to persuade him to leave the house, eventually even his room, for days at a time. His retreat into himself, and into whatever terrors his mind must have held, grew more and more complete.

Back then, from the age of four, when Cora and Karl had taken him to see the specialist in Philadelphia, he'd simply been called autistic. Everyone said the family had coped remarkably well with the burden of having a child like Richard, that they'd handled it all as well as could be expected. Cora's way of coping with the situation was primarily, it seemed, to opt not to talk about it.

Addie, on the other hand, could not be silenced—except in Cora's presence, where, remarkably for her, she eventually learned to keep her bitter ravings to herself. Long before the 1990s, when incidents of autism increased dramatically and a number of people began to raise questions about thimerosol, the mercury compound in which children's vaccines were suspended, Addie got her hands on an obscure article about a quiet little study done in Europe. Mercury poisoning, she started insisting to anyone who would listen (and at that point, not many would). Contaminated fish. Dental amalgams, residue from burning coal, fluorescent lightbulbs, over-the-counter antiseptics. And even more to the point, endless rounds of childhood immunizations suspended in the stuff, absurd amounts of a lethal metal pumped right into an infant's bloodstream. All the evidence was there. And was anyone bothering to do anything about it? Of course not. What was the grief of a devastated mother here and there next to the power of those particular industries, to the American hunger for canned tuna fish and delusions of health and well-being?

It was around this time that Addie's focus as an artist began to shift, from living pelicans, bitterns, and the like to dead birds. Any kind—songbirds, raptors, shorebirds. All that mattered to her was that they were dead—specifically, dead because of what she termed "human interference." And, with an irony that wasn't lost on her or any of those around her, she became, for a time, a regular customer of Richard Schantz, the busiest and best taxidermist in upper Bucks County. Conveniently, Tom had kept the state license allowing him to add newly dead and newly stuffed specimens to the small Burnham collection to keep it up-to-date. A superfluous gesture, he'd always thought; his predecessor had built the yearly renewal of the license into the department budget, and Tom had never bothered to change this. He'd never imagined that it would come in handy one day, for Addie.

Eventually she decided that using Schantz's services was cheating somehow, and she began gutting and stuffing the dead birds that people began depositing at her back steps—pigeons, blue jays, hawks, countless finches and robins, and once, yes, a great horned owl—on her own.

And eventually, when Scarlet could no longer stand it—the piles of dead birds, the constant phone calls and urgent meetings with the loosely affiliated group of conservationists and activists with whom Addie was now associating, the increasingly outlandish "interventions," as they called them, that certain members of the group had begun to stage—she asked if she might stay, for the entire summer when she was seventeen, with Cora and her family in Cider Cove.

In June she took her last eleventh grade exam, packed up the old Volvo her father had bought from a neighbor, and drove to Cider Cove. She worked, throughout that summer, as a maid at a hotel in Cape May. And in August, she decided not to return to Burnham.

There were elements, from those years, that were missing from the most widely accepted version of Addie's life. Most of her small but loyal cadre of fans assumed, for instance, that she had begun working on the dead-bird assemblages at the time of her first bout with cancer. But in fact, she'd been gathering carcasses for a couple years by then.

And most seemed to see her early years of more visible environmental activism as connected with the "transitional years," as one fan called them (in the newsletter devoted to Addie that he published for a few months after her NEA grant was revoked)—the time she spent at the shore in the mid-1980s, the period of rediscovering those species from her stay at Cape May during Tom's sabbatical years before, the newfound freedom of a coastal environment, coupled with her growing distress over the many risks to tidal habitats along the mid-Atlantic. And so on.

Here their timing was a little more accurate, but their reasons were wrong. There were some missing links, things they had no way of knowing. Things like Richard's rapid decline. Like her daughter's decision to leave home, essentially for good, before she'd finished high school. Like a lost boy named Brian Kent from Riegelsville, a town a few miles from her home in Burnham, child of a bitter divorce with a penchant for starting, and watching, fires, who decided to align himself with Addie and her band of Bucks County activists—and who (fortunately for him, unfortunately for Addie) reminded her, somehow, of poor, lost Richard.

Years later, even Cora and Lou would seem to have missed something crucial about their friend. Both assumed that Addie would want to be cremated, her ashes cast into the ocean, or perhaps along the banks of Nisky Creek.

"The shore really *was* her salvation," Lou said through her tears the day before Addie died, when she, Cora, Scarlet, and Tom all found themselves at the beach, gazing out at the sea. She was recalling a visit earlier in the spring, when Addie had still been a bit stronger, and when she, Lou, and Cora had taken a slow, careful walk on the deserted beach.

"She was radiant that day," Lou said. "Wasn't she, Cora?"

Cora nodded, a little absently, it seemed to Scarlet, saying nothing through her tears.

"She looked like a girl again, Tom," Lou went on. "Like when we all first knew her." And then she impulsively grabbed Scarlet's hand. "And when you first knew her too, Scarlet! Lord! Remember, Cora? Remember what a *glowing* new mother she was? She even made *me* think maybe I wanted to have kids, though God knows I wasn't really ready at twenty-two, or whatever the hell she was."

"Twenty-four," Tom said softly, to no one in particular. Only Scarlet heard him.

Lou blew her nose into the tissue Cora handed her and went on, "Of course this is where she should rest, where we should scatter her ashes. Here, in the sand, in the tidepools, with the shorebirds."

No one else said anything. But Tom and Scarlet looked at each other and then averted their eyes, trying to suppress their smiles.

III

proximate and ultimate causes

ten

"I WALKED ALL NIGHT," Lou says, breathless, barely nodding as she accepts the mug of coffee Cora has poured for her. She throws herself into the cushioned rocker by the window, flinging her legs over one arm of the chair and taking a gulp of the coffee. She looks less like someone who's walked all night than a diva who's just stepped onstage. She's dressed in fashionably wrinkled linen pants and a cashmere sweater, and she leaves a clean, haunting scent in her wake; she's a woman who even wears perfume gracefully. Her entrances, as far back as Scarlet can remember, have always been this grand.

Louise Sandrine Begley—she'd kept her own last name when she'd married Ted in 1975; Addie had been delighted by that, impressed by Lou's courage—though maybe it had taken less courage in Washington, D.C., in the mid-'70s than it would have required in Bucks County in 1967. She *could* have been onstage, a diva—maybe not a singer, but surely a powerful actress. She has remained stunning through the births of two daughters and a series of painful betrayals and eventually the bitter implosion of her marriage. Her skin is clear and youthful, even at fifty-eight; her dark hair is so fashionably cut that the wind has only made it look better, her makeup intact despite a night spent on the restless beach and quiet streets of Cider Cove.

"Do you know how long it's been since I've done that? Probably not since Burnham, not since Addie and I took the bus into New York and walked around Greenwich Village until dawn. Remember, Cora? Remember when we used to do that?"

Cora nods distractedly. It's clear she's frustrated to have been interrupted after the bit of news Scarlet has just dropped in her lap. Scarlet is frustrated too, but also relieved. She will have to tell Cora more about her pregnancy eventually, but she's not particularly eager to do so.

Cora picks up her newspaper again. Often she seems to be trying to tune Lou out. Theirs is a friendship Scarlet has never understood, and she wonders if it will continue now that Addie—who seemed to be the one thing they shared—is gone.

"I recall you doing that more often than Addie did," Cora says, pausing to hand the basket of muffins over to Lou. "But I do remember the night you both missed the last bus back. You came back to our room and drank a pot of coffee, and then Addie went off to the Art Building and you slept for twenty-four hours."

"Yes!" Lou bites into a muffin with gusto, then swings her legs to the floor and leans toward Cora and Scarlet conspiratorially. "But not till I'd gone off to find someone to sleep with. New York did that to me, every time; all that art, all that life—it made me just *starving*, for food, sex, everything."

"Ah, yes." Cora nods, remembering this as well apparently, and as always Scarlet is flummoxed by the lack of censure, the same lack of judgment or criticism as in Addie's responses to Lou. Was it her imagination, or was Cora *much* primmer than this? And wouldn't Addie have seen this kind of talk, and this kind of behavior, as hopelessly frivolous?

It's possible that her picture of Lou as frivolous, promiscuous, a bit of a lightweight intellectually—a rather silly, if harmless, woman—came from Tom. It always seemed to Scarlet that he never really warmed to Lou.

"Who might it have been then?" Cora asks, glasses perched on her nose, looking disconcertingly grandmotherly. "You didn't know Ted yet, so it couldn't have been him. Maybe that theater major? Arthur something—what was his name?"

"Oh, who knows? It could have been any of a number of theater majors, art majors. Psychology majors were always the easiest to find, as I recall. *Lord*, that campus was full of beautiful, obliging boys."

They all know this is a kind of show, and everyone is expected to participate. So Scarlet smiles and raises her eyebrows, assuming her role. "*That's* a version of the story I've never heard before," she says.

And then she is torn, as she always is with Lou. Or at least as she's been for the last sixteen years, since that dreary fall when Addie was hiding out in Lou's house, when Scarlet traveled to Washington with Tom to visit her on the weekends, all of them pretending there was nothing all that unusual about meeting up this way, furtively, enjoying Lou's lavish dinners and good wine, making over her pretty, spoiled daughters, Suzy and Liz. Ted was there on occasion too, also trying to act as if this was normal. For people like Addie and Tom.

But the tension was so thick it made Scarlet feel sick. She'd arrive back at Cora's late on a Sunday night and go immediately to bed, not emerging from her room for an entire day, skipping school, talking to no one. Cora never asked questions.

One dinner in particular has stayed with Scarlet, from later in Addie's time in Washington, near the end, when she finally went home to Burnham. Addie seemed more subdued on that visit, almost distracted, and Tom asked Scarlet to join the so-called adults for dinner instead of eating early, with Suzy and Liz.

"Everyone behaves better when you're there," he said, though Scarlet hadn't seen any evidence of that.

It was a particularly oily meal. For years Scarlet would remember the oil of the freshly made salad dressing, pasta swimming in olive oil, some rich cut of meat dripping fat on her plate, its pink center leering up at her. She picked at the food, wishing she could have just had macaroni and cheese with the girls an hour earlier, tuning in and out of the conversation. It was much the same as usual. Ted talking academic politics, Tom trying gamely, at first, to join in. But that night he seemed especially tired.

"I suppose it's a different game at a school like Georgetown," he finally said, apologetically. "Or maybe I'm just too old for the game by now. I don't know, Ted, I mainly teach my classes and do my research."

Then some rejoinder from Lou. "Imagine that, Ted? Teaching and doing research, instead of getting drunk after Friday colloquia and chasing the nearest skirt?"

An awkward silence after this, nothing but the clinking of glasses and forks for a while, until Ted turned to Addie. Scarlet was prepared for this, though she wondered why he kept bothering. Every time Ted (or Lou, or anyone for that matter) tried to reason with Addie about her passions, her despair over unchecked development, the contamination of groundwater, global warming, anything, she'd argue for a while, then put up her hands and say, "It's a simple question really, isn't it? If I'm wrong, who loses? Various multimillionaires. If you're wrong, who loses?" Then she'd pause, and smile. "Your children." Another pause, and then, "So I'm not sure why you're arguing with me."

Her moral superiority, her absolute confidence, were actually admirable, Scarlet sometimes felt. She kind of enjoyed these qualities of Addie's, when she wasn't on the receiving end.

On this occasion, though, Ted took a slightly different approach. "So, Addie," he said, "what *is* it with you and these youthful anarchists you've been consorting with?" He'd had several glasses of wine by this time.

Addie stared at him before taking a slow, deliberate sip of water. "I'm not sure what you mean by 'anarchists,' Ted."

"Well, isn't it a form of anarchy to set several new homes on fire? I can hardly think of a better example, actually." He looked around the table for corroboration. Tom stared at his plate, and Scarlet set down her fork, unable to pretend to eat any more. Lou's lip was curled in a nasty sneer; she was ready for this, it was clear. Probably she'd been waiting for it all day.

"Well, that surprises me, Ted," Addie said. "I'd think you'd have all kinds of time to come up with far better examples, there in your cozy

Georgetown office, far more interesting examples of 'anarchy' and 'dissent' than our little battles up in rural Pennsylvania."

Lou snorted with laughter.

Ted smiled, then tipped his glass toward Addie. "On the contrary, Addie. I'm fascinated by your little battles. And so I really must ask you, how did it feel to strike that match? Or wait, surely you're not going to tell us you didn't actually do it. Why in the world would you be spending all this time at my house if that's the case?"

"Ted," Lou said then, as Tom rose from the table and excused himself. But Ted ignored her.

"Of course, I could understand your enjoying all this time with my lovely wife, the fine wine, the wonderful meals she serves——"

"Ted, just shut up, please."

He looked over at Lou. "Why? Why should I shut up? I'm simply trying to understand Addie's strategy here." He turned to face Addie again. "*Is* this a strategy of some sort, Addie? All part of some master plan you and your friends have?"

Scarlet expected Addie to take her usual approach. So what if Ted was twisting the argument a bit this time, personalizing it, making it a little more uncomfortable for Addie, for everyone? Surely, Scarlet thought, Addie would still find a way to her moral high ground, the perch she always landed on, smiling down at everyone below her. So it surprised her, when she looked over at her mother, to see her staring at her plate, speechless, and—though Scarlet could hardly believe this—seemingly on the verge of tears.

Ted, however, was only warming up. He took a big swallow of wine, then reached up to loosen his tie. He'd grown heavier in recent years, his neck thicker, a slight paunch pressing against the buttons of his well-pressed shirts. He was still handsome, though, his wavy hair peppered with gray, kept just long enough to give him a youthful, casual look. Except for the expensive suits, and the paunch, he could have been modeling himself on Tom. At times it shocked Scarlet to recall that her father had once been this man's teacher.

"You get to be the hero for a while, maybe? Is that it?" He smiled at Addie as he spoke, ignoring her obvious discomfort. "To hell with your husband and daughter, to hell with any kind of normal life for them. What's more important is being a hero for the cause, right?"

Lou, on the other hand, wasn't smiling now. "I said shut up, Ted. Just shut the fuck *up!*"

He turned to her. "Oh, and I suppose you're suddenly ready to *defend* this kind of juvenile behavior? Didn't you just say, at this very table two nights ago, that you're surprised Addie hasn't outgrown all of this by now?"

Now Lou slammed down her fork, then her big linen napkin. It was a shame, Scarlet thought at the time, that all that rich food was going to go to waste; she didn't get the sense that Lou and Ted ate leftovers. For a moment, she let herself get lost in interesting, if irrelevant, questions about how Addie might be dealing with all the excess, and all the waste, in a household like theirs. It was easier to think about that than about what Addie might be feeling at that moment. Or about the fact that, deep down, some part of Scarlet was enjoying this. Weren't these the very questions she had longed to ask Addie herself?

Now Addie excused herself. "Fuck you, Ted," Lou said, and ran after her.

Scarlet carried Addie's and her plates into the kitchen and headed upstairs to say good-night to Suzy and Liz. When she glanced into the dining room on her way past, Ted was eating again, and reading a magazine. Later, when she went outside to get her bag from Tom's car, she could hear Tom and Addie arguing, in the apartment above the garage. No one said anything about that evening for the rest of the visit. And after that evening, Scarlet always ate dinner with Suzy and Liz.

Suzy and Liz, who were only five and seven at the time, were already angry; they were difficult kids. But who could blame them for their surliness? Scarlet thought. They were only reacting to the same things she hated: fake gaiety, too much drinking, all that explosive anger under the surface, occasionally erupting in nasty exchanges like the one that night. Exchanges that, amazingly, no one ever commented on later.

Tom, who mostly sat back and watched, eating well but drinking little, often left for long walks alone: he looked like a confused child himself. How in God's name did we get here? Scarlet knew he was thinking. She felt, watching him, that he must hate Lou. Lou, who kept on making the dinners and orchestrating the museum visits and gathering everyone for movies at night, even though it was clear—because she did, in fact, say it often enough, at dinner, after a cocktail or two and a couple glasses of wine—that she thought Addie's actions were foolish.

Scarlet wanted to hate Lou too, for reasons she couldn't explain. But even then—in the midst of that gray and bitter fall, when her mother fled Pennsylvania, accused of colluding in an ideologically driven act of arson—even then she could see the tenderness Lou felt for Addie. The way she cared for her, despite the obvious strain it put on her already crumbling marriage. Despite the fact that she professed to find Addie's convictions ludicrous.

To this day Scarlet remains uncertain, divided—still torn between impatience with Lou's childish narcissism and admiration for her chutzpah, her thumb in the eye of propriety and womanly sweetness and other forms of wasted energy. For a while she thought she wanted to be like Lou. Beautiful, pampered, sharp-edged, and memorable. What she didn't want was the sadness behind it all.

"What I always heard about was the coffee and the Art Building and the sleeping for twenty-four hours," Scarlet says now, continuing to play along. "Somehow the sex with beautiful boys part got left out."

"Yes, well, you're what, thirty-four now? And enjoying your own series of beautiful boys, I hope. Maybe now you're ready for the awful truth, Scarlet." Lou laughs and swings her legs over the arm of the rocker again. She apparently walked all night in one of the more beautiful pairs of sandals—sleek, strappy things—Scarlet has ever seen. She is admiring Lou's perfect pedicure when Lou points an accusing finger at her.

"I was nearly your age when I decided it was time to put an end to all that and get married and really *mean* it, and have a family and settle and put down roots, and blah, blah, blah." She rolls her eyes and sweeps her hand through her hair defiantly. "It's a trap that *you* can still avoid, if you're smart enough to do so.

"And look at you! You look fantastic—you've got at least ten more years of sex with beautiful men if you keep doing whatever it is you're doing." She takes a lusty bite out of a second muffin, then adds, "Have I told you, Scarlet, that you look lovelier than I think I've ever seen you? Doesn't she, Cora?"

Cora nods, and the corners of her mouth twitch—with either a suppressed smile or a suppressed rebuttal, or both. Maybe, Scarlet thinks, she *does* look better than ever. She's been running faithfully, her skin is in good shape, her hair suddenly seems to have a thickness and waviness it never had before. She is too awash in a sea of unfamiliar hormones to have any real confidence about her physical appearance, but enough people have told her, recently, that she's "glowing" for her to believe everything people say about what pregnancy does for you.

"*What* in God's name are you using to get your skin to look like that, by the way?" Lou asks, reaching for the carafe of coffee.

Scarlet feels the heat rising to her cheeks; a compliment from Lou—the only person from her parents' generation, Addie and Tom included, ever to notice, much less comment on, her appearance—has always had this effect on her.

Cora seems on the verge of saying something, but Scarlet shoots her a look that says no. Not now. Not with Lou. And Cora nods, almost imperceptibly.

"I guess Cider Cove agrees with me," is all Scarlet says, shrugging.

Lou stares at her for a moment, then smiles. "All right, fine. Keep your secrets. But if it's Botox, I want to know where you're getting it." She laughs loudly, then suddenly grows pensive.

Scarlet is stunned for a moment; she can't quite imagine where this has come from. Botox? she thinks. Please, Lou—I'm Addie and Tom Kavanagh's daughter. I've given up caffeine and the occasional joint I used to smoke, and I'm no longer highlighting my hair. I've already scheduled an appointment with a group of midwives in New York, and I'm reading up on breastfeeding. Please, Lou.

"Honestly, Lou." Cora says it for her. "Botox?"

And then Lou is sobbing, her face buried in her hands.

"Why not?" she says as she cries, her voice harsh and needlessly loud. "Why not Botox? Don't you want to talk about Botox and all the other things the women I know talk about—when they aren't talking about their decorators or bitching about the help, that is? Botox, plastic surgery, liposuction. Microdermabrasion. Laser vein therapy. Cosmetic dentistry. We're a fascinating lot, let me tell you. Remarkably diverse in our interests."

She laughs bitterly, then stares ahead of her, as if she's talking to someone else, not to Cora or Scarlet. "What *else* do women have to talk about, at my age?" she asks, her voice dripping with contempt.

She covers her face with her hands again, and when she speaks, a minute later, her voice has suddenly changed. "All I'm saying," she says, so softly Cora and Scarlet both lean forward to hear her, "all I'm saying, Scarlet, is remember what a fucking pack of lies it is, all of it." She sniffs, wiping her eyes on the napkin Cora has handed her.

"Just don't have children," she says then. "That's when it starts, that's when it all crumbles around you. Look at us, look at all of us. My daughters barely talk to me." She points to Cora. "Think of all Cora's gone through. And Addie . . . oh, God, I won't pretend to understand Addie. But much as she loved you and Tom, and of course she did, obviously she did, but still, look how crazy it made her, trapped there at Burnham with all those throwbacks to the nineteenth century, nowhere to go with all that talent, stuck there in that rotten old cabin."

Cora seems to be staring into her coffee cup. "Stop it, Lou," she whispers through clenched teeth.

"It's all right," Scarlet says. "I want to hear this." She turns to Lou. "Go ahead, Lou."

Lou looks up and out the window, then sighs deeply. "Christ," she says at last. "Christ. You have to know I don't mean that Addie shouldn't have had you, Scarlet, that any of us shouldn't have had kids. Or that Addie's life was any worse than mine, or anyone else's."

She turns her gaze to Scarlet. "I have a beautiful house, and I hate it. I'd rather live in a cabin beside a stream, if you want to know the truth. My ex-husband has managed to convince our daughters that our despising each other is entirely my fault. I spend my time, energy, and a good bit of my money on my own appearance, despite the fact that no man is ever going to look at me with anything approaching desire again. And so I channel all my surplus sexual energy into expensive food and art I don't really care about and maintaining the fucking *showplace* of a house I created for Ted, always for Ted, who needed to entertain people from Georgetown, he said, who constantly had his sights set on better things—including a whole gaggle of willing and eager graduate students, all his little political theorists in training and on the make, each of whom he was screwing, one after another right there in his office, then coming home for a cocktail party on our back verandah—can you believe we called it our fucking *verandah*—oozing all his oily charm, talking up the president's wife, glad-handing everyone in the room.

"God, he was good at it. It made me sick, and at the same time, I can't explain this, it turned me on. Even in the midst of all that, even knowing what he was doing, practically right in front of me, I still ached for him; sometimes I think we had the best sex when I hated him the most. At least at the end.

"And so I kept it up—for years I kept it up. I hired the caterers and ordered the wine and decorated, and redecorated, and re-redecorated, until I thought I'd throw up if I looked at one more copy of *House Beautiful* or *Architectural Digest*."

She pauses for a moment, looking out the window. "You know," she says, her voice softer now, "years ago we had a neighbor—crazy old guy, a retired professor of something or other, scourge of the neighborhood, that kind of thing. He had all these hideous overgrown hydrangea and peony bushes—two of the uglier flowers known to man, you have to admit—that were taking over his yard, along with about two hundred species of weeds, ivy going crazy, growing into his window screens. Peeling paint, the whole business. He'd let the whole thing go to hell. Whole families of squirrels were nesting in his two chimneys, and he didn't even care.

"And one day last year I just stood on the verandah and watched the squirrels climbing in and out of his chimneys, gathering their stash for the winter, whatever it is they do, and it dawned on me: I envied him, *really* envied him. I was *dying* to live like that, like my crazy neighbor, to let everything go, let it all just rot away around me."

She pauses, taking a deep, audible breath. Then she says, more quietly, "That was what I said to Addie last night. I said, 'Addie, I'm so tired. I'm so tired, and all I want to do is let it all rot. I want to live in the middle of the rot.'"

"What did she say?" Cora asks.

"Just what you'd expect. 'Rot's vital, Lou. It's teeming with life, a good place to live. You should try it.'" She takes another breath, exhaling with a little laugh.

They're quiet for a moment, and then Scarlet asks, "So why don't you? Let it all go, I mean?"

Lou doesn't look at Scarlet when she answers. "Because I won't give him the satisfaction of watching that happen to me," she says. "He'd use it to try one more time to get at my inheritance."

Scarlet has heard bits and pieces of this, in recent years—details about Lou and Ted's mean, protracted divorce, his contention that he needs access to a portion of Lou's inheritance—which is a sizable one—so that it might be properly monitored and invested, for their daughters' sakes.

"Well, you've already heard my idea about that," Cora says, reaching for a shawl that's hanging on a hook behind her and wrapping it around Lou, who's begun to shiver, despite the warm sunlight that's replaced the chill of the early morning. "Give it away. The girls are adults now, and you've already put aside enough for them. Put aside a bit more for yourself and give the rest away. Then you'd be finished with Ted once and for all." She sits back down and folds her arms across her chest, looking at Lou with a half smile, as if she knows this is a safe suggestion, unlikely as Lou is to take it seriously.

Lou gazes out the window, nodding absently. Her face, in the now glaring light, looks older, and wistful.

"Unless . . ." Cora says, sighing as she turns back to face the table and her newspaper.

"Unless?" Lou turns to face her.

"Unless that really *isn't* what you want. To be completely free of Ted, I mean." She slides her glasses back onto her nose and turns a page. The silence between them now is full and heavy. They know each other, and they knew Addie, in a way she never could, Scarlet thinks. She finds this strangely comforting, which is a welcome change. For years it bothered her, the way she felt so left out of this part of Addie's life.

Years ago, during the year she spent living in Cora's house, Scarlet discovered a book Addie had sent to Cora: the diary and letters of the artist Käthe Kollwitz. She read the book obsessively, fascinated by these day-to-day observations and frustrations of a working artist and mother. Kollwitz herself became a bit of an obsession for Scarlet then, one that would last a number of years.

An artist and a mother. An artist who was, in fact, a champion of mothers, and of the poor. A graphic artist and sculptor with a social conscience, a woman who created realistic depictions of struggling workers and grieving mothers simply because, she said, she found them "beautiful." More beautiful by far than the bourgeoisie. Not attempting, really, to be iconoclastic, to shock—though perhaps she *did* wish to disturb the viewers of her work. Devoted to her children, one of whom she lost in the First World War, and to her husband, despite times of despair over her work. She had found, Scarlet thought, the ideal artist-mother. Why couldn't Addie be more like *that?*

Of course Addie *was* like that. Struggling to make something, in the midst of so much sadness. But it would take some time, and several more readings of Kollwitz's diaries, for Scarlet to see this. And now she can also see that Addie herself wasn't particularly interested in any parallels between herself and Kollwitz. She sent the diaries to Cora, another grieving mother, with the hope that they might comfort and inspire her.

In fact they did provide Cora with a kind of comfort, though she didn't read the diaries carefully until two years after Addie sent her the book, when Karl died, suddenly and unexpectedly, of a heart attack. For the year that followed, Cora locked her door and threw pots and read, day and night—Kollwitz's diaries, other books by and about artists. At the end of that year she emerged, ready, it seemed, to face the world again; in another year she would open her home as a quiet, simple bed-and-breakfast.

When Scarlet visited during those first years of Cora's new business, she had to swallow her disappointment at sometimes sharing Cora's marvelous breakfasts with paying guests, at strangers tossing Karl's old boccie balls in the backyard. She missed Karl's quiet presence, the salami and eggs he sometimes cooked on Sundays, his random piles of books and magazines scattered throughout the house. The way he told the same corny jokes the summer before she left for college that he'd told when she was thirteen. His gentle solicitousness with Cora.

Surely Cora missed all those things too, and more. What had she done to find her way out of her grief and loneliness that year after Karl's death? "I read," was all she told Scarlet. "I worked on my pots."

Presumably she told Addie and Lou more. Or maybe she didn't need to.

They know each other so well, these women, Scarlet thinks. Lou is crying again, quietly now.

"It's pathetic, isn't it?" she says. "That I could still love him."

"No, love, it's not pathetic," Cora says. Her tone is dry, factual, not particularly warm; she makes no effort to reach out to Lou.

"That day I stood and watched the squirrels, something had happened earlier," Lou says, pulling a pack of cigarettes from her pocket and simply holding it for a moment—absentmindedly, almost tenderly—before dropping it on the table in front of her. "I was renting the apartment above the garage in the back—the one where Addie stayed, Scarlet, remember?" Scarlet nods, remembering those clean, nearly empty rooms all too well.

"I was renting it for next to nothing to a friend of Liz's, a student. I'd gotten up early and gone out to the greenhouse to transplant some perennials I'd started, and when I reached the door I heard a sound, an unmistakable one, two people having sex, moaning, breathing hard, really going at it. It was this girl and her boyfriend, and they'd pulled a mattress down there, right there on the floor of the greenhouse, below the geraniums and hibiscus I had wintering in there.

"And who could blame them? It was a wonderful spot, warm and steamy, and of course it smelled heavenly. I'd done it there myself a time or two." Here she pauses for a moment, stopping at a sharp look from Cora.

"What?" Scarlet says, confused. "Now all of a sudden I'm the young innocent again? You have to protect me from something?"

No one says anything for a while, and Scarlet feels, for some reason, suddenly hot and uncomfortable. They've sidled up to something forbidden, and she knows it; she has a feeling she knows more too, somehow. More than she wants to know.

They're silent like this, tense and silent for a long while. Scarlet clears her throat, ready to excuse herself, when Lou speaks again, her voice even quieter now, deep and hoarse.

"No, listen. What I remembered that day was actually something lovely, something from so long ago . . . I stood there at the greenhouse door and watched for a while; I couldn't tear myself away. What I saw between those two was so different from my own clumsy, ridiculous escapades in there."

She and Cora exchange a quick glance, and she goes on, "I knew the difference because I remembered feeling like that. Feeling real passion, I mean. And what I remembered was being in Greece with Ted, when we were still so young. It was right after he dropped out of medical school, and we'd had a huge fight and gone off to screw other people and then come back together, all contrite, the way we always did in those days. And we decided to go to Europe for a while, get away, think about what Ted might do next to avoid the draft. That's how young we were. God, Cora, remember those days?"

Cora nods, watching Lou closely.

"Anyway, we headed pretty quickly for Greece, and we hopped all over the islands. But what I remember was an afternoon on Santorini, one of those gorgeous black-sand beaches, that volcanic sand. We were both naked, everyone there was naked, and we dove in for a swim, and when we walked out of the water we just looked at each other, and I swear to you, I have *never* again felt what I felt at that moment, before or since. He felt it too."

She closes her eyes. "The deepest yearning I've ever felt. Something to do with that sand, and that light and wind and blue-green water. Maybe with thinking he could be sent off to fight in a stupid, meaningless war. I don't know, I don't have a word for it. Passion doesn't mean anything anymore, that doesn't do it somehow, but I'd have to say that's what it was. The real thing. Real passion, pure and simple. He grabbed my hand and we ran, I mean *ran*, for the nearest hidden spot we could find, a patch of sand between some rocks at the base of the cliff behind us. No towel or blanket with us, nothing, we wouldn't have wanted it anyway. And we *dove* onto that sand, and we just tore at each other. . . ."

Scarlet glances at Cora, whose eyes are closed behind her reading glasses. Again she feels uncomfortably warm, sweat trickling down her side. She is trying to understand what's happening in the room.

Lou opens her eyes for a moment, then rubs them, laughing bitterly. "Oh, my God," she says. "I sound like some kind of goddamn Harlequin romance. I'm sorry."

"No, you don't," Scarlet says. Because for once, she thinks, Lou *doesn't* sound like a cheap romance novel. For once she is simply telling the truth. "Go on," she says. "What happened next?" What she'd like to ask Lou is "How did you go from that moment on the beach to the bitterness you've been soaking in for years?" She has her own reasons for wanting to know.

Lou laughs again. "Well," she says, "we eventually fell asleep, and when we woke up it was completely dark, and we had no idea where our clothes were. We finally found them, and then we had dinner at a little restaurant near the hotel we were staying in. And it was so strange—we were almost *shy* with each other then. We'd been having sex for several years by then, but it was clear to both of us that something was different about that afternoon, something had changed. I think it scared us both.

"The next morning we got up early and went to see an exhibit of these ancient cave drawings nearby. And there was one I'll never forget, of two birds, flying, gliding through the air, and one of them seemed to be reaching for the other one, like a lover.

"'Look, it's Addie and Tom,' Ted said. I laughed, but then I just stared at it for the longest time. All of a sudden I felt like I understood, for the first time, what it was between the two of them. I guess I'd always thought she'd just had a crush, the kind I was always having, and of course he was flattered and attracted to this beautiful young girl—who wouldn't have been? But something about what had happened to us on the beach the day before, and then seeing these beautiful, yearning birds . . . There it was again, I thought: passion. It seemed like I'd just never grasped it before.

"There were cards for sale in a little shop there, reproductions of the paintings, and I bought one with a picture of the two gliding birds and sent it to Addie. I think I wrote something about how Ted said they reminded him of Addie and Tom. For some reason I felt embarrassed to tell her the truth, to tell her I felt like I'd seen something about her for the first time. And I think I felt afraid too. Afraid to tell anyone about what I was feeling, for Ted.

"I felt so in love with him that morning it scared me," she says, then covers her eyes with one hand. "Nothing has ever come close to that since."

She lowers her hand to her mouth, and her eyes look almost frightened. Scarlet tries to think of something to say—it seems like Lou needs comforting now, though Scarlet isn't sure why, and she certainly can't imagine what to say to offer her comfort—when Lou lowers her hand and speaks again.

"I got pregnant that day. I didn't even realize it for something like six weeks, and then when I did, two days later I had a miscarriage."

"Lou . . ." Cora says, her voice a whisper, and then she covers her mouth with her hand.

Lou looks at Cora and gives a sharp little laugh. "Can you believe that? Here you and Addie were, back here starting your families and setting up households, and there I was on the other side of the world, acting like some naive sixteen-year-old or something, deciding to overlook the fact that, obviously, I didn't have my diaphragm with me that afternoon. And then drinking and smoking dope and screwing around like I always did, acting like nothing was different because it never would have occurred to me that it was."

She shakes her head, then blows her nose and smiles ruefully. "Ted was sweet about it. 'It's better this way, Lou,' he said to me. But I saw something in his eyes—I could tell he was shaken by the whole thing. And I know he blamed me."

She dabs her tissue at the corner of an eye. "To this day I wonder if things might have been different. If I'd realized it, I mean. And if we'd had the baby we made that day."

Cora stands now, then kneels next to Lou and takes her hands in her own. She starts to say something, then stops, changing her mind.

Lou looks at her and says, "You know I went on to have an abortion another time after that, right? Indeed I did. That was Ted's idea. He said he needed to finish his course work first." She draws a deep, halting breath, then turns to Scarlet.

"I'm sorry, Scarlet," she says. "What a thing to talk about the morning after Addie's death. I can't explain where that came from. I haven't thought about that for years." She turns to look out the window, and Cora goes back to her chair across the table from Scarlet. No one says anything for a while.

"Addie taped that card to the big mirror in the hall outside our bedrooms," Scarlet finally says. "I can still picture it. As far as I know it's still there."

"Ted even knew what kind of birds they were," Lou says. "Of course I've forgotten."

"They were barn swallows," Tom says suddenly, from somewhere behind Scarlet. Instinctively all three women sit up in their chairs, like guilty schoolgirls.

"*Hirundo rustica*. Rusty red throat, white spots on a split tail. Though the flight doesn't look right; barn swallows don't tend to glide like that. And yes, it's still up on the mirror." He pulls a chair up next to Scarlet's, and smiles gratefully as Cora hands him the muffins and a cup of coffee. He looks tired and, Scarlet thinks as she watches him, suddenly much older.

"I'll go make some more," Cora says, rising with the carafe in hand. She is visibly relieved to see him. "Any sign of your plovers, Tom?" she asks before she goes. She's become an increasingly avid bird-watcher herself in recent years.

"Not this morning, no," he answers, as Lou continues to stare out the window.

Scarlet needs to pee, but something has made her reluctant to leave the room. She feels afraid, somehow, to leave Lou and her father alone together. Part of her is desperate to know what they might say to each other. Another part of her can't bear the thought.

"So have you all solved the dilemma of what we're going to do next?" Tom asks.

If she were alone with her father, Scarlet thinks, she would laugh out loud at the question. "No, no," she would say; "first we had to talk about

Lou and her problems. As usual. Yes, Addie's dead, and yes, we have to deal with a few things, just little things, like whether to honor her last request or just do the sensible thing and have her cremated. Nothing too pressing. Of course Lou's sad and desperate love life would come first."

But even as she thinks this, she knows it isn't fair. Who could have guessed that Lou, of all people, would feel something like guilt, and a sense of loss, over a miscarriage that happened over thirty years ago? She loved Ted then, and she probably still does. All she really wanted was what Cora had with Karl, and Addie had with Tom.

But then why in God's name choose someone like Ted? Scarlet thinks of asking her. But she doesn't; she knows she's no authority here. How rational is anyone's choice of whom to love?

"No," Scarlet says. "We didn't get to that yet. Waiting for you, I guess." She smiles at her father, still so handsome, even with his graying hair and a chin that's begun to sag a bit, and now two days' growth of beard. He clearly hasn't slept at all.

"No?" He lifts his eyebrows in mock surprise. Then, "How do you feel, Scarlet?" he asks as he spreads jam on a muffin. He takes a bite, then starts to rub her back. "Did you sleep a bit at least? You should get some rest, you know."

Lou looks at the two of them sharply then, curiously. Probably, Scarlet thinks, she's already figured it out. And then she remembers something Addie said to her last night: "The whole world adores a mother-to-be. Go ahead and milk it." She takes a deep breath, closes her eyes, and leans back into her father's strong, gentle hands.

"Thanks," she says. "That feels wonderful."

She'll pee in a minute, she decides. For now she'll sit here quietly and let her father soothe her, keeping at least a few of her own secrets, for at least a little while.

eleven

ADDIE HAD ALWAYS BEEN MOODY, prone to bouts of sadness, even as a child. Maybe that was it, she sometimes thought; maybe she was depressed. Maybe she had something called "depression." Always, of course, said a certain way—slowly, dolefully, eyes cast down and mouth in a tight line. I have de-*PRESH*-on.

If she had the slightest faith in Western medicine, pharmacology, or the entire field of psychology, perhaps she might have sought such a diagnosis. Then they could have dosed her or shocked her or done something else to ensure, once and for all, that she never again drew or painted *anything* of any value whatsoever. So long as she felt, if not cheerful, at least contented, complacent, unbothered. Optimistic.

You think too much, her mother used to say to her, when she was a mopey child. Also, later, *You read too much.* Or, *You're off in the woods by yourself all day—no wonder you're sad! Why don't you spend more time with some friends?*

And so she had. She'd gone off with friends, danced and smoked and gotten drunk, fooled around with boys. At college she'd found herself a steady boyfriend, and she'd allowed him to fondle her, and she'd done the same for him; they'd always stopped short of intercourse, though, as she'd been urged, in all quarters, to do. Her boyfriend would have been shocked (if delighted) if she'd allowed things to go that far; certainly that would have removed her from the category of marriage-worthy girls.

It hadn't felt like that much of a hardship, forgoing the final act of sex.

She didn't especially mind the kissing and the fondling, sometimes she even enjoyed it—but mostly she did it to keep her boyfriend happy. *She* was happiest, though, when she was with Cora and Lou. Laughing endlessly, baking a cake at midnight and eating the entire thing, arguing about whether God existed (Cora, the science major, said of course not, Addie said she wasn't sure, and Lou feigned shock at both responses—though Addie always suspected the shock was real).

Then came England, Miss Smallwood to steer her, the rush of all those discoveries. And then Tom. And then she discovered what they clearly hadn't wanted her—or any girl—to know about sex. Dangerous to discover it could feel like that—that in fact there were deep, impossible-to-describe pleasures available for her as well. Dangerous, that is, in the hands of someone less careful, less solicitous, than Tom. How had she known, implicitly, without question, from that first day in his class, how fully she could trust him?

Maybe it was what he'd recognized about her, immediately: her longing. It was for him, for his body, certainly; no doubt about that. The first time they'd made love, on the floor of the untouched, nearly rotting cottage, he'd worried he might hurt her. But she hadn't felt a moment's pain, only something that made her feel like singing, like laughing, bubbling over with it, with the impossible delight of his rough cheeks beneath her hands and lips, his tight, wiry body clasping hers, the way he searched and searched until he found her.

But it was more than that physical longing, and he'd known that, and it was he, Tom, who'd told her this: Go back into the woods by yourself. And you'll find it there, again. And for a while she *had* found it again, that thing, whatever it was, that she'd felt in the woods when she was younger. Something hard to name—maybe wonder? Almost a kind of ecstasy? No, too loaded a word—too pious and yet too sexual, both at the same time.

But then, it *was* like God, wasn't it? And also in a way very much like sex? The way she'd felt, as a child of ten or twelve, alone in the woods. Almost trembling, breathless, unaware of herself or of time—seated on a rotting log, smelling wet leaves, feeling the damp air, hearing the silence.

Wonder was better, probably.

When had it stopped?

When she'd had Scarlet?

"It's because nothing is as miraculous as that, and nothing ever will be," Cora said.

But Lou, of course, rolled her eyes. "It's because once you have a child you're never again free to think about yourself, and no one will ever let you forget it. Which means it's never again possible to *lose* yourself. No matter how many yoga classes or meditation retreats you go to. Take my word for it."

Cora didn't disagree. "It's true you aren't free to lose yourself then, ever," she said. "You're needed too much, too fiercely, and you never forget that." Poor Cora, who, for so long, blamed herself.

But to say she had somehow lost wonder, lost the ability to lose herself—in the woods, in her work—after Scarlet's birth felt wrong, too easy an explanation, too much the language of women's magazines, which she hated. Look at Scarlet, after all. She was her own person already, by the age of four—fiercely independent, but also careful, smart. Interested in things. She'd never worried about Scarlet. Her experience of motherhood was worlds away from Cora's, and from Lou's.

So was it Tom, then? Killing wonder with science? Burying her work beneath his? For a while she worried that she'd never find her way back to work of her own that was satisfying if she stayed with Tom, oppressed by his work, his needs, his various demands. Hadn't people immediately started referring to *A Prosody of Birds* as Tom's book—even though her name was right there on the cover alongside his, and even though Tom repeatedly told people that the plates of her paintings were by far the best thing about the book?

So *was* Tom—silent, patient Tom—still somehow, despite all his outward signs of support, to blame for her loss of wonder, and of love of her own work? Sometimes she thought, maybe so. It felt good to be able to blame him, sometimes. Otherwise she might have to think about other things, other possible reasons why she could hardly bear to face a blank canvas, or even a sketch pad.

But of course it also felt faintly ridiculous. All he wanted, he told her over and over, was for her to be delighted, again, by the birds.

She *was* still delighted by the birds at times. Awash in a familiar, comforting warmth when she heard the call of a Carolina wren or a red-eyed vireo and knew it immediately. As instinctively, now, as Tom would. And capable of a different sort of warmth, even a grateful smile, when she heard her first wood thrush in the spring.

But the thing was, the moment she heard it, before she was able to savor, fully, that pleasant hum of knowing, there came another kind of knowing, a voice that hit her like a crashing, freezing wave. That bird's breeding grounds are being decimated, even as you stand here listening. Before long it won't have these second-growth trees, this makeshift habitat, to roost in either.

And so really, why draw, or paint, the thing at all? Some kind of memento mori for all those stupidly cheerful, binoculars-wearing, American "backyard birders"? Those ponchoed men and women racing each other to the longest life list?

"Addie, you're taking this too far," Tom said when she tried once to explain to him what happened to her, more often than not, when she went to her blind to sketch. "All of them, Addie—Carson, Leopold, Edward Abbey—you need to put them all aside now. Read something else, look at it differently. Remember, it's quite possible, even probable, that the damage done through the history of human habitation—if you think of that, say, as half a day instead of several billion years—it's quite likely that that level of damage could be completely turned around in another half day. We've no way of knowing! Why automatically assume the worst?"

"That's the kind of thinking that gave us Agent Orange and arsenic in our drinking water," was her quiet, clipped answer. Tom left the room then, and slammed the door behind him; he was heading for his office, she knew, at eight o'clock on a Friday night. Scarlet was next door at Peter's. And suddenly Addie hated being so alone.

You think too much. You read too much.

That time, when Scarlet was twelve, they took a trip over the spring break, to the Everglades and the Florida Keys.

They'd forgotten, it seemed, about the shorebirds. It revived all of them, watching ibises and egrets in the marshes and tidepools, anhingas rising over the mangroves. When they returned to Burnham, Scarlet raced over to show Peter her new collection of shells and sea glass. Tom, tanned and rested, gathered his notes for another five-week offering of Biology of the Birds.

And Addie set herself up in an empty studio in the Burnham Art Building, two doors down from the studio she'd used as a student, thinking it might do her good to get out of the house, and away from the creek, for this next attempt at new work. She got going on an Audubon-inspired painting of an anhinga, and each day she climbed the hill to the campus, sketchbooks and a sandwich in a pack on her back. All morning she worked, day after day, sipping at a water bottle, struggling over and over with the neck, which looked, she felt, like something in a *Road Runner* cartoon. All morning she tried to capture the hazy Florida light that somehow both brightened and dulled the sheen of the male's wing, struggling to hold on to the smell of salt and fish, to tend only to that particular remembered smell, fighting to hold it there above the encroaching ones of dust, and mildew, and memory, there in that tiny room that reeked of her past, of a self she could barely recall, one she no longer trusted but longed for all the same.

In the end it took her five months to paint that anhinga, a problem she couldn't solve until one hot July night, the night before her departure, with Tom and Scarlet, for the coast of Maine. They'd been invited to spend a month there, in the home of a former student and his wife, who was an avid bird-watcher and a passionate admirer of *A Prosody of Birds.*

She couldn't recall the particulars of the dream, only the oppressive feeling it left her with, as if someone were sitting on her chest and covering her mouth, suffocating her. That, and its *colors*—lurid pinks, greens, oranges, all there in a kind of particle-soaked light, fluorescent or neon, maybe. They were, she knew immediately when she woke, the colors of Florida—of the roadside motels, T-shirt and fast-food stands, makeshift shops selling guns and fireworks. And the suffocating feeling: She recognized that too. It was the feeling she'd had, first paddling in a canoe alongside impossibly tangled mangrove roots, next on a rocky inlet off Big Pine Key at dawn, each time Tom had suggested they plan another sabbatical, this time in Florida.

They couldn't afford to spend another year, or even a semester, in England after all, especially—and this was understood, if unspoken—as no funded research opportunities were likely to be forthcoming for Tom, who'd been immersed, again, in his teaching and note-taking in the field, and who hadn't published a thing since the *Prosody*. Neither of them had thought, or spoken, much about another sabbatical; Addie hardly felt her work could justify that long a trip, away from home, from her illustrating income and her local activism. And Tom was Tom—happy and content to go on teaching, piling up more notes, to what end he could not have said.

So it surprised her when he proposed the idea, not once but twice, each time, of course, in the midst of a particularly satisfying time in the field. But each time he suggested a longer stay in Florida, and she pictured them setting up house in some tiny hamlet in the Everglades or, worse, someplace like Key West, all she could see were those same flashes of neon, those overly bright, falsely cheerful colors.

"I don't think so, Tom," she said the second time. "I just can't see it somehow." And he only shrugged, willing enough to let it go; every suggestion of time away from Burnham was more for her sake than for his, after all.

But if she couldn't see a year in Florida, what she *could* see, waking from her dream on the verge of dawn that morning in July, were those colors, there in her painting of the anhinga. Of course; there it was, the thing the painting needed, handed to her in the middle of the night when she'd finally stopped struggling. She dressed in the still shadows of their bedroom at the back of the cabin and scrambled up the hill to the Art Building. She'd planned to leave the painting behind, hoping a month away might somehow free her from the thing, free her either to finish it at last and move on or just to let it go. Now she packed it carefully, and throughout the endless drive—around New York City, up through Boston, staying the night with an old graduate school friend of Tom's in Woods Hole on Cape Cod, then inching, it seemed, along the ragged coast of Maine—she could hardly stand the wait.

It was the first—and only—thing she unpacked; she left the rest to Tom and Scarlet. And that evening, much to Tom's chagrin and embarrassment, she declined to go to dinner with his former student and his wife, their great fan, who'd driven up from Boston to welcome them. "I'll meet her another time," she insisted, oblivious to Tom's discomfort with going alone. "I can't stop working now."

Twenty-four hours after they arrived, it was, she knew, finished. The changes were, at least superficially, fairly simple ones. Behind the anhinga, which was caught in a sudden, jerking rise into flight, was a pinkish-purple background, cloudlike and billowing: a poison sky. And in the bird's eye—and how she managed to paint this so accurately, Addie could never explain; it had just poured from her brush somehow—was a look, an unmistakable look, of cold terror. Something beyond panic; what one critic would eventually, to Addie's infinite satisfaction, call "a clear awareness of impending, and grisly, death."

She painted happily, ecstatically, for the entire month. She drew on all her old sketches, from Florida and other trips, from her Nisky Creek blind. In each painting—of a red-tailed hawk, a rough-winged swallow, a brown pelican—there was *something*, whether that same look in the eye or an unnaturally bent wing, feathers somehow gone lackluster and coarse, that hinted at imminent violence, imminent pain. Yet there was nothing in the painting to attribute the pain and suffering *to*. Nothing except a garish, neon-saturated background that spoke of something in the air, more pervasive than smoke, a cloud of it surrounding the helpless bird.

Addie's exuberance that month pleased Tom and Scarlet, of course. But it unnerved them a bit as well. What to do with a happy wife and mother like this—singing while she cooked their dinner, tackling and splashing her husband and daughter on their daily walks along the beach at sunset? Here she was again, suddenly: the Addie of Scarlet's earliest memories, and of Tom's fondest ones. Better not to question it, they decided, both of them knowing they'd be wise to hoard the happy moments while they could.

It was Tom's idea to visit Cora and her family in New Jersey on the way back to Burnham. A few days before they were to depart, a letter from Cora had arrived, forwarded to them in Maine from the Burnham post office. She and Karl and the boys were moving in a week, Cora said (she'd written the letter at the end of July), to a town on the New Jersey shore called Cider Cove. She described it as a quiet old fishing town only a few miles from Cape May that had somehow (maybe because it lacked a boardwalk) managed to escape the taffy stands and ski-ball shops that filled the beachfront streets of most of its neighbors.

They were moving there, Cora wrote, for the boys. Even though it meant a hard commute for Karl, and a house that was going to require a lot of work. Childhood teasing was one thing, she said, but junior high school had been absolutely brutal for Richard. And now that he was almost fifteen, even adults in their comfortable, affluent suburb—at the shopping mall or the swim club, at school events, in restaurants—were less than subtle about their discomfort, and distaste, at sharing space with someone like Richard. It was one thing to be a cute, freckled boy who twirled his hair or flapped his arms and spun in circles obsessively, who never looked anyone in the eye and yet, at the same time, had a habit of standing uncomfortably close to people he hadn't even met. But for a tall, gangly young man with facial hair and, suddenly, a deepening voice to do such things—well, that was different. Decidedly different. They hoped things might be better, Cora wrote, in a low-key, blue-collar town like Cider Cove, especially in the quiet, off-season months of the school year.

It had been hard on Bobby too, of course, she said. In fact the move was actually Bobby's idea. "Won't you mind giving up the swim team and the mall and your friends at school?" they'd asked him. His answer had been a terse "What friends?"

Though she felt terrible about not responding to Cora until nearly a month after she'd written, it was good, Addie knew, that Cora's letter had taken so long to reach her. She certainly wouldn't have been able to work with such energy if she'd gotten it earlier. It made her immeasurably sad and then, as was usually the case with things that made her sad, immeasurably angry. How could disorders like Richard's still be happening? she raved to Tom, after showing him the letter. Was *anyone* looking into this, into the obvious links with toxins from burning coal, for instance—didn't Tom remember that research she'd found, when was it, maybe back when Richard had been diagnosed?

"He was *conceived* right there along the Lehigh River, for Christ's sake," she hissed. "Right there in the shadow of those monstrous Bethlehem Steel smokestacks."

They were seated on the back deck, looking out over the steep, rocky slope between the house and the beach below. In the distance they could make out the orange sweatshirt and long, blowing hair of Scarlet, who'd stayed behind on the beach after their walk that afternoon. Breathless from their climb up the path to the house, Tom and Addie had discovered Cora's letter under a rock on the deck, left there by a neighbor who had gone to the post office to pick up mail. Watching Addie's face as she read it, Tom had feared something far more dire and gone inside to fix her a drink.

"Addie," he said now, reaching over to take her hand. "Addie, don't."

But she wouldn't be quieted. She rose and started pacing the length of the deck, taking quick, angry sips from her drink as she spoke. "And then from there to probably the most toxin-filled state in the whole country. Maybe things will be better at the shore, but I sincerely doubt it. How likely is that, really, when you consider everything that gets dumped into Delaware Bay?"

"Addie." He stood now too, and reached for her arm to stop her pacing. He was growing exasperated, and he couldn't stop himself from saying, "If it *was* a product of their environment somehow—and you know I'm convinced it's a genetic disorder, not something that could have been prevented—but if it was, as you insist, somehow connected with where they were living, where they live now hardly matters. The damage is done."

She stared at him then, and when he saw the fury in her eyes he wished, yet again, that he could learn to keep to himself these explanations that so incensed her. She slammed her drink down, spilling it, and turned toward the door.

"Addie, please. You know it doesn't help to—"

And then, suddenly, she was crying. She stopped in front of the door and lowered her head, her shoulders shaking as she sobbed. He went to her, and she buried her face in his shoulder.

Because yes, of course, she knew it didn't help, all her raving. It didn't help, and it had, in fact, hurt her relationship with Cora, this anger, this rage about possible causes of Richard's illness. For years now their contact had been sporadic, even a bit formal; since she'd become involved with the Bucks County Mothers for the Earth ten years before, both Cora and Lou had, she knew, found it hard to endure her angry rants, her clear disapproval of everything from where they lived to what they allowed their children to eat.

In this stunning place on the heels of a solid month of gratifying work, she could see that more clearly now. And she could see how much she missed her old friends, particularly Cora.

"I don't know how to begin to respond to this," she finally said, wiping her nose and holding up Cora's letter. "What can I possibly say?"

"Why don't you call and say you're happy to hear about their move, and that we'd like to stop to see them on our way home from Maine?" he said. He wiped the tears from her cheeks, then kissed them both. "We could stop by the lighthouse at Cape May too," he said. "For old times' sake."

She tried to smile. "Just please don't start talking about sabbaticals again," she said. "Imagine what a wasteland Cape May must be by now, with all the damned tourists, all that development along the coast. It will be completely different, you know—overrun with all those Gore-Tex-clad birders, none of them with any idea of what it was like there twenty years ago—"

"Addie," he said again, his voice quiet and tired. Also warning her.

She swallowed whatever it was she was on the verge of saying next, took a breath and looked out at the sea. "I'll be careful," she said then, quietly. "I'll call her now and ask if we can stop through. I won't say anything else."

When Addie went inside, Tom sat down again. Surely that had been the right suggestion, he hoped. Better for her to see Cora in person; she'd be less likely to go off on one of her harangues then.

He watched as Scarlet turned and began climbing the rocky, winding path. How much easier would her own imminent high school years be? he wondered. No one like Richard to deal with, but they were not, he knew, the easiest parents. Or so he feared. And yet she never seemed to mind the way they lived; she loved traveling as much as they did, and Nisky Creek and her neighborhood friends still seemed to fill her days and satisfy her. But how much longer would she travel contentedly with them, laugh with them, climb into their bed in the morning to read the comics?

As she rounded a curve below the overhanging deck where he sat,

Tom lost sight of his daughter for a moment. He held his breath, seized, suddenly, with something like panic.

Then there she was, climbing the last steps up to the deck—her wild, windswept hair, her wind-chapped face and open brown eyes, like her mother's, like his own.

"Cormorants can't hold a candle to great blue herons," she said, plopping down in a chair, then pulling off her sand-filled sneakers and emptying them, one by one, over the deck's railing. "They are downright *boring* to watch, if you ask me."

"Boring?" he gasped in mock horror. "You find cormorants *boring?*"

Such happiness was what Tom thought then, reaching over to pull playfully on his daughter's tangled hair. Such beauty and such happiness. How in God's name might he make it last?

twelve

THE VISIT TO CIDER COVE surprised all of them. Cora and Karl and the boys were happy in their new home, and happy to share its old, sloping-floored rooms, where Addie, Tom, and Scarlet slept soundly on old mattresses piled on the floor. They ended up staying for a week.

Each day of their visit Tom pushed away thoughts of all the work facing him back in Burnham before classes began, in a matter of days. How could he drag his laughing, suntanned daughter away from this bliss? And something powerful was happening with Addie too, it was clear. She was peaceful, quiet, seemingly content, but her mind was working too—he could see it—as she walked along the beach or sat on the screened porch with Cora in the evenings, drinking wine, sometimes talking, sometimes only listening to the sounds of the sea.

Finally they drove home to Pennsylvania, the night before Scarlet had to return to school—lacking, as usual, the required notebooks and binders, the shoes and uniform for gym, and so on; for a week Addie or Tom wrote vaguely apologetic notes, asking that their daughter be excused from gym class, and Scarlet spent those periods contentedly reading in the cafeteria.

Neither parent could be bothered, that first week, to shop for school supplies—at least not for ones that they could see their daughter neither wanted nor needed. Tom was wrapped up in meetings and the first days of classes. And every day after their return, from early morning until dusk, Addie was holed up in her Art Building studio, painting.

The work she produced that fall was different and, in Tom's opinion, far more powerful than the paintings she'd done in Maine, with their circuslike colors, their expressions of exaggerated, distinctly *human* emotions projected onto birds. Cartoonish, he might have said, though he understood—theoretically, if not in his mind or heart—the power these paintings would hold for many viewers.

The paintings after their week in Cider Cove were disturbing in a far more immediate, and visceral, way, and at times weirdly comic. Some were realistic, like the one of a robin below the cavity nest inside a purple martin's house, unable to walk on its deformed feet. Others, though realistic in execution, had elements of the surreal: a female scarlet tanager feeding her young, not via her beak, but from a nipple rising from a small, round breast in the middle of her yellow front.

She'd taken to carrying her twenty-year-old course notes from his Biology of the Birds class to the studio with her. Tom asked, once, to see that notebook; it was, as he'd expected, a scattershot affair, like her field notes, where she'd reveled in flouting the conventions he'd presented to the class. Not so personal as her field notes, but every bit as eccentric, the notebook was filled with rough sketches (often of him), along with trenchant observations of her classmates and plans for her next painting, or for the weekend. And occasionally, a fact or a remark from one of his lectures that had, apparently, struck her for some reason. Now, more than fifteen years later, she'd gone back to this notebook, highlighting certain of those facts and observations:

> *Alfred Russell Wallace grew disillusioned with the tenets of organic evolution late in life; he later became a spiritualist. One thing he objected to was forced vaccinations, especially for the poor.*
> *Photographs always have distorted colors—which is why artists' renderings are better.*
> *Brood parasites (e.g., cowbirds) do not build their own nests. Phoebes are "acceptors."*

There are two types of false nests: (1) cock or dummy, and
(2) refuge.
Passerines (e.g., robins) have to be raised in cup nests—or their feet
will be deformed.
The ancient Egyptians considered birds winged souls.
The hormones that cause milk letdown in the crops of birds are similar
to those that cause letdown in human mammary ducts.
Birds: male by default. Mammals: female by default.
Waves of migration are triggered by changes in the weather in the
eastern U.S.
Genetically, birds like plovers know where to go and how to get there,
even though the young travel separately from their parents.

When, in the early spring, Addie was gathering the work she would include in a show at a gallery in New Hope, whose owner—another former student of Tom's—was in love with her new paintings, Tom suggested she use relevant passages from her notebook as accompanying captions. He was worried, of course, that the many levels of her work would be lost on most viewers, and worried too about negative reactions setting Addie back. Wouldn't it enrich the experience of seeing her work, he asked, for its viewers to know about the effect on passerines of being raised in false nests? Or that milk letdown in a bird's internal crop is triggered, like the letdown of human milk, hormonally?

She smiled indulgently at his suggestion, then kissed him. "I'll think about it, Dr. Kavanagh," she said, patting his cheek. She was more affectionate, in the weeks leading up to her show, than she'd been in months, maybe years.

In the end, she'd opted for simple titles instead. The painting of the robin with deformed feet she called *False Refuge*, the one of the scarlet tanager with a human breast *Female by Default*.

Reactions to her show were mixed. A reviewer from the Allentown newspaper called the Florida series "goofy." But the show was also re-

viewed (several pages into the Saturday "regional" section) in the Philadelphia *Inquirer,* whose critic called the work "troubling and powerful"
and "suffused with the environmentalist passions that inform the artist's
work in her husband's quirky, but seminal, 1969 book *A Prosody of
Birds.*"

Another far-flung fan, apparently; it angered Tom to see Addie's work
subsumed like this and, on top of that, credit for the book given only to
him (though this had been common enough through the years). But to his
surprise, she was delighted. "What matters," she said, "is that he *gets it.*"

Yes, he thought, it's good that he and others get it, and yes, these are
important things that no doubt need to be said. But what, Tom sometimes
wanted to ask her, about their *songs?* Have you completely forgotten
about these creatures' beautiful music? And how we used to love to hear
it, together?

Obviously you can't paint a bird's call. Some, though, were so doleful,
so filled with sorrow—the very thing she might have painted. Tom wondered if he might persuade her to try. Those sad songs—of the mourning
dove, of course, but also, to his ear, of the hermit thrush, the eastern
wood-pewee, and particularly, that year, the long-eared owl; that was
what he kept hearing, waking and sleeping, throughout the summer and
fall of 1983, in the months after Addie's show in New Hope.

They talked, once again, of another sabbatical; they'd spend this one
in a rented house in Cider Cove, they said, at the Cape May lighthouse
and other birding sites in the early mornings and at dusk, spending time
with Cora's family in the afternoons and evenings. There were sales of a
few paintings, there was talk of other shows, a gallery in Philadelphia had
expressed some interest. Through it all, she kept on painting.

Then one day a small notice appeared in the local newspaper. Bert
Schafer had purchased three hundred acres of land, mixed woods and
farmland, two and a half miles south of Burnham College, on the rolling
hills winding west from the Delaware River; his plan was to build a high-
end housing development there—large "country estates," each with a

few acres of land, marketed as the perfect escape for Philadelphia suburbanites whose towns were growing too crowded and for New Jerseyans exhausted by their state's high taxes.

Tom knew that parcel of land well; it was in those woods, during the last two summers, that he and other area birders had spotted a pair of rare long-eared owls. He immediately set to work on a letter to the editor, and called up some of the local Audubon Society members to do the same— all the while wondering how long he'd be able to keep the news from Addie, who had been too busy, of late, to read the local paper.

Maybe he should have just told her right away. But he wanted to protect her somehow, protect her recent productivity, and her happiness; protect her from her ragtag band of activist friends. And he couldn't think of birds, even these remarkable owls, the way she did—as scapegoats, sacrificial victims, symbols of human folly and excess.

Yes, they inspired poetry, music, art. Yes, their singing could still, all these years later, make him as giddy, as shivery with delight as he'd been as a boy of twelve. But they were, in the end, *birds*. Members of the class Aves. Subject to, even victims of, human meddling, of course. But continually, and *successfully*, evolving in response to that meddling, and to countless other influences, affected by causes both proximate and ultimate. He'd seen the terms scratched in Addie's nearly illegible handwriting in her notebook from his course—these not, unfortunately, circled more recently in red: *Two kinds of causes in biology: proximate (mechanical causes, like weather) and ultimate (unrelenting pressures placed on populations over time)*.

How could he see all animal life—mammals called humans included— otherwise? he'd asked Addie many times. How could he *not* perceive his beloved birds as evolving rationally, responding as each species must to human and other interventions? Of course he was concerned about habitat loss, about global climate change and disruptions in migration, about increasingly toxic water and air—about a planet that, to its own peril, was rapidly snuffing out the diversity of life it would need to survive. Hadn't he written about these very things?

But humans are only one species, after all—one species early in its evolutionary history. And "nature," "the natural world"—terms he was learning to hate, their increasingly careless and cavalier use setting his teeth on edge—is anything but balanced and kind. Nature is a death machine, a cauldron of brutal extremes that, in the largest sense, only a handful of hardy individuals have *ever* managed to survive.

And yet they do, miraculously, survive. Look at them! Look at all the remarkable species of birds that have made it this far (consider too that their early ancestors may have been *dinosaurs*). Despite untold millennia of fierce predators before humans even appeared on the scene. Despite the damming of rivers, the clear-cutting of forests, the polluting of waterways, the reckless spraying of pesticides. The spill of so much human clutter in the middle of their natural homes.

Addie did, of course, learn of Bert Schafer's plans for the land to the south of them, home of the presumably breeding pair of long-eared owls, only a few weeks after Tom did. Though the Bucks County Mothers of the Earth were long gone by the early '80s, Addie had since allied herself with a loosely affiliated group of environmentalists, fringy types from Philadelphia and surrounding areas who'd grown impatient with the quieter efforts of their local Audubon Society or Sierra Club chapters. It was the self-appointed leader of this small, rather disorganized group—a twenty-one-year-old UC–Santa Cruz dropout who was living with his parents in suburban Levittown—who called to tell Addie about Bert Schafer's purchase of the farmland south of Burnham College.

On hearing this news, Addie started by reading everything about Schafer's plans that she could get her hands on. She laughed at the pointlessness of the letters written by Tom and his fellow birders. She neglected to respond to messages from the gallery owner in Philadelphia, who eventually stopped calling. And once again, she stopped painting. By September she was living in a tent on Bert Schafer's newly acquired land.

There were five of them that time. At first they camped in the woods, and for over a week no one noticed they were there. They never left their campsite. In the evenings Tom brought them food. Scarlet came with him the first couple times, but on the third night she declined when he asked if she wanted to come along.

"It's just too weird," she said.

"Yes, it is," he answered as he packed sandwiches and apples, then lifted the car keys from the hook by the door.

He was relieved when, arriving at the sad little cluster of tents that evening, he learned that the group's meals were now being delivered by a teenager named Brian Kent, son of one of the now scattered members of the former commune near New Hope. He'd shown up on the third day of their squat and announced that he wanted to help out. When she'd learned that he was only sixteen, Addie had argued against allowing him to camp with them. Instead, each morning when he appeared at their campsite in the woods, they gave him money to go buy them food.

It was clear to Tom, and, he was sure, to Addie, that there was something wrong with Brian. His eyes, on the rare occasions when they met anyone else's, had the same glassy, faraway look as Richard's. But there was something angrier, something more desperate, about Brian Kent.

But then, none of the five people sleeping in those tents—with the possible exception of Addie—would have been considered "normal" in most circles. There was Bob, the angry and disaffected, and clearly lonely, retired engineer from Bethlehem Steel; when Addie had learned about his recent lung-cancer diagnosis, she'd nodded knowingly, and Tom had chosen to keep quiet about Bob's multiple-pack-a-day smoking habit. There were Kate and Nicholas, the Penn undergraduates with oddly shaved heads and assorted piercings and tattoos ("It's called punk, Dad," Scarlet had said), camping out until classes started in a week.

And then there was Kyle, the new, self-appointed organizer of this local group. He was dreadlocked and rather loutish, usually stoned, and—it became immediately apparent—annoying to everyone in the group, who seemed to look more to Addie for leadership and encouragement. So she became the group's de facto leader, through their series of small, makeshift squatters' camps on Schafer's newest piece of leveled, clear-cut land. The first happened that fall of 1983, when Addie learned of Schafer's purchase of the land. The second came the following year, when Schafer's bulldozers and backhoes arrived, and the whole slash-and-burn process of turning a farm into a newly seeded "model community" got under way.

When they arrived to pitch their tents yet again, at the end of the summer of 1985—Addie, Bob, and a new handful of cohorts, including an elderly Quaker couple from Bethlehem—it was Addie who was doing the organizing. A number of the new houses on Schafer's land, now called Burnham Estates, were nearly completed (though none were yet occupied), and Kyle was back in California.

And so he missed the conflagration. Two days after Addie and the group were once again arrested and released on bail, three of the newly built homes were set on fire. Perhaps if Kyle had still been in Levittown, things would have been different. Perhaps it would have been his door the police knocked on at five A.M. the day after the fire, instead of Addie and Tom's. Perhaps it would have been Kyle, not Addie, who, only an hour before the police arrived, had urged Brian Kent to drive south and not stop until he'd crossed at least two state lines.

Perhaps, but probably not. Surely only Addie would have made it her mission to protect poor, lonely, dangerous Brian Kent. Addie—sweet, young, charmingly innocent Addie Sturmer Kavanagh. Tom's sweet Adeline.

Tom had imagined their lives so differently. Of course it had been pointed out to him, many times, that it was naive, at best, to imagine that Addie could remain content with the roles of secretary and transcriber, and occasional illustrator, of his work. But he'd never seen her this way. As he'd said in the Acknowledgments in *A Prosody of Birds*, he considered her his partner and his peer, her sharply attuned observations in the field every bit as crucial as anything he might eventually record.

That was how he'd pictured it: a collaboration. The two of them, and when Scarlet came along the three of them, driven by their own *Zugunruhe*, following their own migratory path up and down the eastern seaboard and then, with the start of each academic year, coming home to roost in their Nisky Creek cottage.

That was what all the trips—to Florida, the Eastern Shore, Cape Cod, Maine, even one summer as far north as the noisy breeding grounds of the Canadian Boreal Forest—had been about. The same with the talk of further sabbaticals. All of them his idea, and each trip or imagined sabbatical usually in response to one of Addie's low periods, to a time when, for some reason, she'd stopped drawing and painting. All his way of trying, again and again, to re-create what had been, for him, their magical year, their purest and simplest period of shared work, in England and Ireland, before Scarlet was born.

Was he wrong, then, to attribute the changes in Addie, and the loss of that magic—as well as Addie's growing, and (to his mind) increasingly irrational, fears about environmental damage—to Scarlet's birth? To *motherhood* somehow?

The bond between Addie and Scarlet stunned him at times—its rawness, its complexity. Of course breasts are objects of fascination, for all of us, he often told his students; their power, for mammals, is profound. Yet he'd never truly understood this until he'd watched his own daughter suckling at Addie's breast. Scarlet clung adoringly to Addie, who nursed her daughter completely instinctively—without, from all appearances, a moment's hesitation or resentment—until the day Scarlet turned three and announced she would be giving up her "Addie milk" now, in favor of the cups and spoons and such of adulthood. Then suddenly she *was*, it seemed, a little adult.

And there could be such a coolness between them, or so it seemed to Tom—hours spent together in the same room, not speaking, barely acknowledging one another. It wasn't really coolness, Addie told him; to call it that was to misunderstand what went on between them, and the way Scarlet understood, from an early age, her mother's need for peace, for at least a taste of solitude each day. *What is that if not coolness?* he'd sometimes thought of asking, but never did.

He preferred noisier times with Scarlet—hiding and chasing, singing along with Pete Seeger records, splashing each other in the creek. Nothing thrilled him in quite the same way as his daughter's bubbling laughter.

And yet, after a day of quiet at home with Addie, then an hour or two of loud, laughing roughhousing with him before dinner and bed—after all that, always, it was her mother's arms she sought, Addie's gentle soothing that eased her toward sleep. Even long after she'd given up her mother's breast. For years, until, at around age thirteen, she suddenly preferred him. And eventually, a year or so after that, neither of them.

"What is it you feel for her?" he asked Addie sometimes, late at night in their bed. "What is it you feel for *me*, now?" He couldn't ignore his sense that something had changed.

"You want me to name it so you can *measure* it somehow, quantify it," she answered him once. "Measure it and compare it to some standard you have for the species or something."

"No, no, that's not it. I only want to *understand*. Are you different now somehow, are we different than we were when I first knew you? Are our lives fuller or less full, or somehow both?"

"Yes and no and yes and no, and what difference does it make anyway?" was her answer. Other nights, when he tried to raise such questions, she simply kissed him, turned off her light, and turned her back to him.

And what difference *did* it make? But of course what he really wanted to understand was their sexual life together, its rises and falls, its odd turns. At times, still, five, ten, twenty years after they'd met, she was as avid a lover as she'd been that first spring and summer. At other times— and not necessarily her sad times, or the times when her work was going nowhere; it was never as predictable as that—her indifference left him baffled and cold.

It seemed to him that in all the years he'd known her, his longing for her had never abated in the least. Pregnant, she was a revelation to him, and he cradled her belly between them like the sacred, delicate egg it was. Sad and distant, she was a lost girl that he longed to comfort; happily drawing and painting, she was the passionate young woman he'd first fallen for.

When she withdrew from him, he didn't know where to turn. "Maybe another child?" a friend suggested when he hinted at his frustration once, when Scarlet was twelve. But that wasn't the answer, he knew; they had, it seemed, an unspoken agreement about that. He feared he couldn't love another child as fully as he loved Scarlet, and when people asked Addie if they didn't want to provide Scarlet with a brother or sister (and it was shocking, really, how free people felt to ask such a thing), she always answered, "One is the only responsible choice in a world on the brink, like ours."

Surely it was this—this bottomless despair at the plight of the earth— that took her away from him, and from her work, Tom always concluded. Not Scarlet, not motherhood. Though later, after Scarlet's decision to spend her final year of high school in Cider Cove, he'd assumed there was, then, this other thing behind Addie's sadness and anger. A sense that her daughter, at only seventeen, was lost to her now. But he'd never suggested such a thing to Addie.

That was the dreadful autumn in 1985, when Addie was hiding out in the apartment above Lou's Washington garage. A fugitive of sorts, fleeing the Pennsylvania state authorities, as absurd as that was—as absurd, and strange, and miserable as that whole time was. The obscenely lavish meals with Lou and Ted, the drinking, the ugliness between them, and Addie's own drinking and arguing; she had never been farther away from him than she was on those weekends when he visited her in Washington. Lou seemed to treat the whole thing as a lark, maybe because it clearly angered and unnerved her husband. And Addie, so clearly innocent but stubbornly silent, refused, every time he spoke to her, to listen to reason. The more he tried ("You can't save this boy, Addie—and you can't keep protecting him at the expense of your own family" he told her, over and over), the colder she grew.

"*You're* the one who insists on these visits, Tom," she said, "dragging Scarlet down here from Cider Cove, where she's so much happier." It was maddening to him, this refusal, on Addie's part, to acknowledge what it meant, and how it felt, to see Scarlet choose Cora's home over that of her own parents.

"You should just stay home and tend to your work," she said. "Both you and Scarlet would be better off not coming here at all. Let me just wait this out here. Let me just stay here quietly until the whole thing blows over."

"Blows *over?*" He couldn't stay calm and rational when she said things like that. "Addie, you're on the verge of being charged with *arson* here. This isn't going to simply 'blow over.' "

And yet, almost six painful weeks later, that was essentially what happened, when Brian Kent returned to Bucks County. This time he made several mistakes. He chose an occupied (though vacant at the time he lit the trail of gasoline) home in an established development instead of one of the homes in Schafer's new development. And he set a fire without someone like Addie to run to.

When Tom learned of Brian Kent's arrest and his confession to setting the Burnham Estates fires as well, he immediately canceled his classes and drove to Washington to deliver the news to Addie in person. It was the middle of the afternoon when he arrived, and he found Addie reading in the apartment; no one was home at Lou and Ted's house.

Tom knew Addie would be more concerned about Brian's well-being than relieved to be free, finally, to return to her home. But he couldn't hide his *own* relief and happiness. Nor could he suppress the visceral longing for his wife that he'd felt through the entire three-hour drive. His mistake was taking her in his arms and kissing her, fully revealing his desire to her, before saying, "It's over, Addie. Brian Kent's confessed."

She stared at him blankly, as if she couldn't understand his words.

"He set another fire. When they arrested him, he confessed to the Burnham Estates fires as well. You can come home now, Addie. It's over."

He'd never seen her look so distraught, and then so thoroughly disgusted—absolutely rigid in his embrace.

"Addie, they'll try him as a minor. Surely he'll get some help now, the help he clearly needs."

With that she tore free and ran out the door. She didn't return for hours.

Lou was back within the hour. Seeing his car, she came up to the apartment to see what he was doing there. And something in him broke. She saw it in his eyes immediately; she'd been looking for that response from him for years, she told him, really since taking his course twenty years before.

She took his hand and led him downstairs to the greenhouse, "the most private place in this whole compound," she quipped—"no one's ever in here but me." They spoke very little; there wasn't much to say really. *What choice do they give us, these impossible spouses of ours?* Or maybe, *They must both want this to happen, on some level, don't you think?*

Her body was still remarkable, and he chose not to think about how she'd kept it that way—long-legged and strong as she wrapped herself around him, full-breasted and hot everywhere he touched her, almost too rough for comfort when she took him in her mouth. Not at all like Addie, he realized, and at that thought he pulled her to the blanket she'd tossed on the floor, and he entered her quickly and came almost immediately, suddenly eager for it to end, there amid the potted geraniums and leggy, overgrown petunias.

Convenient that she'd only just moved those pots indoors, at the first threat of a frost, she said, after he rolled off her. They made a nice little bower of sorts, didn't they? And then she rose and left him there.

Through the years he'd wondered, on occasion, what might have happened if, back in May 1965, he'd taken the clear and ready offer there in front of him, asked the willowy, dark-haired and dark-eyed Lou— seated there next to the mysterious girl he called "the artist"—to see him after class. Impossible to imagine such a choice, of course. And when, through the years—after one of those drunken dinners in Washington, and once earlier, when they'd all visited Cider Cove together—she'd made it clear to him that the offer still stood, it had been equally clear to him (even in the midst of feeling undeniably flattered) that her interest now had more to do with her rage at Ted than with any real awareness of Tom or who he was.

Addie only laughed when he mentioned it once, casually remarking on Lou's unabashed come-ons. "That's just Lou," she said. "Sometime you should just take her up on it—end the mystery for both of you once and for all."

He couldn't tell if she meant it. But now, maybe as enraged, finally, as Lou (certainly tired, certainly more tired and confused about his relationship with Addie than he'd ever been), he'd done it. It was surprising how little guilt he felt, how few Catholic demons seemed to rise to haunt him afterward. On the other hand, he hoped he might never see Lou again.

Later they showered—separately—and Tom refused Lou's offer of dinner, choosing instead to wait alone for Addie in the apartment. When she finally returned, well after dark, and walked into the room where Tom sat reading, she looked at him briefly before beginning to pack her suitcase. He was certain she knew.

"I'm sorry," she said, holding her hastily packed bag and staring at the floor as she stood by the door. "I needed to clear my head. I just kept walking, and I lost track of time." Without saying anything, he took her bag, then steered her out of the apartment and into their car.

She'd noticed immediately: he'd had a shower. Instantly she'd known why. And she'd known that she'd driven him to it. Reading too much, thinking too much, trying to say to someone, *anyone:* Please notice this! Already our groundwater is tainted, laced now not only with arsenic but with countless other toxins, all leaching down from another Schafer construction site. And when those houses are occupied, it will be far worse. Every time it rains, pesticides from those two- and three-acre, weed-free lawns will seep down to Nisky Creek, to the river, and make their way into Delaware Bay. Then everyone will wonder why so many people have cancer, and why the doctors can't just *do* something about it. Because God forbid we have to look at anything we might be doing to *ourselves*.

But a lot of good she'd done. Brian Kent was in jail, her daughter couldn't bear to live with her, she was slowly but surely driving her husband away. What *had* she thought would happen, really? For a month and a half it had simply felt good to be quiet. To hide and be quiet and hope that she might at least be able to protect *one* person.

Well, that was only part of it, of course. There was also the fact that she knew she was seriously ill. She'd known since the first week she'd been at Lou's, when she'd first noticed the lump. Since then it seemed to have grown, or at least that was how it felt to her, when she made herself feel it again, each morning when she woke up. She'd told no one. It confused her, baffled her really, when she tried to think about what to do next. She couldn't quite believe this was happening to her. As long as she stayed at Lou's, she thought, she could pretend it wasn't. Except in the morning, when she made herself feel it.

She hadn't a clue what she was going to do now.

Riding next to Tom on the drive back to Burnham, she looked out the windshield at the clear, brilliant sky—the stars sparkling, she suddenly recalled, as they had the night before Scarlet was born. It was after midnight that night when, her contractions still mild and widely spaced, she'd walked with Tom, up the quiet dirt road to the campus, then over the paths between the buildings, looking at the stars, listening for owls. The students had left for the summer the day before, and everything was perfectly silent, perfectly still.

She'd been exquisitely happy then. And she'd known so little. Hence the happiness, of course. What *was* she supposed to do with everything she'd learned since? With what she knew, for certain, now?

They said nothing to each other through nearly the entire drive home. But at the turn-off for the river road, ten miles from Burnham, she turned to him.

"I've found a lump in my breast, Tom," she said. "Much as I hate to, I suppose I'm going to have to see a doctor. What do people say about that new guy who comes to the campus health center now?"

Pity me, she heard, behind her carefully casual words. Pity me, take care of me. Never mind how I might have hurt you. She hated the sound of her own voice.

By the time they reached the cabin on Haupt Bridge Road, he was crying uncontrollably.

Journal—Field Entry

30 May 1965
Sunday

Fisherman's cottage on Haupt Bridge Road, Burnham, PA (Near the convergence of Little and Nisky Creeks, 1 mi. from campus, where Addie Sturmer and Tom Kavanagh first made love, on a lumpy old mattress below a nearly full moon while a screech owl circled overhead.

> With sweet abandon.
> Listening to frogs.
> With no apparent cover of clouds.
> Picturing a life spent together, and with birds, while they stared
> into each other's eyes.)

Time: 9 P.M.–2 A.M.
Observers, Habitat, Weather: See above.
Remarks: Please sing Robert Burns songs for me, again and again,
forever.
Comments: Your eyes are the deepest brown I've ever seen. I could spend
my life trying to capture the scarlet tanager, and you. And yes. I will.

thirteen

EVENTUALLY, THEY SAY, ALL your old loves come back, in one way or another. Certainly a lot of Scarlet's seemed to do so. For instance, when she moved to New York at twenty-eight and published a book of poems, there on her answering machine one day was a message from her old friend Peter Gleason. And from that point on the two of them had a regular Sunday-night date, always spent watching television in Peter's apartment, eating Chinese carry-out and crying into their cheap white wine over their wayward boyfriends.

Both Addie and Tom, Scarlet's first great loves, eventually came back too. Or, more accurately, she found her way back to them, though this took a while.

And then there was Bobby.

Though she wouldn't have called Bobby one of her great loves. Those first two summers in Cider Cove, she found him alternately goofy and annoying, then wild and reckless in a way she hadn't realized she needed. Together they broke into abandoned buildings, and rode their bikes through back alleys and gated cemeteries and other people's backyards. Bobby's fearlessness in the ocean inspired her. She wanted to do everything he did. At first.

Then, during the summer of 1984, when Scarlet was sixteen and Bobby was fifteen—the summer when Richard seemed lost to everyone—Bobby grew strange to her. She was sure it was her fault. It was her idea, after all, to kiss him one night, as they sat in a booth in the boarded-up diner in the middle of town where they often went (instead of to the movies or the arcade, as they'd told their parents). And when he kissed her back with a strange forcefulness, and bumblingly reached for her breast, she didn't pull away. They might have gone on to have sex that night, if either of them had known what to do.

After that Bobby was wildly unpredictable, sometimes bolting from the house in the morning, the old screen door slamming behind him, without so much as a word to Scarlet, other times watching her almost tenderly at the breakfast table, offering to get her more juice, asking what she wanted to do that day. And if she minded if he asked Richard to come along.

"Of course not," she always said. And she didn't mind. It was one of the things that drew her to Bobby, his way of caring for Richard. And she was Bobby's one friend who understood, and who never minded, who his brother was.

They also shared the same eclectic tastes in music then—a fondness for a strange mix of Bob Dylan (even in his mystifying born-again Christian phase), Pink Floyd, the Clash. Sometimes, at night, they'd sit with Richard in his room, all of them eating a stash of junk food from the corner convenience store and listening to "Blood on the Tracks" or "The Wall," over and over. Even at sixteen, when Scarlet might have been driving (had either Tom or Addie thought it worthwhile to teach her), she preferred careening over the hills in the Cider Cove cemetery on bicycles with Bobby and Richard, screaming the lyrics to "London Calling."

A kind of arrested development, perhaps. Scarlet had been happy, she thought, at twelve, thirteen, even occasionally at fourteen. Why not keep doing the things she'd done then?

Cora finally took it upon herself to teach Scarlet to drive that summer. Maybe to keep her and the boys out of cemeteries in the middle of the night, or maybe because she saw Scarlet's sadness on the mornings when she sat at the breakfast table alone with a book, watching Bobby gallop down the stairs and out the door without even looking at her.

Scarlet did pine for Bobby that summer, at least at first. It wasn't that she found him particularly attractive; he was smaller than she was, scrawny really, and his curly, brown-black hair was always a wind- and salt-dried mess—though when he combed it, or on the rare occasions when he agreed to let Cora trim it, it only looked worse. After their one failed make-out session, he and Scarlet agreed not to try that again.

"I think it's better for us just to be friends," he said to her a few days later, and even then she could hear the clunky, romantic-comedy cliché in such a remark.

But all she said was "Sure, that's fine." Because that was all she wanted—all she longed for really—as well. She didn't particularly want to kiss him again; she just didn't want him to leave her behind. "We're misfits," she might have said to him if she'd had the courage. "We need each other."

Eventually, on days when Bobby didn't want her around, Scarlet set her sights on driving. Cora was a good teacher, and Richard, who sometimes joined them, was even better. Though he never drove himself (it made him far too nervous, he said, to think of attempting to maneuver a four-ton steel box in the midst of a sea of people maneuvering their *own* four-ton boxes), when he rode in the backseat of Cora's car during Scarlet's lessons, he was a remarkably calm and observant passenger.

"You should start braking about twenty yards sooner, about five seconds after you pass the yellow curve sign," he told her after she careened wildly around a curve on the outskirts of Cider Cove, failing to slow down in time. "Then start to accelerate again right at that blue mailbox," he added. When she followed his instructions the next time they were out for a practice drive, she took the curve perfectly.

Richard also gave her precise, mathematical instructions for merging onto a busy interstate, and for parallel parking. By the middle of that summer, when she was back in Burnham with Addie and Tom for several weeks, Scarlet had a Pennsylvania driver's license. Years later, every time she slid a car into an impossibly small Manhattan parking space on the first try, she said a silent thank-you to Richard.

The following fall Scarlet persuaded Addie and Tom to let her drive their rusted old hulk to school each day, so that she could leave after her five periods of classes and drive to the job she'd gotten in the kitchen of a nursing home in Doylestown. By Christmastime she had both a driver's license and a bank account that was growing steadily, and she was plotting her escape. Somehow, she'd decided, she'd get through her final year of high school; working—and making money—would help, as would reading more Allen Ginsberg and Anne Rice and John Fowles (her reading was as eclectic and undisciplined as her tastes in music).

And somehow she would survive another year with her embattled mother, who'd spent a good part of the fall of 1984 once again camped out on the land south of Burnham, where foundations had already been laid for several new Burnham Estates, and from which the pair of long-eared owls that Tom had spotted the previous year had long since disappeared. She would apply to college somewhere far away, she decided, buy a car, and finally, *finally,* leave Burnham and her crazy, outsider, outcast life behind. The only thing she'd miss, she thought, would be the beach at Cider Cove.

Then, early one morning between Christmas and New Year's, the phone rang. It woke Scarlet, who tried to roll over and go back to sleep, but then she heard her father's voice, strangely breaking in the middle of a sentence. He was crying, she realized. A relative in Ireland, she thought at first, and then, panicking, she became convinced that her grandmother, Addie's mother, was dead. She'd been living on her own for several years by then, since Addie's father's death; she still lived in the old farmhouse in the northeast corner of the state, looked after by Addie's brother, John, who lived in Scranton.

But when she heard Addie wailing in response to whatever it was Tom had told her, she knew that wasn't it. Addie loved her mother, but in a distant way, Scarlet knew; she wouldn't have responded with such primitive keening to news of her mother's death. That, Scarlet thought, could only mean Cora.

And then Tom was in Scarlet's room, while Addie sobbed in the kitchen.

"Scarlet, my love, listen," he said as he sat on the edge of the bed and reached for her hands. "Don't be alarmed. But listen, there's something I have to tell you. That was Karl on the phone. Richard shot himself yesterday."

"What?" She was up then, suddenly, fumbling ridiculously for her slippers and robe. She raced for the kitchen, with Tom following her.

To see Addie like that terrified Scarlet. Certainly she had seen her mother sad, even quietly crying, on occasion; in recent years she'd made Addie cry a few times herself, with a spiteful remark or a deliberate snub. But this was different—unimaginable depths of grief contorting her mother's face. Scarlet stood helplessly in the middle of the room, not knowing where to look or what to do, while Tom held Addie, whose body shook with sobs.

"Who found him?" Scarlet finally asked. When they both looked at her, she knew the answer. Both of them tried to reach for her then, to hold her. But she ran to her room, to cry in her bed, alone.

At the funeral, Bobby didn't speak to Scarlet, or to anyone. Cora looked distant and gaunt, her hair suddenly far grayer than it had been only six months before, when she had sat next to Scarlet in the front seat of her car, calmly talking her through a sharp curve in the road, laughing gently when she ground the gears yet again. Karl greeted all the mourners and steered his shell-shocked wife and son through all the proceedings—the service in the old Congregationalist church, the graveside remarks at the cemetery where Bobby, Richard, and Scarlet had raced on their bikes only two years before.

Later, back at the house, Cora handed Tom a box full of the birds'-nest models he'd worked on with Richard. And Bobby handed Scarlet a stack of albums. "I can't listen to these anymore," he said, and Scarlet nodded silently, wishing she knew what to say.

Lou was there too, with Ted and their two young daughters. She and Addie stayed with Cora for a week after the funeral. When Addie got home she looked thinner and grayer too, though the gray was less visible in her shoulder-length blond hair, cut shorter now, Scarlet supposed, to make it easier to care for on her extended "camping" excursions.

Addie didn't draw or paint—or camp—for a while after Richard's death. She began her collecting of bird carcasses at that point, carrying the more intact ones to Richard Schantz for stuffing and preserving. Mostly she read—more treatises on the environment, more accounts of pesticide contamination and the like. And Tom did what he had always done: He worked.

Scarlet never mourned, openly, after that morning when Karl had called with the news. But every morning that winter, she woke up with the same image in her head: Richard's dark, unshaven face and down-cast eyes as she'd passed him each morning in the hallway the summer before. Then, in a kind of painful, punishing ritual, after seeing Richard's face in her mind, she forced herself to imagine Bobby walking into his brother's room, probably after an afternoon of surfing with his friends, and finding him there, slumped over in a chair, blood splattered on the wall behind him.

Every morning Scarlet did this. Addie, she knew, must have been con-ducting her own private ritual each day as well. (What might *she* have forced herself to see? Scarlet sometimes wondered. Richard, so sad and desperate, placing the gun in his mouth? Cora, arriving home to an oddly quiet house, finding Bobby sobbing on the stairs, then running to Rich-ard's room, pulling herself free from Bobby's grasping arms at her an-kles?) Because when Brian Kent showed up on her doorstep one morning in early April, saying he was planning to drop out of high school and hitchhike somewhere, anywhere—anywhere to get far away from his drug-addicted mother, his cold and distant father and stepmother who wanted nothing to do with him—Addie invited him in and gave him a cup of coffee and got on the phone with her fellow squatters from the previous years and said Bert Schafer's contractors were getting ready to complete the building of the first Burnham Estates, and so hadn't they better get busy?

"So you see, Brian," she said, when she got off the phone, "you can't run away. We have work to do, and you're needed here."

And so by May, when Addie was once again gathering gear and supplies and holding planning meetings—this time with Brian and Bob the disgruntled engineer and a few new recruits—in the kitchen of their house on Haupt Bridge Road, Scarlet had made up her mind. If they would have her, she would spend the entire summer in Cider Cove with Cora and Karl and Bobby.

She knew it saddened Tom to watch her, the day after school ended, packing the old car he'd helped her buy. He hugged her, saying nothing, and then opened the car door for her—and as he did, she saw the tears in his eyes. For the first half of the trip to Cider Cove, she drove too fast along the winding country roads, windows open and the car's old radio turned up as loud as it would go, willing the rushing wind and screaming guitars to burn away that image of her father.

Addie's good-bye, on the back steps, had been more stoic: a quick, tight hug, a kiss on each cheek. "Give Cora a kiss for me," she'd said. The other thing Scarlet didn't let herself do, on that bright June morning as she drove toward the Jersey shore, was to repeat the question she often asked herself through those sad, busy years of her late teens: Why did Tom appear to love her so much more than Addie did?

It wasn't Bobby who kept her in Cider Cove at the end of that summer. She hadn't seen much of him, really. Or of Karl. They all seemed to be working constantly. That, according to Bobby, was how his father was dealing with Richard's death—by working outrageously long hours, struggling to keep up with the "young Turks" at his job, all of them so much more at ease with new technologies than he and the other engineers of his generation.

"He seems almost panicked," Cora said, on one of the rare evenings when she, Bobby, and Scarlet were all home together for dinner. "I really think he's afraid he could lose his job—and that's a bitter pill for someone who's been the breadwinner for twenty years."

Bobby took a long drink of iced tea and stabbed at the food on his plate. "It's not that, Mom," he said, refusing to meet either Cora's or Scarlet's eyes. "It's that he just doesn't want to look at us. We remind him of Richard."

Cora stared at her own plate then, tears rolling down her cheeks, and at that moment—and at several other moments that summer—Scarlet hated Bobby.

Bobby, who might have been speaking of himself when he described his father this way, who worked late every night at one of Cider Cove's innumerable pizza joints, then slept most of the day, only emerging from his room to eat a quick meal in the late afternoon before joining his friends—suddenly, that summer, a new, "cool" group, very much the Cider Cove in crowd—to get high before work. He hardly went to the beach at all anymore.

Cora spent much of her time at her pottery wheel. She had taken one class, before Richard's death, and now she worked for hours each day, teaching herself more. Though her pots were getting better, she hadn't yet achieved the dark beauty of the mugs and pots she would eventually make—the black raku with a hint of fiery red below the rough glaze. That summer, in 1985, she was "only dabbling," she said. Still, Scarlet loved to hear her talk about how it felt when the clay moved perfectly in her hands, when the rhythm of her foot on the wheel hit that perfect groove with the shaping that was happening at her fingertips.

Even Scarlet was out of the house most of the time, leaving early for her two jobs in Cape May, cleaning rooms in one of the beachfront hotels in the morning, scooping ice cream in a shop on the boardwalk in the afternoon. She'd get back to Cora and Karl's around six, too tired to move, and Cora would rise from her wheel to serve her a home-cooked meal. Then, revived by her food and her company, most evenings Scarlet would join Cora for a walk along the beach. Cora was, really, Scarlet's only friend that summer. She felt, to Scarlet, like the only friend she needed.

As they walked they'd both point out birds. Scarlet talked about Addie and Tom, and Cora listened, offering no judgments or defenses. The only topics they avoided, throughout that summer and after, were Richard and Bobby.

In the fall Scarlet got a better job, waitressing at a pancake house in Cape May, and she dutifully attended classes at Cider Cove High. What a solace it was, coming home to that silent, often empty old house, after those dreadful weekends with Addie and Tom at Lou's in Washington— Addie and Lou drinking and laughing as if they were having a giddy college reunion, Tom sitting in miserable silence, staring at his uneaten food, Ted choosing a different fight to pick, with Lou or Addie or both of them, every night. But back in Cider Cove, the only sound Scarlet would hear, when she turned her key, was the whir of Cora's wheel. It might have been the silence of denial—Richard's sad and angry ghost, hovering there above Karl the workaholic, Bobby the aimless pothead, Cora the isolated artist with a sixteen-year-old loner for a friend. But it sounded good to Scarlet.

"It's hard to explain," Cora said to her once, her eyes gleaming, "but it's just a very *visceral*, bodily thing, when a pot finds its center on the wheel. You feel it in your body, and yet it's as if you had nothing to do with it at all."

Scarlet envied Cora then, longing to feel that way—that grounded, that exuberant—about something, *anything*, in her own life. Years later, at work on a poem in the middle of the night in her rented room in Amherst, she found the connection, both verbal and visceral, she was looking for in a poem she was trying to write, about Richard. She'd been listening to a CD of birdsongs Tom had lent her, and when she heard that eerie, completely unmelodic, almost *drowning* sound the American bittern makes, she knew she'd found it: a bird that sounded as strange and disconnected as poor, lonely Richard had been. What she felt, at that moment, was such a clear *physical* sensation: She'd found the poem's center on the wheel, she thought. It was all she could do not to dial Cora's number then and there. She'd certainly called her for wilder and sillier—and also more desperate—reasons than this, over the years. But, she reminded herself, it *was* three A.M. And she knew how dearly Cora valued her sleep. Also, this would mean bringing up Richard, which was something they simply never did.

They were all together in Cider Cove for Christmas that year Scarlet lived with Cora, Karl, and Bobby, after Brian Kent's arrest and Addie's return to Burnham. Tom and Addie seemed subdued, for reasons Scarlet thought she could imagine but had no interest in pursuing. Cora and Karl, though still mourning Richard's death a year before, worked to be gracious hosts; there were carols on the stereo and hot mulled cider. It even snowed. By the day after Christmas, Bobby and Scarlet were both desperate to get out of the house and away from their parents, and he proposed a trip to the mall to redeem their gift certificates.

Driving home in her old Volvo, Scarlet chattered, nervous in Bobby's brooding company, about her college applications. She had applied to three colleges in Maine, none of which she'd visited, or even knew very much about, simply because Maine was the last place she could recall feeling happy—purely, uncomplicatedly happy—during the month she, Tom, and Addie had spent on the coast, when she was fourteen.

Apparently Bobby wasn't troubled by Scarlet's fairly flimsy grounds for choosing a school (a year and a half later he himself would, after all, choose SUNY-Albany because that was where his best supplier of marijuana planned to go). He only nodded and stared out his window before turning to her to say, "They'll talk about Richard, you know, now that we're not there." For all his dark silences, Bobby was always a remarkable reader of people, of their emotional blind spots, their ducks and dodges and blunderings.

"Really?" was all Scarlet could think of to say at first. Then, "What do you think they'll say?"

"Oh, all about whose fault it was—my mom will say it was hers, my dad will get all restless and uncomfortable and go work on building up the fire or something, and your mom will probably start talking about how toxic New Jersey is, and then your dad will try to calm her down." They both laughed then. It was an undeniably accurate portrait of their parents.

And indeed, back at the house, they walked into an eerily quiet living room: fire actually dying down, cider cold in half-filled cups, nothing playing on the stereo. Both Cora and Addie had clearly been crying. Karl sat in his recliner, chin resting on his hand, staring into the fireplace. And Tom stood at the window, staring out, as if willing a bird, *any* bird, to alight at Cora's feeder.

Bobby and Scarlet exchanged a quick glance and, without a word, hurried upstairs to their respective rooms, to listen, on their respective Walkmans, to the music they'd just purchased at the mall. While Scarlet had no memory of what it was, Bobby would later insist that he'd bought REM, and she'd opted for some dreadful compilation of piano classics.

"You said you didn't want to hear any more words," he told her, and she believed him; she could hear her seventeen-year-old self saying that very thing.

The winter that followed brought a lot of snow, and calls back and forth to Burnham to get various financial aid forms completed. At Christmas Tom and Addie had asked if Scarlet wanted to return to Burnham with them for her last semester of high school. "I think it'd be easier just to finish here," she'd told them, rather coldly it seemed to her later. Neither of them tried to change her mind.

Scarlet could see that something had happened, at Christmas, between Addie and Cora—presumably something about Richard, if Bobby was right. Cora said nothing, and Scarlet didn't ask. But a few weeks later, when a package arrived for Cora from Addie, Scarlet prowled around the first-floor room (not yet called her studio) where Cora spent her days to get a glimpse of what it was: *The Diary and Letters of Kaethe Kollwitz*. Scarlet read it, secretly and hungrily, late at night, after Cora had gone to bed.

When she went to Burnham for her spring-break week in March, Scarlet was amazed to see the work Addie was doing with the dead birds she'd been collecting for more than a year. Amazed, but also a little sickened. And completely unable, at that point, to make any kind of connection between her mother and Käthe Kollwitz—who, along with Cora, had become the ultimate artist-mother in Scarlet's eyes.

During her last summer in Cider Cove Scarlet cleaned hotel rooms again in the mornings, then waitressed several evenings a week. Bobby seemed to have turned almost nostalgic at the thought of her leaving, and he found time to go to the beach with her now and then, for old times' sake. So she arrived for freshman orientation at Bates with a suntan, like many of her peers.

Most of those tans, though, had come from summers spent in places like Mount Desert Island, Martha's Vineyard, Cape Cod. Scarlet learned quickly, that first year, to keep quiet about her summers on the lowly Jersey shore. She also went on to spend some summers of her own in tonier beach climes—Provincetown that first summer, Nantucket the next. One could always waitress, she discovered; that was a skill that translated well, even from New Jersey.

But she never lost her love for Cider Cove, for what had always been, for Pennsylvania girl Scarlet, the glorious, not the lowly, Jersey shore. The sleepy, overlooked quality of a town like Cider Cove (it was no accident that one of the most romantic locales of Scarlet's lonely, dreamy adolescence was the boarded-up Main Street Diner), the faded-glory feeling of so much of Cape May, the taffy and fudge and ski-ball joints, the smells of dead fish and cotton candy and whipping sea air: She loved it all.

It was the new development at the edges of both towns—the Days Inn and Denny's in Cider Cove, the pricey condos in Cape May—that she hated; she *was* her mother's daughter, after all. And her father's as well, and so she loved watching diving cormorants on those evening walks with Cora, and scanning the roped-off sections of dunes and beach grasses, glowing orange in the setting sun, for a rare glimpse of a family of nesting plovers.

That curving, crowded shore, that embattled bay—so much complicated coexistence. Addie might have considered New Jersey one of the more reckless, poisoned states in the union, but she loved that shoreline too; in the end, when she, Tom, and Scarlet ventured beyond their sheltered valley along Nisky Creek, across the wide, wide Delaware and to the coast, none of them could ever quite stomach the pristine beaches they found elsewhere.

"The domain of the entitled," Addie would say on a pure white beach at the tip of Long Island or along the northeastern edge of Cape Cod. Though of course it was hard to argue when Tom pointed out, on their various excursions through the years, that only the entitled had the resources to preserve such stunning pieces of habitat.

"Imagine having been able to buy that piece of land before Bert Schafer had even sniffed it out," he said once, looking downright wistful. "There could have been a whole family of owls there by now."

By age seventeen, and for a couple years after, Scarlet thought that what she needed, more than anything, was to find a place of her own on those clean, protected, entitled grounds—to leave behind her peculiar Pennsylvania childhood, her period of hiding on the Jersey shore, those years of nothing, really, but books, and work, and Cora, and sometimes Bobby. A change of habitat.

She also decided she should arrive for her first semester of college life armed with not only a suntan, but also the shield of her lost virginity. And so the night before she left Cider Cove, she asked Bobby for help with this particular task. They'd spent the afternoon and evening on the beach; he'd been sweet and solicitous, dribbling sand over her belly, watching a ladybug make its slow course over that smooth brown expanse. Scarlet had grown daring enough to wear a bikini that summer; she was thin and tanned, and she wanted something to happen. Bobby agreed that she shouldn't enter college a virgin, and he gallantly offered to spring for condoms when Scarlet acknowledged that she had no other form of protection. That night they carried Scarlet's old sleeping bag with them to the still boarded-up diner.

Bobby had learned some things since the last time they'd ventured into this strange territory, the year before. While Scarlet had moved on from gangly young outcast status to a sullen retreat into work and books, Bobby had embraced his new status as a cool stoner—dark-eyed and brooding, ironic and hip. And suddenly, very cute. He was now in demand, and those fast—and older—Cider Cove girls had taught him well.

Scarlet often thought she couldn't have asked for a better first time. Despite the distance between her and Bobby that last year, she trusted him, and she could tell, when he kissed her, that he was—for just that moment, just those couple hours that night—letting down his guard. They kissed, seated together in a crowded booth, for a while, just as they'd done a year before. But their tongues and teeth were a little less in the way this time, and it felt marvelous to Scarlet to explore Bobby's mouth, which tasted of mint and a trace of smoke.

She could have gone on kissing much longer, but eventually Bobby pulled away from her, stooping down to unroll her sleeping bag. When he looked away from her, Scarlet felt her nerve eroding; she had to will herself not to collapse in nervous giggling and tell him she'd been joking.

But then he looked up at her and grinned, his sweet, goofy grin—the most soothing sight in the world to her. She grinned back, and said, "I think I'm nervous."

He shrugged. "Me too," he said. "But if we can't trust each other, who can we trust?" And when he said that, she was out of the booth in an instant, kissing him again, pulling him onto the sleeping bag, pulling off her clothes, reaching for his.

"Slow down," he told her, laughing. "We've got time." And so she did slow down, and she let Bobby finish undressing her, slowly, and watched as he explored her naked body, slowly, then grinned at her again. We've got time, she thought; maybe this night won't end. In the years that followed, Scarlet found that few people seemed to understand the value of taking time the way Bobby did that night.

After they'd slept for a while, wrapped tightly together inside the sleeping bag, they woke up and talked about Richard. Scarlet didn't ask Bobby what it had been like to find Richard's ruined body; she didn't have to. Eventually, at dawn, they crawled, shivering, out of each other's arms. While Scarlet dressed and Bobby rolled up the sleeping bag, they both cried. And they both tried to hide their tears. They were quiet as they walked back to the house, and he held her hand.

Later Scarlet ate breakfast with Cora while Bobby slept. He was still asleep when she threw her last things into the Volvo and pulled away, driving to Burnham for a night at the cottage before Tom and Addie would drive her to Maine the next day.

It was strange to keep a secret like that from Cora. But Scarlet never told her. Beyond the obvious reasons, there was this sure awareness on her part: Cora would know it was all really about Richard somehow. And it would make her terribly sad.

And eventually, seventeen years later, Scarlet had another secret. The one she'd kept from everyone but Tom and Addie, who held her daughter's face in her thin, dry hands and gave her her blessing and, before she died, cried because she wouldn't get to see her grandchild.

IV

zugunruhe

fourteen

"I CALLED JOHN THIS morning," Tom says when Scarlet returns from the bathroom. She has never been close to her uncle—he and Addie rarely spoke—but still she feels a pang at hearing his name, realizing she has barely thought of him over the past few days. Shouldn't a brother and sister, a niece and her uncle, shouldn't any and all family members, share a stronger connection than this?

She tilts her head expectantly and looks to Tom for more. "And?"

"He wanted to know when the service would be, and where to send flowers."

Lou lets out a snort of laughter, and Cora smiles.

Scarlet is standing in the doorway between the kitchen and porch, feeling restless, reluctant to sit again. A few minutes ago, when Cora had returned with a fresh pot of coffee, she'd felt free, finally, to take a bathroom break, knowing she wouldn't be leaving Tom and Lou alone. She wandered through the rooms of the old house—filled now with old farmstead furniture and thick rugs, beds made up with crisp white sheets and warm duvets, Cora's bowls and vases tucked discreetly into corners here and there, a few adorning the mantels over the three fireplaces. Now, as a bed-and-breakfast, the house is in considerably better shape than in the days when Scarlet, Tom, and Addie first visited Cider Cove—the walls painted a clean white, new windows installed throughout, the old wood floors polished and gleaming.

The floors still creak and slope, though, and sand still gathers in the cracks between the smooth planks. Breathing in as she roamed through the rooms, Scarlet savored the house's familiar smell—the mix of coffee and something baking, and behind that the fresh sea breeze. No matter the season, Cora always opens up the windows first thing in the morning and hangs everyone's bedding out to air in the sun, or the fog, even on occasion a light snow. After her upstairs tour Scarlet stepped outside for a moment, careful to avoid Dustin and his ceaseless sawing and hammering. She listened for the sound of the waves and watched all the quilts (most, if not all, from beds that hadn't been slept in last night) flapping in the breeze, like so many flags of surrender.

Now, back on the sunporch, Scarlet is surprised to see the three of them, still in the same chairs as before, still drinking coffee, as noon approaches. Her stroll into the yard has reminded her that there's a world outside, and time is moving on. How long can they hide out here, lazily talking, avoiding what has to be faced now?

"But you know," Lou says as Scarlet steps onto the porch, "some sort of memorial something-or-other would be good, don't you think?" She's leaning forward in her chair, serious now. "I mean, she did have her various and sundry friends and admirers, from all over the place, especially these last few years. We could do something at my house, maybe. . . ."

Cora laughs. "You little Washington hostess, you," she says.

Lou looks mildly annoyed for a moment, then shrugs and smiles, leaning back again and kicking off her sandals.

"Addie was adamant about not wanting anything like that," Scarlet says, recalling her mother's remarks from two days before. "No taking turns 'eulogizing' me or something ridiculous like that," she'd said. "No public reading of poems—not even yours, darling, much as I love them. And for *God's* sake, no cut-flower arrangements."

In fact Scarlet did read two of her poems, but only to Addie and at her request, yesterday morning—the two Addie loved most, not surprisingly: "All the Bilge and Ruin" (Scarlet's tribute to Käthe Kollwitz, and indirectly to her mother) and "American Bittern," that poem of the middle-of-the-Massachusetts-night revelation. This, Addie said, was surely preferable to a reading for a roomful of listeners without the proper context. And a reading that, being dead, she herself wouldn't even get to hear.

"In fact," Scarlet says now, thinking it's time they finally get to the business at hand, if—surely—that's what they've gathered there on Cora's sunporch to do, "she was very explicit about what she did and didn't want to have happen now, and I think we'd better try to figure out what we're actually going to do about some of her ideas—" She is silenced by a look from Tom.

"We know what we're going to do, Scarlet," he says softly.

We *do?* she thinks. She can't imagine what he means. Can he mean that they are going to break laws in two states (not that there's been time to research this at all), and put his entire career and reputation at risk, all because of Addie's fury at Bert Schafer and Burnham College, her need to make one final point, even when she's *dead?*

"Have you been talking about this?" she asks.

"Well, no," Tom says, giving her a look that she can't decipher. "Not specifically. We've just been remembering Addie, 'memorializing' her in the way I think she'd like, sitting and talking and reminiscing. I do think this is the sort of thing she'd want, don't you, love?" he says, patting the chair next to him. Signaling his daughter, apparently, to sit down and be quiet about less pleasant topics.

"You know," he goes on as Scarlet takes her seat next to him, "John also reminded me that their parents had purchased burial plots for both Addie and me, next to theirs."

"In *Scranton?*" Scarlet can't imagine a less likely burial site for either of her parents. "Did you know about this?"

"Yes," Tom says, calmly sipping his coffee, "I did, though I'd forgotten about it. Addie told me about it a long time ago. They bought plots for the whole family, back when your grandfather became ill. I have to say her reaction to the whole thing surprised me. 'Don't you want to tell your parents we'll surely prefer to be cremated?' I asked her, and she said no. 'Why trouble them with thinking about that,' she said. 'They're likely to die well before we do; they won't know what happens to those other plots.'"

In fact both had died before Addie, her father when Scarlet was twelve, her mother three years ago.

"It always surprised me, how protective she was of her parents," Cora says.

"Or afraid of them," Scarlet says.

"Well, neither of those seems quite right to me," Tom says. "But I do think she cared more about them than she ever let on." He takes another sip of coffee, then says, "There's even a plot for you in the church cemetery in Scranton, Scarlet."

At hearing this, Scarlet laughs, then abruptly stops. She's actually never given it a thought—whether she'll be cremated or buried, or where. Were these the kinds of things she needed to start thinking about, she wondered, as a parent-to-be? Pondering it now, briefly, it occurs to her that next to her sweet old grandparents, in a cemetery in Scranton, might not be so bad. More feasible, certainly, than a place next to her mother— if Addie has her way.

"Can you sell a burial plot back?" Scarlet asks then, only half kidding.

"I don't know," Tom answers, sounding genuinely puzzled. "I never thought to ask."

"Maybe you get less on the resale," Cora says, and they all laugh, a little awkwardly.

"But why?" Scarlet asks. "It's not like it's going to be used."

"Right." Cora laughs. "It won't even be dug yet. Just an untouched piece of land."

"But of course, nicely mowed and watered and fertilized," Tom adds.

"Do they fertilize cemeteries?" Scarlet asks, incredulous. "I mean, do they really need to?"

"Do you think a corpse shot full of embalming fluid, vacuum-packed in an armor-plated coffin, is going to add a single nutrient to the soil?" Tom asks.

And then Scarlet isn't laughing anymore. Clearly Tom and Addie had been discussing this, she thinks, for who knows how long. Perhaps this *isn't* one of Addie's typically outrageous plans. *Could* Tom have been in on it all along? He's the one, after all, who's been insisting for the last year that he spotted a cerulean warbler—and keeping mum while Addie contended that *she'd* seen a long-extinct or even made-up bird—on the ridge above their home. He's also been writing endless letters designed, presumably, to shame Burnham College into refusing Bert Schafer's offer and thus prevent development of the land surrounding Nisky and Kleine Creeks. "What kind of institution of higher learning would fail to give sanctuary to an unbelievably rare species of bird, would sacrifice this real possibility for one more strip mall and a hundred new McMansions?" began his letter to the editor, published in the Philadelphia *Inquirer* last fall—a publication that didn't exactly endear him to members of the college administration, or, for that matter, to the significant number of faculty members who support the sale.

But despite all this, despite his efforts on behalf of two birds, one of which most people are certain Addie didn't actually see, and the surely irreparable doubt this has thrown on all of his work, even among many of his longtime fans and supporters—still, Tom *has* always been the sensible one. Sensible and practical, in the midst of all Addie's excesses. Surely that's who he'll be now, Scarlet tells herself, deciding to ask no more questions. She leans back in her chair and smiles back at her mysteriously smiling father. It does feel good simply to laugh about it all, this quandary of the proper resting place for Addie's restless body, to imagine that Tom has come up with a perfect solution, and that Scarlet can just relax and go along with her father's careful handling of it all. Which surely means, she

thinks, that they'll be arranging for cremation. Despite Addie's contention that that's nearly as unsound, environmentally, as a traditional
burial.

"That isn't true, you know," Tom said to Scarlet two weeks ago, after
Addie had made her request and then fallen asleep, and Tom and Scarlet
had stepped out of her room.

"What isn't?" Scarlet was still reeling from the conversation they'd
just had, from hearing Addie speak, barely above a whisper now that she
was so weak, so matter-of-factly about the finer points of her death.

"What Addie said about cremation. I'm sure some toxins do get
released, but it's not actually that bad. I think she has other reasons
for this."

At that point, Scarlet felt overcome with exhaustion, and also very
sick. It was late in the afternoon, the worst time of the day for her; she
seemed to have afternoon, not morning, sickness. "I can't talk about this
anymore," she said, and fled to the upstairs bathroom.

Now, remembering what Tom said, she wants to ask him more about
this, about Addie's—and his—views on cremation. Why, for instance,
couldn't they simply scatter Addie's ashes on the ridge between the
creeks? But she can't ask this now, not with Cora and Lou in the room. So
she stews in her own thoughts for a while, worrying, again, about how
they'll resolve this. Obviously, they can't actually honor Addie's wishes.
Can they? How could they possibly bury her illegally—and not just that,
not just bury her somewhere other than a cemetery, but on land that she
and Tom don't even own?

But if Addie truly had strong objections to cremation, what else could
they do? Bury her in the cemetery in Scranton, maybe—where, presumably, she'd have to be embalmed. Scarlet's stomach pitches, sending
something sour and dangerous toward her throat, at the memory of Addie's description of embalming. She closes her eyes and swallows hard,
willing the memory away.

Tom and Cora are laughing again, at some other memory of Addie presumably; Scarlet has stopped listening. But Lou, she notices, isn't joining in the general merriment anymore. She's become noticeably restless, shifting in her chair, fiddling with her sweater.

She turns to Tom. "So what *did* you talk about with Addie during these last few days?"

There's a sudden silence in the room; it's well past noon now, and the air is still—no birds calling or singing anymore, and even the waves seem to have quieted. Scarlet feels herself start to sweat again. When Tom turns to Lou and says, "We didn't dwell on the past, Lou," Scarlet looks to Cora, whose smile has faded. And there it is again: the uncomfortable, unnamed something that was in the room before.

Scarlet decides to leave the porch again. In the kitchen she pours a tall glass of water; as she drinks it, slowly, she can hear Lou sniffling in the silence.

"But dwelling on the past—on all the silly little details of the past— that's all we've been doing for three days," Lou suddenly says, her voice rising to an unfamiliar pitch. "There was so much I wanted to say, I should have said, but there was never *time*. And do you know why? Because we spent all our time doing *this,* just this very thing—laughing and joking and reminiscing, like we always did, carrying on like nothing was wrong, like we were just here having a little reunion on the beach. And my God—she was *dying*. And there were things I should have said to her . . ." She chokes on a sob. "And now I'll never have a chance to talk to her again."

Scarlet moves to the doorway, watching as Cora tries to hand Lou a napkin. But Lou, rocking back and forth with her eyes closed, doesn't see it. There are tears on Cora's cheeks as well. Maybe, Scarlet thinks, she should be crying too.

But she doesn't feel like crying now. She is staring at Tom, who is staring at the floor. Probably she has always known this, Scarlet realizes—

known that something happened with Lou. It was just there, after Addie came home from Washington. Somehow she could tell that something had changed between her parents. There was a strange quality, something in the air, it seemed—a heaviness, something that made it momentarily hard to breathe—when they were together in a room after that. It was *that*, that fleeting but insistent gasping for air, as much as Addie's various exploits, that had made Scarlet decide not to return to Burnham after Christmas that year she stayed in Cider Cove.

Of course, there had also been this other thing between her parents then—the first lump Addie'd discovered, the scare over her health. But they'd kept that from Scarlet; she hadn't learned about it until three years later, when Addie's cancer was full-blown. That may have been the first time—that time of the horrible gathering in the oncologist's office, followed, a month or so later, by their family trip to New York, to the Kollwitz show at a gallery on 57th Street—that it dawned on Scarlet: There were things about her mother and father that she didn't know.

Lou goes on, still rocking, her eyes still closed. "Do you know why I think it's *really* tragic, the way we laughed and joked and acted like nothing was wrong these last few days? It's this feeling I have now, that I'd known Addie for over thirty years by the time I sat with her last night, and now today, the day after she died, I feel like I know no more about her—about who she *really* was, what *really* went on inside that beautiful, stubborn, maddening head, than I did when we were twenty!"

They are quiet for a moment then. When Scarlet looks at Tom again, she sees that he looks peaceful, almost detached. It startles her when Cora speaks.

"Would knowing all that really make a difference, Lou?" she asks, staring at the table in front of her, fingering a pile of crumbs.

To her surprise Scarlet finds that she wants to defend her mother—her stubbornness, the ways in which she seemed unknowable. "When you tried to ask her things like that," she says—"you know, 'What's this really all about, Addie? What is it that makes you want to spend your time with lonely teenagers, fighting these battles with some local land developer?'—you could pretty much count on just getting another one of her lectures. Maybe about the dangers of too much pop psychology, too much energy wasted on trying to understand 'the self.'"

Tom smiles. "Often a lecture complete with recent scientific and pseudoscientific references," he says, looking at Cora, then signaling Scarlet to sit next to him again.

"It's why I liked the laughing and reminiscing," Cora says, finally dusting the crumbs she's been stacking in front of her into her palm and dropping them onto a plate. "I wouldn't change a thing about my last hours with Addie." She shrugs. "Call me a Pollyanna."

When she says this, Scarlet realizes, with a rush of relief that feels like an ocean breeze, that she also wouldn't change a thing about her last moments with Addie. Unlike Lou, she said what she wanted to say. And unlike Lou, she doesn't feel bothered by the mystery of Addie. Not now.

Two nights ago she'd held her mother's hand and looked into her eyes, which were remarkably clear, despite her obvious pain; she had declined the medication the hospice workers offered for as long as she could, saying she wanted to stay as clear-headed as possible. As she gazed into those remarkable, impenetrable eyes, Scarlet said, "You've taught me so much." It seemed that the words came, unaccountably, from her chest, which ached with a very real pain.

Because Addie *had* taught her a great deal, and at that moment she could see it, and she longed for her mother to teach her more. Who else, after all, had given her permission to be a poet? Who else, besides Addie, and also Tom of course, had let her search for, and find, a voice for all those years—and use it, without apologies or regrets? Who had let her fly from home to the shore that year, with no cajoling, no arguing, no burdening with guilt?

And now, on the verge of being this whole new thing, *a mother* (something far more mysterious to Scarlet than being a poet), she longed desperately for Addie's brand of certainty, her angry wisdom, her hard-won knowledge. No matter how maddening she had found it through the years.

It's true that you can feel your heart breaking, she found herself thinking, astonished. And despite herself, she was suddenly envisioning a poem.

Addie read her mind. "Don't waste precious ink writing poems about me," she said. Her voice, though so quiet Scarlet had to put her head next to hers to hear her, was as clear as her eyes. "Write about your child, write about all you learn and feel as a mother. . . ." Her voice trailed off, and Scarlet could see her retreat into the pain. It was clear this was exhausting her, and Scarlet tried to tell her to stop. *Be quiet now, Addie,* she tried to say with her eyes.

And then Addie smiled, the most heartbreaking, beatific smile. "You'll be a wonderful mother, Scarlet," she said. She looked gloriously beautiful, even as wasted and gaunt as she'd become. Scarlet had forgotten, she realized as she stared at her hungrily, just how beautiful her mother was. "Whatever you feel through it all," Addie went on in her breathy but clear whisper, "whatever ridiculous things people say to you, hold on to this: You will love your child as deeply as I've loved you, and that will be enough."

That will be enough. Scarlet closes her eyes now, smiling as she remembers Addie's words.

"That's what I said to Addie last night too," Cora goes on. "'I know you think I've always been a hopeless Pollyanna,' I said. And she said, 'No, Cora, you're an artist. And it's the artists who are the optimists, not the scientists, no matter what Tom always says.'"

Lou has gone over to sit next to Cora now, squeezing into her wicker chair with her, reaching her arms around her, leaning on her shoulder. "Do you know what Addie told me?" she says. "She said, 'If I had half your money and half your confidence, think what I could have done to that bastard Bert Schafer.'"

They are all crying and laughing then, except for Tom. Whatever happened with him, alone with Addie when she died, it is clear—from his quiet smile, his dry eyes, his Buddhalike composure—that all was well, for Tom and Addie, when she died. Tom is clearly at peace. At peace and, it seems, harboring no need to share anything about his last moments with Addie.

So his voice, when he finally speaks, surprises everyone. "A few weeks ago she told me something similar to what she said to you, Cora. 'You were wrong, you know,' she said. 'I'm more of an optimist than you've ever been.'" He is still smiling, though there is clearly pain, now, behind his smile. "I said to her, 'You're right, my love.'" His voice catches, and he pauses for a moment before he goes on. "'You are now, and you always have been.'"

At that moment, Scarlet sees it. Of course, she thinks. Of course they are going to honor Addie's wishes. How could she have thought otherwise? She can't quite imagine how they will do it, but it's clear to her, looking at Tom, that they will. Already they've begun following her instructions. Addie's body is safely resting on dry ice, and Dustin is at work on a simple, homemade coffin. What's next Scarlet can't quite imagine, but clearly Tom knows. She will simply need to rely on her father, Addie's one great love. On him, and on their strange, unknowable bond.

Thinking of it, suddenly Scarlet feels bold. Now, while they are all sharing everything, revealing what they said, or wish they'd said, to Addie: Maybe this is the time for her to reveal her own bit of news. *The last thing Addie told me was that I'll be a fine mother,* she could say, surprising Lou. And then, when Lou inevitably asks, immediately, about the baby's father, she could take this opportunity, this strange, still moment of remembering her mother, to break that other news too.

But as she opens her mouth to speak, they all turn at the sound of someone opening the screen door. It's Dustin, who steps quietly into the porch, still clutching his saw.

"The coffin's finished," he says. "What should we do now?"

Tom rises from his chair and walks over to pat Dustin on the back. "That was quick work, Dustin," he says. "Thank you. And now you should get a tall glass of water, and we should all eat some lunch." He looks to Cora then. "Did you say your friend the fisherman could also provide us with a refrigerated truck for the next day or so?" he asks her.

"Until Monday morning he said, yes," she answers. She looks puzzled, but it's clear she won't question anything Tom says, or asks for.

Lou, on the other hand, scoots to the front of the chair and looks over at Tom. "But Tom," she says, "you know you don't need a refrigerated truck. Whether you decide to cremate or not, whoever you call will transport Addie's body now."

He takes Scarlet's hand and pulls her from her chair. "We won't be calling anyone," he says, smiling at his daughter. And then he turns to Lou and Cora. "From now on I'm afraid you're going to have to leave things to Scarlet and me. It's what Addie wanted. We'll be fine," he says, nodding in Dustin's direction, "with Dustin's help."

Looking at this thin, angular boy, with his sweat-stained T-shirt, sawdust and wood shavings coating his arms, and his long brown hair, Scarlet is shocked by how much her feelings have changed. Suddenly she is filled with gratitude. To Dustin the idealistic young environmentalist coffinmaker, and to Tom, as always her strong and smart—if not always sensible—father. Of course they will take care of Addie's body now. How could they possibly let anyone else do it?

Standing, Scarlet realizes how exhausted she is. And she decides, with relief, that her own news can wait until another visit.

Tom walks with her to the foot of the stairs. "Go and lie down now," he says, stroking her hair. "I'll bring a sandwich up to you."

She has never been this tired, Scarlet thinks as she climbs the stairs to her room. With each step she remembers another time, a lifetime ago, climbing these steps as a bewildered teenager, meeting a sullen Richard or, later, a stoned Bobby—each seemingly oblivious to her presence—on his way down the stairs and out the door.

Below her she hears the three of them, Lou, Cora, and her father, banging pans, laughing and chattering, putting together some lunch.

Dustin turns on the shower in the bathroom next to her room. As she drifts to sleep she thinks of Addie's face, more peaceful in repose, there on the cot in the restaurant cooler where Scarlet and Tom laid her at dawn, than Scarlet could ever recall seeing her when she was alive.

"That's how she looked when I first knew her," Tom said as they positioned the bags of dry ice and tucked the sheet around her. An odd thing to say, considering that Addie had wasted away to dry, ashen skin shrunk over sharp bones, her long blond hair now gone completely gray, cut to just above her shoulders. And yet Scarlet understood what he meant; there was an innocence in her face, a kind of youthfulness in its stark lines. They lingered for a while before covering her fully, reluctant to leave her.

Remembering this, on the edge of sleep now, Scarlet thinks of Addie as a fevered twenty-one-year-old, floating free of everything she'd known before, deeply in love with Tom, with birds, with art. And then, only two years later, sailing home from Europe, and pregnant.

And finally, she lets the full flood of all that she lost last night wash over her.

fifteen

THE LUMP ADDIE DISCOVERED that time, in the fall of 1985 at Lou's, turned out to be benign. But the others that eventually followed were not. This time, though, Addie felt ready for them. It energized her, this feeling that the battle—against the cancer, yes, but also against what was, she was sure, its source: the ruining of the land—was suddenly more personal than ever.

Around the same time, Bert Schafer began cozying up to high-level administrators at Burnham College, a hopelessly cash-poor school whose founders had found it distasteful, not to mention morally suspect, to make ambitious investments with what little funds they had. Unfortunately for Burnham, several subsequent generations of administrators had shared this reluctance, and by the early 1980s, the school was teetering on the brink of insolvency.

If only those canny Quakers had reached their grasp just a little farther north, Tom liked to say. It was true that in the 1930s, the first time the school had nearly folded, a group of Quaker businessmen from Philadelphia had considered rescuing Burnham College, reopening it as a kind of Haverford North, but in the end, they'd decided against it. That time Burnham's savior had been a wealthy and eccentric alumnus, for whom both the library and the student center were named after he paid for the building of both at the end of the Second World War.

This time, apparently, the self-appointed savior was to be Bert Schafer. He wasn't an alum, but by the mid-1980s, with all the money he was making as a real estate developer, his tax situation demanded that he find some form of philanthropy, and soon. Preferring, he said, to keep his money "close to home," he went looking for a place in Bucks County—someplace where they would name things for you. By then another developer, some carpetbagger from Philadelphia named Driscoll (Schafer made much of the fact that he was a local Bucks County boy who'd grown up on a farm near Doylestown), had already beaten him to the county's two major hospitals, one of which now had a wing named for Driscoll's parents, the other a wing named for his wife. So Bert Schafer turned his attention to quiet little Burnham College. And in the fall of 1988, on the dreary November day when Addie learned that she had not one but two malignant tumors, the college ceremoniously dedicated the new Walter Schafer Gymnasium, named for its proud donor's grandfather.

But of course there was more to Bert Schafer's interest in Burnham College than plans for a few buildings bearing the family name. The one thing the college *did* have, thanks to several generous German farmers a century before, was land—acres and acres of meadows and second-growth woodlands, on rolling hills and along the banks of the two rushing creeks, all of it surrounding the village center and the heart of the campus, with its several intact colonial buildings, dating back to the time of the Revolutionary War. All of it quite lovely. And, with new access to a major east-west interstate just twelve miles north, below Easton, all of it increasingly valuable, and *very* desirable, to a developer like Bert Schafer.

The squatting and the arrests, Addie realized finally, had accomplished little or nothing in the end. In fact, even before the Burnham Estates fires, Bert Schafer had used the protests to his own advantage. "It's a free country," he'd been quoted as saying in an article in the local paper, following the squatters' second arrest in 1984, before construction of the new homes had even begun. "I respect these people's right to express their views. And I am truly sorry that those two owls might have to find a new place to live. But I wish these folks could understand that it's to *everyone's* economic advantage for our county to grow in this way."

Never mind that the day before he had driven his monstrously large pickup truck right to the edge of their tents, stepped out long enough to call them a few obscene names, then warned them that if a single one of them got anywhere near his contractor's equipment when it arrived later that day, he'd have their asses in jail faster than they could climb one of those goddamn trees they were so fucking in love with.

Addie enjoyed quoting him to Tom and other friends at Burnham. But unfortunately, no one from the local paper had come to interview *her*.

Schafer followed through on his threats, arranging for their arrest that afternoon, even though none of them, and none of their gear, was anywhere near the access road the contractor's workers used to drive in their trucks and cranes and bulldozers. They had deliberately set up camp inside a patch of woods on the border of the farmland Schafer had purchased, a woods that the farmer who'd sold him the land had, so far, refused to include as part of the sale.

But that farmer was now in a nursing home in Harrisburg, where, according to Bert Schafer, his two sons were "trying to get him to see reason" (to the tune of another twenty thousand dollars). The sheriff wasn't interested in splitting hairs. "Either way it's private property," he said as he steered Addie and her comrades into his and his deputy's cars, "and that means you're trespassing."

One rainy day the next June, Brian Kent helped Addie and Bob the engineer pitch their tents, brazenly, in the middle of the already pesticide-drenched lawn in front of the shell of one of the new model homes. They camped there, in the rain, for a week, during which there was no sign of the builders. Ten days later, when the sun finally returned, they were back in the county jail. This time the only coverage they got in the local paper was three lines in the daily log of arrests.

When three of the completed model homes burned to the ground, Bert Schafer achieved not only a public relations coup but a hefty insurance settlement as well. Two months later Brian Kent was in jail. Addie never heard from him again.

The winter that followed left her certain, at forty-two, that she didn't have long to do something, finally, that might make a difference, maybe even, somehow, make amends. For what, she wasn't able to say exactly. Something to do with Richard's sad life and death, Cora's silent suffering, Brian Kent's aimless unhappiness. Even, perhaps, her own cancer scare. Her strange distance from Tom and Scarlet, from her own work as an artist. She needed, somehow, to find a way to atone for all of that, and more, it seemed. Why it was her responsibility to do so, she certainly couldn't have said.

There was also that horrible exchange she'd had with Cora, the day after Christmas, in Cider Cove. All winter she dwelled on it, replaying everything that had been said, and, true to form, she read everything she could get her hands on, to help her understand what Cora had told her.

"I can't begin to tell you what it's like," Cora had said, "the way you keep on blaming yourself, the way other people let you know, sometimes subtly and sometimes not, that this whole thing has to be your fault." She laughed bitterly, then covered her eyes with her hands. "As if you needed anyone to add to all the blame you've already heaped on yourself," she said. "Over and over I asked myself, why didn't I recognize it earlier, why didn't I somehow protect Richard, why didn't I somehow manage to love him more?"

While she talked, Karl busied himself with building up the fire, refilling everyone's drink, going outside for more wood, whatever he could come up with to take him away from the conversation.

Tom could see the fury building up inside his wife, who rushed to Cora's side, embracing her. "How could you possibly have loved him more? You did *everything* for him. Why listen to all that ridiculous nonsense that passes itself off as science—as if all the horrors of this world could be explained by the so-called discipline of psychology!"

"Like that fool Bettelheim," Karl said then, drawn into the conversation despite himself. "Tell them about that ridiculous book."

Cora wiped her eyes. "A woman at our church recommended it to me," she said. "*The Empty Fortress,* it's called. It's about autism. He says the mothers of autistic children are like the SS guards in Nazi concentration camps—that cold and brutal—and that's why their children have become the way they are."

Karl rose again to poke at the already blazing fire.

Tom looked at Addie and realized there'd be no containing her now. Her face was flushed, and tears filled her eyes. He knew it was pointless, but he tried to keep talking, hoping she might have the sense to just leave the room.

"Seems odd that someone who thought children needed to hear the grisliest fairy tales, all that blood and gore and such, would come down so hard on mothers," he said.

That, it turned out, had been exactly the wrong tack.

"Of *course* he's going to blame the mothers," Addie snapped, her voice dripping with contempt. "They *all* do that, *always.*" She shook her head then, disbelievingly. "Jesus Christ! Nazi SS officers. At least he had the courage to say what all those goddamned fools really think. They *never* look at where and how their patients live, what they're exposed to on any given day, the garbage they're fed and the particles they're breathing in at school, the radioactive waste they're routinely exposed to, the absurdly contaminated water they're drinking."

"Or the genetic packages they've inherited," Tom said quietly, though by now it was clear no one was listening to him.

Addie didn't even look at him. She went on, ticking off a list of evils on her fingers, "Coal residue from industries like the steel industry. Contaminants in the water. Lead and arsenic and mercury in products children are exposed to every day."

"Stop it, Addie." It was Cora saying it this time, barely audibly. Not Tom.

But Addie was too caught up in her list-making to hear her. "Paint. Gasoline. Seafood. Dental fillings, antiseptics, thermometers, blood-pressure gauges. Fluorescent lightbulbs."

"I said *stop it!*" Cora rose from the sofa and walked briskly across the living room, toward the door to the kitchen.

She stopped, but didn't turn around, when Addie called after her, "Cora, wait—listen! Don't you see how all these things beyond your control were at the root of Richard's problems? Not *you*, for God's sake, not something you did or didn't do."

Slowly Cora turned to face her, her hands balled into fists, her eyes closed below her furrowed brow. "And don't you see," she said, slowly, her voice rasping and choked. "Don't you see that every time you do this, launching into all your research and statistics, regaling me with your litany of all the poisons my sons were exposed to every day of their lives— every single time you do this *you* blame me too, Addie? Maybe more than anyone, you blame me—for living where we lived, for feeding my family what I fed them. For letting them drink the water. Jesus, for taking my children's temperatures, for letting them be vaccinated!"

She stopped then, walking over and lowering herself into a chair beside the fire. "I know you mean well," she said. "But I don't think I can listen to this anymore. I simply don't want to hear it."

Tom had never seen his wife—his hotheaded, righteously angry, impetuous Addie—look so stricken. For quite a while she only stared ahead of her, first at Cora, then, it seemed, into the fire.

When she finally spoke, her voice was so soft and broken that Tom wondered if Cora could even hear her. "I *don't* blame you, Cora. I don't." And then they were all silent, for how long no one could say. And this was how Scarlet and Bobby, returning from their trip to the mall, found them.

They didn't speak of it again. But clearly that exchange had changed Addie somehow. Later, back in Burnham, when she returned *The Empty Fortress* to the college library, she complained bitterly to her friend Candace, the head librarian, about Bettelheim's treatment of mothers.

"Well," Candace said, "no surprises there. Who *doesn't* blame everything on their mom?" Then she led Addie to the art stacks, a section of the library Addie had known intimately back in her days as a student but that she hadn't spent any time in, really, for years now. There Candace pulled *The Diary and Letters of Kaethe Kollwitz* off the shelf. "Here's a healthy antidote to all that mother-bashing," she said.

Addie raced through the book that evening, and at the college bookstore the next day she asked Mrs. Hodges to order two copies. When they arrived, she sent one to Cora—secretly hoping that Scarlet might take a look at the book as well. She wanted both of them to read it, though she couldn't have said exactly what message she wanted to send them with this account of a life as mother and artist, cheerful and productive one day, the next filled with despair and self-doubt.

With the book she included a note that read simply, "I'm sorry." She hoped Scarlet might see the note as well; it could have been addressed to either her friend or her daughter. This was her attempt, however indirect, to apologize to both of them.

In the months after that painful Christmas in Cider Cove, Addie devoted much of her time to collecting, stuffing, and preserving dead birds, using Tom's state license and the tiny Burnham College "museum" of specimens to justify her work—at first. For years people had been bringing dead birds to Tom and her, convinced that the shining blue-black grackle or the flamboyant downy woodpecker corpse they'd found in their backyard (the former left there, no doubt, by their cat, the latter probably done in by a confused flight directly into their big bay window) was some rare and exotic species, tropical, maybe, based on those dramatic hues. Others, more thoughtful and aware (and often older), did bring less common species—a meadowlark, a Swainson's thrush, a sharp-shinned hawk—assuming Tom or Addie might want to stuff and mount it for their work. Dead birds had always been part of their life together, an occupational hazard of sorts for an ornithologist and a bird artist.

How did they die? Lots of ways. Cats. Still the occasional brush with a boy with a BB gun. Confused flights into large plate-glass windows—

like those stretching above the front doors and illuminating the cathedral-ceilinged foyers of Bert Schafer's Burnham Estates. And some—in fact most, Addie was convinced; certainly far more than anyone wanted to admit—had been sickened by eating plants or insects that were poisoned by pesticides, or by drinking water contaminated by runoff from the new developments popping up everywhere.

At first she simply decided to take the more intact ones to Richard Schantz, to have them stuffed and mounted; this was, after all, what the people who brought most of them seemed to expect. Before long she found herself collecting them on her own—a dead Canada goose she found along the canal towpath, two gulls from a weekend visit to the Eastern Shore; she wasn't looking for trophy birds.

One morning in early May, Addie arrived at Schantz's shop with a great blue heron someone had left on her doorstep. He laughed and said, "You ought to just learn to do this on your own, you know."

"Could you teach me?" she asked. She'd been thinking the same thing herself.

"I could, yes," he said. "But I'd say you're probably smart enough to figure it out on your own," and he pulled his dog-eared copy of Leon Pray's *Taxidermy* out of a drawer in his desk. She borrowed the book for a few weeks, eventually ordering a copy of her own. Even Mrs. Hodges, who thought she'd seen everything in ordering books for Addie through the years, raised her eyebrows at that one.

For a long time she couldn't have said what she was doing—gutting the poor things, disjointing their knees and tails, hanging them on a savage-looking chain-and-hooks contraption so as to pull their skins down over their heads and shoulders more easily. Perhaps she should have been a surgeon, she thought on occasion, contentedly immersed in the delicate work of trimming away ear and eyelid linings, removing eyeballs and brains. She set up shop in the tumbledown garden shed behind the cabin—a space both Tom and Scarlet, when she was home for visits, began to avoid assiduously—stocking it with tools ranging from scalpels and forceps to claw hammers, heavy thread and baling twine, galvanized wire, cotton batting, excelsior, glass eyes.

And there she worked through that winter and spring, and on into Scarlet's first years of college, with a dogged enthusiasm she could never explain to her husband or daughter. Sketching the stiff corpses from various angles. Using her paints and brushes, now, to touch up patches of bare skin and give bills and feet more lifelike color. Treating skins and dusting feathers with borax powder. She liked Pray's bluntness, his praise for borax—a recent replacement, at the time of his book, in the 1940s, for the formerly much-used arsenic—as taxidermy's "greatest boon—mothproofing that will not kill the operator."

One morning, well into her second year of this new obsession, Tom asked Addie if he might join her in the gardening shed (which he'd dubbed the "charnel house"), to watch her at work.

She raised her eyebrows over her cup of coffee. "You're sure you want to?" she asked. "You've always seemed kind of squeamish about it."

He shrugged. "Well, I've handled the finished product nearly every day for the last thirty years," he said, acknowledging the various stuffed and mounted specimens that were part of every ornithologist's laboratory. Necessary evils, Tom might have said, though he himself had never felt compelled to add anything to Burnham's inventory.

"If I start to grow faint you can wave some turpentine under my nose," he said, and she laughed.

Tom watched quietly through the morning, while she worked on shaping and stitching the false body of a red-tailed hawk that had been shot in the woods nearby, presumably by a bored teenager with a hunting rifle.

"Better a hawk than a bunch of kids at the high school, I suppose," said the owner of a nearby orchard, who'd found the dead bird and delivered it to Addie and Tom's house a couple days before.

Addie shuddered when he said it, relieved that Scarlet's years at the area high school were over. And thinking too of the photographs of nearby Hawk Mountain in the 1930s, its crest spread with hundreds of dead hawks, all laid in neat rows below a group of smiling hunters with their rifles held aloft. Now, as Tom examined the hawk's skin while she tucked, wrapped, and stitched, she said, "This one was harder. I haven't had to deal with too many shot holes or dried blood."

"You've cleaned it up quite well, I'd say," he said, turning the drying skin to examine it more closely. Then he walked over and sat down beside her, watching her work in silence for a while. Finally he said, "You know, I don't know why this never occurred to me before. You've turned to sculpture now. You're sculpting."

Of course. That was it. And how odd that for all these months it hadn't occurred to her, either, that this was what she was doing. But then, Tom had always had more confidence in her and her work than she'd ever had in herself. It may have been, in the end, her lack of training. Or her sense that she was trying, somehow, to do something else—to change people's minds, maybe, about how they chose to live—however much she might fail. Still, if she could never bring herself to say that what she was doing was "making art," she also could never stay away from the work for long.

Pointing to the two gulls, which she'd mounted in an awkwardly splayed position, he said, "Those you've crucified, haven't you?" He walked over to examine them more closely. "Two of the 'untouchables,' the underclass. They could hang on either side of a peregrine falcon, maybe. Or our sorry long-eared owl." He laughed quietly.

But she stared at the gulls in silence, her mouth open. How had she failed to see it? She looked then at the stuffed body of the hawk in her hands, and saw something else she'd only been feeling, moments before: a mother's body, soft and mournful, curving inward. She'd felt, as she shaped it, how she would mount it: as the anchor for a kind of feathered pietà. All these Catholic images! Of course Tom would see this immediately; for her, though, they'd been echoes of something else: Kollwitz's sculptures and engravings.

Her fingers, sticky with papier-mâché and bleeding at the tips, where she'd pricked them with the raw ends of wire, suddenly tingled. That night the dreams started again. And once again, the images washed over her faster than she could even begin to sketch them, to store them somehow for the months of work ahead.

She worked ceaselessly after that; every dead bird set off something like visions in her. If she still wasn't certain *what* she was making, it hardly mattered; all that mattered, now, was doing it.

If Tom had not forced her to go for a checkup in the fall of 1988 (making the appointment, dragging her from the shed to the car, driving her there), who knew how advanced her cancer might have grown? As it was, by the time the three of them, Tom, Scarlet, and Addie, sat in the oncologist's office two weeks later, there were already several lumps in Addie's breast. And they were not benign. At Tom's request, Scarlet had come home to accompany them to Addie's appointment with the oncologist, who urged her to begin chemotherapy as soon as possible.

Tom had hesitated, at first, to involve Scarlet in this way. But in the end he was glad he had. Clearly it was Scarlet's tears that convinced Addie to agree to the conventional rounds of treatment—Scarlet's tears that saved her; he was sure of it. Scarlet often said it was Addie who chose to fight the first time. But he remained convinced that Addie had fought for Scarlet.

She had never been able to bear her daughter's tears—bringing Scarlet to their bed at night at the first whimper, allowing her to stay home from school whenever her feelings were hurt by another child or, later, an unfeeling teacher. It was peculiar really, how powerfully it affected tough, steely Addie, seeing her daughter cry. Maybe, Tom thought, it was because Scarlet so seldom did, at least in their presence, past the age of three or four.

"You're going to make her incapable of getting on in the world," he sometimes warned his wife. Lamely, of course; he couldn't bear to see Scarlet's sadness either. Somehow Tom's tenderness when it came to his daughter made more sense. It was stranger in Addie, this unexpected softness, this hidden capacity for pain and sorrow in a woman whose *own* tears always seemed connected, not with sorrow, but with a bottomless rage. Strange, but there it was: It was Scarlet's tears that did it. Scarlet's tears, which cut her mother more deeply than every round of pesticides, every felled woodland, every diminished species of bird.

sixteen

PEOPLE SENT HER THE most ridiculous things during that year of chemotherapy, followed by a dose of radiation—and, lest she miss out on *any* of the horrors late-twentieth-century medicine had to offer, years of follow-up hormone therapy to wreak its own brand of havoc.

Books on visualization and "psychic healing." Endless arrangements of hideously tinted cut flowers. Even a newly released recording of birdsongs—two volumes, on compact disks (though of course she and Tom did not own a CD player). This even Tom had to laugh about ("All we have to do is open a window to hear most of these," he said, reading over the liner notes). Though he *did* borrow a machine from the college and listen to both volumes, pronouncing the recordings, in the end, "not that bad."

But Addie couldn't bear to listen to it. Even birdsongs, even Tom's beloved dawn chorus, had taken on a menacing timbre for her of late, linked, as she'd grown convinced those riotous songs were, with competition over shrinking territory; one study she'd read posited the dawn chorus as nothing more than a hostile choir of male birds signaling their aggressive intentions by mimicking each others' songs. So much for the friendly, playful banter she'd imagined she was hearing as a love-struck coed twenty-five years before, wandering aimlessly through the English countryside and the Pennsylvania woods.

She tried, though, to be grateful, to thank visitors for the flowers, read the books and articles Tom brought for her, enjoy the show of Käthe

Kollwitz's prints that Tom took her and Scarlet to see during that year's Christmas break. But never, in her life, had she felt so tired. So tired, and so sick—and so convinced, this time, that it wasn't going to end.

"You can't think that way," Tom told her with tears in his eyes. "You have to try harder to be optimistic, Addie. Or you really never will get well."

Suddenly Tom, the rational scientist, had turned into Norman Cousins.

He worked tirelessly to boost her spirits in any way he could. For years he'd been envisioning another sabbatical—maybe spent at Hawk Mountain, then Cider Cove, again. Nothing elaborate. Of course now they needed to be near the hospital in Philadelphia, at least for the months ahead. It also seemed to him less pressing to try to get Addie away from Burnham, now that she had work that, however different from the work of their early years together, was clearly satisfying to her. Or at least had been satisfying to her, before this setback.

He wondered about the following year, when Addie's course of treatment would be over. But he hesitated to ask her, fearing her grim response. Maybe, he sometimes thought, resting at home would be better for her than a sabbatical trip somewhere. Maybe Cider Cove would hold too many difficult memories for her. She seemed peaceful, now, at home in Burnham—too resigned for his liking, yes, but at least peaceful for a change.

Still, the machinations of Bert Schafer were always there on the horizon, buzzing or humming there like an out-of-tune fiddle, throwing everything out of whack. In recent years—and especially since Schafer had set his sights on the college, dropping money almost tauntingly here and there, clearly with his greedy eyes on all that land—Tom had come to dread the very sound of his name, reacting as strongly as Addie had years before.

Teaching satisfied him less too, in these waning years of Ronald Reagan's decade; students seemed to have become complacent consumers with little interest in learning, bored by everything—and boring themselves. He was turning, he realized with despair, into a jaded old boy of the faculty—one of those perpetually disgruntled geezers, lecturing from their yellowed notes, filled with a deep and abiding contempt for their students: the kind of colleague who'd both amused and annoyed him in his early days of teaching. It was time for a change, he knew.

But something or someone interfered with his plans, every time. First there'd been Addie's presumed connection with the fires at Burnham Estates, then Scarlet's choosing to live apart from them, in Cider Cove. Then, the next year, Karl's death and Cora's retreat into herself had made a stay in Cider Cove seem wrong, for everyone concerned. And of course now there was Scarlet's tuition to contend with—still a strain for them, despite her healthy scholarships.

But then, with Addie's sickness and exhaustion there in front of him each day, and—more disturbing than that—her apparent resignation, her inability, or unwillingness, whatever it was, to *fight* the damn disease, he thought, again, of trying to make it work anyway. In December, after the first dose of cytotoxins, he said to her, "What if we spent next year in Cider Cove? Would you like that? Wouldn't it be good for you to get away from here? You might rest better somewhere else."

Actually, all she did now, it seemed, was rest. Reading no longer seemed to interest her; even the trip to New York for the Kollwitz show appeared not to have reached her.

She stared vacantly at him for so long that he wondered if she'd even heard his questions. She sat in the rocker by the woodstove where she spent most of her days, dressed in a sweatshirt and jeans that hung loosely on her now. She'd lost a good deal of her hair as well, but it was her empty eyes, Tom thought, not her thin frame or nearly bald head, that made her look more like a corpse than like anything resembling the stubborn woman he'd loved for twenty-five years.

Finally she turned her gaze back to the window, to the light snow that had begun to fall that morning, dusting the feeder Tom had erected outside the window earlier in the fall. He'd set it up with the vague (and slim) hope that Addie might, at least, pick up a pad to sketch a bit through the difficult weeks ahead. Now it appeared that she didn't even see the junco below the feeder, doggedly pecking at seeds, though she was staring directly at it.

"Addie," he said finally, "do you hate the feeder too?" He knew some part of her surely did hate this clear emblem of connection to the cult of backyard birders—those who can't be bothered to walk into the woods, who expect the birds to come to them. But he'd hoped, since she was too weak to make her way to her old blind, that a feeder might somehow soothe her.

She turned back to him, her gaze a bit clearer now, he thought. "What?" she said, then shook her head. "I'm sorry. Cider Cove—you asked about Cider Cove. We can go there if you'd like, Tom. Whatever you'd like." She stood then, slowly, and turned toward the bedroom. "I'm going to lie down for a while."

It was Scarlet who helped him see what Addie needed. Not the blind, not a feeder. Scarlet, who'd been transformed, somehow, through some mysterious alchemy triggered by her time, the preceding summer, on Nantucket, and the writing course she'd taken during the fall when Addie had been diagnosed, into what he could only describe (in a phone call to Cora) as a contemporary version of her mother at this age. To which Cora had only replied, "Hmmm," then mumbled something about Scarlet's being, perhaps, a bit more independent than Addie had been. He'd decided not to take that as a criticism of him.

"I think you need to get her back into her charnel house," Scarlet said during her Christmas break, when they returned from the Kollwitz show in New York. And so one weekend after the holidays, when Scarlet had returned to school and the snow had melted, he set to work, installing a small woodstove, putting in sturdy windows, and—before he wrapped her in her old down coat and led her there—depositing, on the new work table he'd set up in place of the rickety old card table she'd been using before, two dead crows. He'd found them that morning, below the ridiculously oversized window above the entrance to Burnham College's newest building, the Mildred Schafer Auditorium.

Later Addie would credit Tom with pulling her through that very bad time, at the end of her first round of chemotherapy, and getting her back to work. "Everything I've done has been in collaboration with Tom," she would say in an interview; "he's been my teacher for thirty-five years, since the day I walked into his classroom." By that time, when *A Prosody of Birds* was being reissued in its millennial edition, it was Addie everyone called for pithy quotes about the dire state of the planet. To Tom's amusement, she worried that he might mind.

Gradually, in the winter of 1989, accustomed now to the nausea and fatigue, she got back to work. By springtime she'd begun painting a bit as well. In June, after another family gathering in the oncologist's office, Scarlet's tears once again working their magic, Addie reluctantly agreed to a follow-up round of radiation. In August she didn't even object—she seemed, in fact, hardly to notice—when the oncologist urged her to follow *this* up with hormone therapy: that daily pill. By then she seemed too engrossed in her work, maybe even too determined to go on living, to argue.

Meanwhile Scarlet, home for a month's visit and traveling back and forth between Burnham and Cider Cove, read them a draft of a poem she called "All the Bilge and Ruin." Here she was, their beautiful grown daughter, long legs filling the entire front-room sofa, long hair falling loose from a ribbon tied carelessly at the nape of her neck. A poet. She made them sit behind her, where she couldn't see them. "I can't see you looking at me while I read; I'll start laughing if I do," she said, and blushed. Her voice filled the room like honey, as gold and pure as that.

The poem seemed to be about everything from cormorants and herons flailing on some nameless shore, their faulty wings slick with the rainbow hues of an oil spill, to the struggles of Käthe Kollwitz, to the hidden lives of illegal immigrants. "A mystery, what or whom the artist loves" was one line Tom would never forget.

By the winter of 1991, after graduating and then moving to Vermont, into some sort of communal something-or-other in an old farmhouse outside Burlington, Scarlet had begun working on "Sick with Certainty," her blood-for-oil elegy in response to the Gulf War.

"Trust me, there's more than grand utopian visions going on there," Lou said, a few weeks after Scarlet and a pack of her friends ("neohippies," Lou dubbed them) had camped out at her house after marching against the war—protesting by day, relishing their host's food and wine by night. "Yes, they want to get back to the land and share the labor and the wealth and so on," she said. "But they're sharing more than that. And I could tell you exactly which one Scarlet's sharing hers with, if you'd care to know."

"That's her business, Lou!" Addie chirped in response. She had been pronounced clear of cancer the month before, and finally they were all together—Lou, Cora, Addie, and Tom—in Cider Cove, to celebrate. Addie was working steadily on several new pieces. "Assemblages," she called these new works, some of which incorporated paintings, both old and new. And all of which included models of actual birds that she'd gutted and stuffed—many of them found in or near newer housing developments, most of these Bert Schafer's, in southeastern Pennsylvania. And most of them, in all likelihood, poisoned by pesticides, a point Addie planned to stress in her accompanying artist's statement.

"That would be Kevin you're talking about, Lou," Tom said. "We've already met him. Seems like a terrific guy."

"Better than the Nantucket playboy, is he?" Cora asked. Though of course she knew the answer; Scarlet had spoken to her often, about both young men.

"Well, more to our liking, yes," Tom said, prompting Lou to roll her eyes.

"Seems to me a Nantucket playboy might set her up better than some sweet organic farmer boy in Vermont," she said. "A wealthy patron's not a bad thing, for an artist or a poet." She looked pointedly at Addie, who only laughed at her friend and shook her head.

Actually, Addie seemed circumspect about Kevin, as she had, also, about Scarlet's previous boyfriend, Nate. Tom had imagined that it would be harder for him to tolerate this—his daughter becoming a young woman, and clearly a sexual one. But in fact he'd liked both Nate and Kevin; it made him happy to think that his daughter found pleasure with these engaging young men, both of them like students he'd enjoyed through the years. And he'd been undeniably proud to watch Scarlet grow into such a beautiful girl, hints of red brightening her long brown hair, her former gangliness transformed into a graceful, long-legged frame (where her height came from was anyone's guess), so wonderfully at ease in her filmy peasant skirts and lacy camisoles.

He also adored her friends, the ones connected, now, with her confident new poet self—the girls, Kira and Gianna, who sang old Joni Mitchell songs in breathy harmony, Kevin with his guitar, clownish Mike who kept excusing himself to go outside to smoke. (Did he really think, Tom wondered, that they didn't know what he was smoking?) When Scarlet and several of these friends had visited for a few nights, en route back to Vermont after marching in Washington, he'd pulled out his fiddle, and they'd all drunk beer and danced and sung until the middle of the night. Their visit had even energized his teaching, grown so routine and stale in recent years. The morning after they'd left, he'd carried his fiddle to class, leaving his lecture notes behind in his office—something he hadn't done in years.

But a mother—and Addie in particular, he supposed—surely has her reasons for not completely trusting the men in her daughter's life. It pained him to think of it.

Did she ever speak of her fears or doubts to Scarlet? Not that he could see. It seemed to him that they barely spoke at all. And through those years of Addie's getting back to work and Scarlet's finding herself as a poet, it seemed particularly strange to Tom that his wife and daughter never spoke to each other about their work. Clearly they were influencing, even inspiring, one another—both of them making repeated references to Kollwitz. But it was Tom that Scarlet spoke to about poetry during those years, late at night, sipping scotch beside the woodstove, or staring at the moon and slapping at mosquitoes as they dangled their feet in Kleine Creek. Mostly they joked and teased, Tom insisting on the superiority of birdsong, Scarlet berating a typical passerine's limited emotional range.

With Scarlet, he thought, Addie seemed almost shy. The same was true of Scarlet with her mother.

Yet, though credit always seemed to be given to him, for helping Addie through the first cancer, for steering her back to her work, the truth was it was Scarlet who seemed to keep making the right suggestions. First it was getting Addie back to her charnel house, a place Scarlet would never have stooped to mention by name just a couple years before. Then, home from Vermont for Christmas in 1991 (and clearly mourning, but tight-lipped about, her recent breakup with Kevin), she suggested Tom call his former student, the owner of the gallery in New Hope where Addie had had a show of her paintings eight years before.

He balked at that idea at first. "You mean a show of these new things, the assemblages?" This work was so radically different, Tom thought; what might the gallery owner who'd loved her earlier work think of it? And if he declined, what might that do to Addie? "I don't know, Scarlet. I'm not sure what he'd think of this stuff."

"He'll be interested if there's a collector who's already interested," Scarlet said.

He stared at her blankly. "Well, sure," he said. "You have someone in mind?"

"Call Lou," she said then, with a casualness that he somehow didn't trust. What exactly had she and Lou talked about last winter, when Scarlet and her friends had stayed at Lou's house?

She squatted down to examine something at the edge of the canal; they were walking the old German shepherd named Jinx (Tom and Addie's most recent stray, found foraging in their compost pile three years before, on the morning when Addie's doctor had discovered several new lumps in her breast). No, he decided as he watched her; she doesn't know. If she did, she'd never have suggested such a thing.

"How'd you suddenly become so clever and conniving?" he ventured, clearing his throat.

She shrugged and smiled as she stood, reaching to take Jinx's leash from him. "I've been talking to Cora. It was her idea. A good one, don't you think?"

He didn't really think so, for a lot of reasons. Addie would never go for that, he thought, and Lou was such a loose cannon; who'd want to have to deal with her? But then he realized that all it really came down to—the main reason, really, that he didn't like the idea—was that it meant he would have to call Lou.

"Why doesn't Cora ask her about it?" he said. As soon as he asked, he realized that of course Cora had to know; both women had surely told her. How could he have imagined otherwise? And now, presumably, she'd come up with a way for them to make up for the mistakes of the past.

"She thinks the idea should really come from you, Dad," Scarlet said, yanking Jinx away from another dog's recent deposit. "Maybe you could invite Lou up to see what Addie's been doing, that kind of thing." She winked at him then. "You know, flatter her. Court her a bit!" With that she shook the leash and clicked her tongue, running ahead of him, pulling Jinx into a reluctant trot.

He watched her gamboling with the dog, looking—from this distance—like she had as a thirteen-year-old, all arms and legs and boundless energy, running ahead of him on whatever trail they were traveling. Well, he thought, now of course he'd have to make the call. How could he not?

Through the years that followed, he did wonder whether Lou had truly loved Addie's new work as much as she said. The piece she chose to buy, via Tom's former student the gallery owner, was the one that would eventually cause all the trouble—or all the excitement, depending on how you saw it; Tom could never quite decide.

Titled *After Kollwitz*, it was based on an 1896 etching of Kollwitz's called *From Many Wounds You Bleed, O People*, a triptych of sorts. In the center panel, a traditional Christian lamentation scene, a man with a sword bends over a nude male corpse; on either side are nude female figures, bound to columns, crucifixion-style.

In Addie's assemblage, the female figures were replaced by lifelike models of two stuffed ring-billed gulls, hideously splayed and nailed to miniature crosses. Between them was a painting—a large one, four feet by five feet: a self-portrait of Addie on a hospital bed, bald, gaunt, and nude (the likeness is impressive, and eerily prescient), an IV tube attached to her arm. Above her is a window, a view onto the world outside: rows and rows of Burnham Estates–style McMansions. In the center of the window is a gate before this hillside clogged with new houses as far as the eye can see, and on the gate is a sign—a photograph of the actual sign at the entrance to the real Burnham Estates. Eventually Addie's show in New Hope—centered on this piece, along with a *Pietà* depicting a wounded juvenile hawk and its mother—generated a bit of a fuss, a flutter of indignation here and there, and some admiration too.

But reactions in New Hope in 1992 were nothing compared to the trouble, or excitement, to come two years later, when Lou pushed Addie to apply for a grant from the National Endowment for the Arts (and pulled some strings to make sure she got one). Then she helped arrange for several of Addie's assemblages, including *After Kollwitz* and *Pietà*, to be included in a show at a prominent gallery in Washington. And one cold and dreary day in 1994, Bert Schafer invited the conservative Republican senator Howard Swenson—a devout Catholic from western Pennsylvania, to whose last campaign Schafer had made several sizable contributions—to join him in viewing that show.

Schafer must have thought he'd won the battle when Swenson and his cronies in the Senate had succeeded in getting Addie's grant rescinded. He'd made much of the fact that he'd chosen *not* to sue her for libel. "It's not about money, or about the defaming of a wonderful, small-town neighborhood," he said. "The shocking thing here is this so-called artist's despicable use of the most sacred images of Christianity."

"Libel?" Lou screamed with laughter. "*Libel!* Against what—a goddamn *housing development?* Against Jesus Christ?"

They all laughed then, and clinked their glasses. They were all together again—Addie and Tom, Cora, Lou—now in the fall of 1994, this time seated on the plush sofas and chairs in Lou's living room, celebrating once again. This time Scarlet was there too, taking a break from her graduate work in Massachusetts.

They were celebrating because suddenly *After Kollwitz* was worth well over ten times the amount Lou had paid the New Hope gallery owner two years before. And now plans were under way for a show in New York.

Tom looked at Addie that evening, trying to read her dazed smile. *Was* she enjoying this? Certainly she *looked* happy, glowing really, lovelier than she had in years. And why shouldn't she be happy? Suddenly her work—and her passionate anger—was reaching more people than she would have ever dreamed. For her sake, then, he sipped his champagne, kissed his wife's cheek, and smiled.

His kiss woke her from a kind of reverie. She'd been thinking, almost dreaming really, behind her glazed smile, about her twenty-one-year-old self, roaming the Burnham hills and woods with Tom. She felt like that now—as if she were twenty-one again, her life just beginning, but know-

ing a bit more. Knowing this time, for instance, that it couldn't last. Because of course the cancer would return; she knew this with absolute
certainty. The sense of urgency this gave her made her giddy, like she
might bubble over some edge at any moment, like the champagne Lou
kept uncorking.

It was all she could do not to take Tom's hand and lead him, right now,
up to their king-sized bed in Lou's "guest suite" upstairs.

The more she smiled, barely able to suppress whatever this was—
perhaps only the hormone therapy, she thought—the more they all smiled
back at her. Seeing this made her giddier still, and she bit her lip to keep
from laughing. Of course she knew they thought, Lou particularly, that
she was only grinning and giggling over all that had happened in the last
few months—the success of the show in Washington, all the attention
and acclaim once the grant had been rescinded.

In truth, she could take or leave all the attention, though the money
was certainly nice. She and Tom were planning to travel; already there
were invitations, from a foundation in Santa Fe, from an artists' retreat in
Florida, from a private collector who wanted to host them at his home in
Costa Rica. And it pleased her, of course, that suddenly her work, and all
she'd been trying to say for years, was finally reaching people. But she
doubted this was going to change that many minds, in the long run; she
was still convinced it would take more than art to do that.

She'd known that Lou had not loved *After Kollwitz* half as much as
she'd claimed. Since their days as students—since, maybe, the earliest
days of her crush on Willem de Kooning—Lou's tastes had run more toward Abstract Expressionism and the like. She'd always hated "art with a
message."

But Addie had gone along with Tom and Lou and all their plans. For
them. For their sakes: finally to soothe their guilty consciences, to free
them.

Meanwhile, all she wanted was to get back to work. To make love to
her husband, get out of bed early, and take a big mug of coffee back to her

shed. But for now she'd swallow her restlessness and tip her glass and join in the merriment.

Lou was ebullient, and Cora was happily passing around pictures of her first grandchild, now a month old. And there was Scarlet, watching them all and smiling, her hair cut short, dressed in jeans and a T-shirt, fresh from her simple life in her simple room in Massachusetts (a celibate life, she'd told Addie, with a peculiar sort of pride). Even as she watched the rest of them, smiling absently, Scarlet was thinking about a poem, Addie was sure of it; she recognized that faraway, happy look and the way her daughter's fingers tapped a rhythm on her knee.

Even Tom was smiling happily, seated in this richly decorated room that she knew he hated, sipping champagne, which he also hated, from Lou's expensive crystal.

And she, Addie Sturmer Kavanagh, was alive and, for the moment, well. She took Tom's hand and squeezed it. She didn't tell him, then or later, that she'd stayed at that and countless other parties and receptions and tributes in the years that followed, for him.

seventeen

THE SUMMER AFTER SCARLET'S sophomore year at Bates, she worked as a waitress in the restaurant of an old inn in 'Sconset, on the eastern shore of Nantucket. 'Sconset was a glorious town, with wild roses blooming along every perfectly weathered fence row and with beautiful beaches, populated mainly by summer residents, some of whose families had been summering on Nantucket for generations.

Other families—like her boyfriend, Nate's—went even further back, to the original English residents of the island, whalers from Nantucket Town. It was Nate who'd gotten Scarlet the job at the inn; the owner was a friend of his father's.

Every moment that she wasn't waitressing that summer (and there were precious few of these, as the summer wore on; by early August, most of her fellow college-aged waiters and waitresses had quit, happy to burn through the money they'd earned so far, partying and beach-hopping on Martha's Vineyard or the Cape), Scarlet spent sailing with Nate. This, she thought at the time, was to be her future: summers spent sailing with her handsome, suntanned husband at the family compound on the outskirts of 'Sconset, winters in Boston or New York with her husband the successful lawyer, which was Nate's plan, if he could get his grades up.

Never mind that that summer, while Nate barhopped with his friends, Scarlet was working two shifts a day at the inn, serving endless plates of artfully arranged swordfish and scallops, opening bottle after bottle of chardonnay. And that she was staying not at the family compound—his parents wouldn't really approve, Nate had said apologetically—but in a T-shirt- and underwear-strewn room above the inn's kitchen that she shared with two other "summer girls," girls whom she rarely saw and whose names she had forgotten by the end of the summer.

Still, through June, July, and into August, Scarlet persisted in this belief: She would marry, if not Nate, then someone like him. And eventually she and this husband would live, with their two perfect children, in a big, spotless house in some old, tasteful, and moneyed suburb with good schools. They would have a television, two nice, new, and rust-free cars, and a big, tidy backyard without a single bird carcass visible anywhere. At last she would be normal. Marriage would give her that, at last.

This vision persisted through not one but *two* women's studies courses, in which Scarlet did quite well. Which wasn't to say that anything she read, talked about, or wrote about in those courses actually reached her. So she had every right to expect to earn as much as, or more than, her male peers at Bates. So what? she thought. At that point, she knew that what she wanted to do was write poetry, a profession that would leave her equally destitute were she male or female. Marriage seemed the only viable route.

It wasn't women's studies that changed Scarlet's mind. It was Käthe Kollwitz—and, indirectly, Addie and Cora. Addie, who surely knew that if she'd sent a book like Kollwitz's *Diary* to Scarlet directly (she'd tried, often enough over the years, with Rachel Carson, then people like Aldo Leopold, Jessica Mitford, Wendell Berry), she wouldn't read it. And Cora, who might have left the book out in plain view on the coffee table in the living room, but chose instead to leave it—along with Addie's brief, cryptic note—half hidden in a pile of books in her study. So of course Scarlet found it, and read it in secret.

In 1941 Kollwitz wrote in her diary that "originally pity and sympathy were only minor elements leading me to the representation of proletarian life; rather, I simply found it beautiful." Scarlet might have found this impossibly smug and patronizing if she hadn't, on some gut level, also found it true. If she hadn't found the busboys and dishwashers and maids at the inn, many of them illegal immigrants from Guatemala, kinder, more interesting—and yes, more beautiful—than Nate's friends and family, truthfully even than Nate.

And if she hadn't, one morning in August, awoken bleary and hungover from a night of drinking with Nate and his friends, sickened by that morning's mechanical sex with her still drunk boyfriend—who, Scarlet felt, could have been humping a piece of furniture, for all the interest and affection he displayed. Later that morning she stepped into the motorboat she and Nate were to take out to his sailboat, anchored farther out in the bay, took one look at the oil-slick puddle of bilge below her feet, and immediately vomited over the side.

She and Nate had little to say to each other after that morning, when Scarlet stepped out of the boat without a word, went back to her room, and fell asleep. That night, after her shift in the restaurant, she climbed out the window of her room and sat on the folding chair on the fire escape where her roommates, both of whom had quit their jobs and moved on by then, had gone to smoke. It was a gorgeous night, a full moon and a sky blazing with stars, and Scarlet sat there, notebook on her knees, scribbling away until dawn.

That was the beginning of a change in Scarlet—or maybe less a change, she sometimes thought, than a simple acceptance of who she truly was. A would-be poet. Tom and Addie Kavanagh's daughter. Not particularly normal. Addie's cancer contributed to this acceptance, though Scarlet spent a good part of her junior year in college, the year of Addie's diagnosis and treatment, pretending it wasn't happening. But each time there was to be an appointment with the oncologist—a loaded one, a "what do we try next" one—at Tom's request, Scarlet was there.

Not surprisingly, Addie had no use for pink ribbons and pink teddy bears, or for walks and runs "for the cure." "No cure is going to come from making the damn disease look cute and pink," she said when Scarlet came home with a breast-cancer awareness T-shirt and mistakenly wore it into the kitchen one morning.

Scarlet had been running since her last summer in Cider Cove. She wasn't a competitive runner, but during the spring semester of her junior year at Bates, as Addie's chemotherapy was winding down and she was once again immersed in her work, Scarlet signed up for the local Race for the Cure. It would be, she decided, her own personal vigil for and tribute to her mother, whom she'd barely recognized when she was home for Christmas break.

Scarlet hadn't gone with Addie to a single session of her treatment. She liked to think this was because Addie refused to let her. This might well have been the case, had Scarlet offered; Addie was adamant about her daughter going on with her life at school, and not making extra trips back to Burnham to be with her parents during that time. But in fact Tom never asked her to go, and she never offered.

For some misguided reason Scarlet wanted Addie to see her Race for the Cure T-shirt that morning in the early summer, on her first visit home in two months. There were no teddy bears on it at least. But there *was* an image of a big pink ribbon, the words "Race" and "Cure" in neon-pink letters. When she heard Addie's response to the shirt, she thought about running again, this time out of the house and into her car—back, maybe, to the relative safety of Cider Cove.

"I'm sorry, Addie," she said, stepping back from the stove, where Addie stood stirring a pot of oatmeal. "I wasn't thinking—I'll go and change."

Addie reached over to stop her, her thin hand resting on Scarlet's shoulder. Scarlet glanced at the band of pale skin on Addie's ring finger; she'd removed her one piece of jewelry, her gold wedding band, now too loose for her bony finger. She'd never seen her mother's hand without it, Scarlet realized.

"You don't have to change, Scarlet," Addie said, covering the oatmeal and then sinking into a chair at the kitchen table and reaching for a section of the newspaper. "I'm sorry—that must have sounded thankless and cruel." She whipped open the newspaper, then put it down in front of her and rested her head on her hand. "Do I sound that way a lot?" she asked, looking up at Scarlet. She knew the answer, of course; Tom had repeatedly pointed out to Addie, in recent months, that she ought to at least try to express gratitude for people's gestures. Scarlet stared at the table, uncertain how to respond. Cooing, comforting noises of reassurance wouldn't sit well with Addie, she knew.

"Sometimes," she finally said.

Addie smiled, staring at Scarlet, who suddenly realized there were tears in her mother's eyes. "I really am sorry, Scarlet," she said. "It's just that I feel like we're all sick, so sick with all our certainty about this disease, all our silly self-assurances. Our teddy bears and pink ribbons. And meanwhile we go on living like we always have, poisoning ourselves and our children, just setting ourselves up for more."

It was the first time Scarlet realized how deeply all this truly pained her mother. How preventable her own suffering, and that of every other cancer victim, seemed, to her, if only people would open their eyes and see.

Less than a year later Scarlet watched "smart bombs" coursing across a television screen, video-game-style, masking the reality that most of the bombs used in the Gulf War—like the one dropped on the Ameriyya air-raid shelter in Baghdad that killed over two hundred civilians, many of them children—weren't, apparently, all that smart. She thought then of her mother's words. "Sick with certainty," she kept muttering to herself. She'd read somewhere that birds can, somehow, anticipate the shocking arrival of a bomb, rising and fleeing in panicked flocks, seconds before the explosion. Actually, she couldn't recall whether she had read this or dreamed it. Wherever it came from, she realized that what she had, suddenly, was the rough outline of a poem.

She didn't finish "Sick with Certainty" for a year and a half—not until after her sweet, bearded boyfriend, strong and sensitive Kevin, announced one day that he would be moving into the bedroom two doors down from theirs, in the drafty old Vermont farmhouse they were sharing with six other recent college graduates. To share a bed with Gianna, into whose room he'd apparently been sneaking, after lulling Scarlet to sleep with his sweet lullabies, for the past three months.

For a while Scarlet worried that *real* poems—good ones, not the countless discardable ones she kept tinkering with in her notebook—were only going to come to her when her heart was broken. But her experience after moving out of the farmhouse and, in the fall of 1992, enrolling in a graduate program in writing, suggested otherwise. During those three essentially celibate years of graduate school, she wrote the rest of the poems in her book. It all came to her in a rush: her life with Addie and Tom, Cider Cove, Richard, Cora—and many of those poems came to rest, somehow, in the body, or the song, of a particular bird. She hadn't realized how much of Tom and Addie's great passion she'd absorbed.

She actually thought of titling her book *Ontogeny Recapitulates Phylogeny*, in a kind of tribute to Tom. But also as her own private joke, her way of asserting that we all become our parents eventually—though this wasn't, of course, what Ernst Haeckel was saying at all.

"Don't call your book that, whatever you do, my love," Tom said when she ran the idea by him. "You're still not really understanding Haeckel, I'm afraid."

They were sitting in a café on Greene Street in Soho at the time; around the corner, in a gallery on West Broadway, Addie was busy with the mounting of a show of her work. It was the winter of 1996, and Scarlet had moved to New York the summer before, into a small but comfortable apartment on the Upper West Side that she rented for a song. This was yet another perk of being the child of Addie and Tom Kavanagh: The apartment was owned by one more bird-crazed admirer of her parents. Her book was to be published the following fall.

Scarlet chose not to be insulted by Tom's reaction to her idea for a title. He hated New York, she knew; something about the city always made him short-tempered.

Even Addie seemed exhausted, during that week of mounting her show, by all the fuss and attention that had followed her since the Senator Swenson brouhaha two years before. Tom and Scarlet were both worried about her health, though neither was saying anything; it was a relief when, once the show was up, Addie announced that she wanted to get out of New York, even to skip the opening. "Lou can play gracious hostess," she said; "she'll do a far better job than I would." She also proposed to Tom that he apply for that long-deferred sabbatical for the following year. "Let's hide out someplace far away from all this for a while," she said, "and let Scarlet bask in her new life and her book, without us breathing down her neck."

It was Addie's fame that Alex, her editor, wanted to capitalize on, Scarlet felt, when he suggested she try for a title having to do with birds. "It's part of your work, after all, this whole bird thing," he said. Alex had actually been a good, and sensitive, editor of Scarlet's work. They'd been working together since Scarlet's prize for the book had been announced, in the spring of 1995. And they'd been sleeping together since the summer that followed, when Scarlet moved to New York and he took her out to dinner, two days after she arrived.

In the end, they settled on *All the Bilge and Ruin* as the title, with a Morris Graves painting called *Little Known Bird of the Inner Eye* on the cover. Alex agreed with Scarlet that anything by Kollwitz, or by Addie, for that matter, would be too obvious. In fact he seduced her by finding the Graves painting and showing her a picture of it that night he took her to dinner.

Alex's marriage hadn't held much energy or passion for a long time, he told her at that first dinner; he and his wife stayed together, he said, out of some sort of loyalty, as much to their families as to each other. She was in publishing as well, a high-level executive at another house, and at one time she'd been *his* editor; he'd published a couple books of poems him-self. By the time Scarlet met him, though, he and his wife rarely saw one another; she worked around the clock, and traveled constantly, without him. They'd each had a series of affairs, and they seemed to find that a workable arrangement.

Like others in that series, presumably, Scarlet imagined, for quite a while, that she would be the one to make him change his loyalties at last.

For one thing, he told her, often, that he truly wanted children. He and his wife had considered it for a while, but when she didn't become preg-nant after a year of infertility treatments, she decided her heart really did belong to her work. For the first few years, Scarlet continued to harbor the fantasy of having several little poetry-loving babies with Alex. It was easy enough to replace the highly paid lawyer with a house on Nantucket from her college years with a well-enough-paid editor who had a number of friends in the Hamptons.

Perhaps he was a father figure as well. This was the argument of some of her friends, Lou among them—less because of his age (he was only ten years older than Scarlet) than because of his appearance: He bore a striking resemblance to Tom. He could have been a "black Irishman," as Tom liked to call himself, with his dark eyes and curly dark hair, though in fact he was Jewish. He also had the most sensuous mouth Scarlet had ever seen—far fuller in the lips than Tom, as she pointed out to Lou on several occasions. That first night he took her to dinner, she couldn't take her eyes off his mouth, this mouth that was talking, in hushed, nearly reverent tones, about how powerfully her poems had affected him.

He could seem arrogant, Scarlet knew, even cold. Lou was quick to point this out as well. "Since when do you find arrogance unappealing in a man?" Scarlet finally asked her, and that silenced her for a while. Cora, of course, was more understanding, as Cora would be. "You'll figure out what to do," was all she said to Scarlet during her many tearful visits to Cider Cove after she became involved with Alex. Scarlet knew what Cora meant by this was that she'd eventually figure out a way to leave him. Cora was considerably more confident about that than she was.

Addie and Tom stayed out of it—their way always. For the first year or so, Scarlet hid her involvement with Alex from them; she feared their disapproval, which seemed strange to her later. Eventually hiding the affair seemed pointless—it was such a large part of her life by then—and so one evening when Addie and Tom came to see her in New York, she invited Alex to join them for dinner. He was charming, of course; she could see that Tom liked him, though Addie was (as always, when it came to the men in Scarlet's life) a bit more reserved. When Scarlet told them, the next time she saw them, that Alex was married, Tom was visibly shaken by the news. Addie only nodded and said, "I thought so."

A few months after that, Alex spent a weekend with Scarlet at Cora's; there was probably no safer place to go with her than a quiet, nondescript town on the Jersey shore, after all. Lou was there that weekend too, as were Addie and Tom. Everyone treated Alex cordially. Before long, everyone seemed to think of him as Scarlet's boyfriend, plain and simple. Even she could forget, sometimes, that he was not fully available to her. Sometimes it seemed to Scarlet that life simply conspired to make her stay with him. There was the time, for instance, not long after her book was published, when she came home one day to find a hauntingly familiar voice on her answering machine. It was Bobby, and he sounded surprisingly like he had that summer before she'd left for college. She'd seen him on a few occasions after that, when they both happened to be visiting Cora in Cider Cove. He'd gone on to college in Albany, as he'd planned, and a year after he'd graduated had married his college girlfriend, a pretty, dark-haired girl named Cynthia, from Long Island; Scarlet had gone to their wedding at Cynthia's father's house in Patchogue.

Over the years Cora had worried, Scarlet knew, about Bobby's drinking. She didn't know if Cora knew about his drug use; she imagined, knowing Cora, that she had willed herself not to know. But Bobby seemed to be doing all right during those years after college; he had a good job as an investment adviser, and he and Cynthia had bought a house outside Princeton. They had one young daughter, and when Bobby called Scarlet that day in December 1996, Cynthia was pregnant with their second child.

They met for a drink a few days later, at a bar near his office in the World Trade Center. Scarlet hardly recognized him when he walked through the door; he could have been just one more of the clean-cut, gray-suited, postwork crowd. But then she saw his face—the same dark, brooding eyes, so unlikely above the carefully tuned smile he gave her.

They hugged each other, a little awkwardly, and then he said, "I'm sorry I haven't read your book yet, Scarlet. I'm going to—it's just tough right now, you know, with work and the family and whatnot. I'll get to it, though. It must be pretty exciting for you, having a book out."

Scarlet waved his praise and apologies away; she was used to this sort of greeting by then.

Then he pulled a copy of the book out of his coat pocket and placed it on the table between them. "Will you sign it for me anyway, before we go?"

She was used to this as well. "Sure," she said, trying to smile as gratefully as she could. "It was really sweet of you to buy it." Thinking, all the while, And what do I write on the title page of this copy? "To the love of my lonely teenage years; thanks for deflowering me"?

They made polite small talk for an hour or so—about his family, Scarlet's time in New England, Cora and her business at the bed-and-breakfast, Addie's sudden fame.

"Now she just seems to want to hide out in Burnham, with Tom," Scarlet said. "I think all that attention wore them both out. I'll go there to see them in a couple weeks," she said, "for Christmas."

Bobby nodded, then flagged the waitress for a third drink. Scarlet was still on her first beer.

"Will you go to Cora's for Christmas?" she asked, grasping at straws. What were you supposed to talk about with an investment adviser?

He took a sip and nodded. "Yeah, well, actually we'll just be there on Christmas Eve. Then we'll go to Cynthia's family on the Island for Christmas day. Mom says that's fine, that she likes her solitude on those big family holidays." He shrugged. "Who knows if she really means it? You know my mom."

That sounded more like the Bobby Scarlet used to know, she thought— too aware for his own good, and cynical in the face of all that awareness. They bumbled on then, laughing as they recalled the Christmas eleven years before, when they'd returned from the mall with their newly purchased music to find their parents mysteriously silent, locked in some sort of miserable tableau, both their mothers wiping away tears.

She was struck by the fact that despite having polished off four vodka tonics in the hour they'd spent in the bar, Bobby showed no signs of being drunk. It seemed there was something he wanted to say to her but for some reason couldn't.

When the check came he whipped out a credit card, pushing away the five-dollar bill Scarlet proffered. While he signed the slip she pulled on her coat and gloves, eager to escape into the cold air of the Manhattan evening. If this is what married life and a house in the suburbs look like, she was thinking—the drinking, the gray suit, nothing interesting to talk about—she wanted nothing to do with it.

She was standing to go when he reached over to take her hand. "Wait," he said. "You haven't signed my book yet."

"Oh, right!" She laughed nervously and sat back down. "I completely forgot." In fact she hadn't forgotten, but she'd been hoping he had. She pictured the book on Bobby and Cynthia's spotless coffee table in their spotless living room, unopened and unread. Then, while she fumbled in her purse for a pen, racking her brain for something innocuous, but friendly enough, to write, Bobby reached for her hand again. When she looked up at him, his eyes looked haunted.

"Do you ever think about Richard?" he asked.

Scarlet stared at him, shocked, for the moment, into silence. "Yes," she answered honestly, when she finally found her voice. "Yes, Bobby, I do. Not as often as I did for a while." And not in such horrific detail, she thought but didn't say. "But I still think of him, and of you, and of our summers together."

He let go of her hand then, but he continued to stare into her eyes, as if he were searching for something. She had no idea what he was thinking. His breathing suddenly seemed inordinately loud—loud and fast.

"There's a poem in here that's sort of about Richard," she said at last, looking away and opening the book to sign it. "The one called 'American Bittern.'"

"To Bobby," she wrote inside his copy of her book then. "Remembering Cider Cove, and Richard, and our midnight rides through the cemetery."

"I *will* read it," he said when she handed the book back to him. "I know you don't believe me, but I will."

She stood up and kissed him quickly on the cheek. "I believe you," she said, even though she didn't.

She stopped outside the door of the bar and took a few deep breaths. A light rain had begun to fall, and the narrow streets of the financial district were slick and gleaming with light, crowded with cabs and people huddled under umbrellas. She had written those poems, she told herself as she stood there breathing it all in, and she had put that time—Bobby's daily rebuffs, Cora's silent tears alone at night, Addie's madness, her own nightmare visions of Richard's death—behind her. She needed to go home now, to go home and forget about this whole evening.

When she turned to walk to the subway entrance at the corner, she glanced in the window to her right to see that Bobby had taken a seat at the bar, another vodka tonic in his hand.

It was years before she heard from him again. And Scarlet put that odd visit behind her and fell into a peaceful enough routine for those last years of the millennium. A routine that was punctuated, occasionally, by sudden bouts of loneliness—late nights when she'd suddenly be filled with

despair at her situation (no poems written for months, nothing but dron-
ing freelance work and a strange sort of thrall to this man who *seemed* to
love her, yet would not, or could not, make a move to be with her). Those
were the nights she rented a car and drove to Cora's, arriving at some ungodly hour. Every time Cora would answer her call, rising to let her in
and make up her bed upstairs, greeting her with a cup of coffee in the
morning, ready, once again, to listen, saying little or nothing, while Scarlet cried about her sorry state.

From time to time she'd try dating again. It wasn't that hard to meet
men, really. New York offered ample opportunity: other runners in Central Park in the morning, readings at neighborhood bookstores, even,
once, during a tour of jury duty, where she met a songwriter and a com-
puter programmer, each of whom asked her out for coffee—that safest of
all first dates—within five minutes of each other. There was also the occasional publishing-world party she went to with but *not really with* Alex;
they'd arrive separately, and on the several occasions when his insistence
on secrecy was particularly irksome to her, Scarlet got a nasty sort of
pleasure from giving her phone number to another man, right under his
nose.

"You are missing a *rollicking* good time," Lou said to her on New
Year's Eve, 1999. She and Scarlet were spending the night in Cider Cove;
Addie and Tom, seemingly newly in love—with each other and, once
again, with birds—were spending the holidays in Costa Rica. Scarlet
had wanted to get out of New York, less out of a sense of end-of-the-
millennium menace than a feeling that life was somehow passing her by.

"Not to mention squandering the years of your sexual *prime*," Lou
added. Scarlet rolled her eyes. As if it wasn't bad enough to hear her use
terms like "sexual prime," she had to deal with the rather embarrassing
fact that Lou was slurring her words. But then, she was hardly sober herself. Hence, perhaps, her decision to fight back for a change.

"Lou, I've tried dating, and sleeping around, and you know what?"
she said. "I *hate* it. Okay? It's empty and soul-depleting, not to mention

dangerous. You know, it's a different world now than it was when you were my age." (There were few things more effective, Scarlet knew, than bringing up Lou's age when you wanted to silence her.) "Maybe you've heard of an inconvenient little illness known as AIDS?"

Lou stared at her for a while then, saying nothing. Finally she shook her head. "Good Lord, Scarlet," she said, "you sound like some puritanical old Republican. What in God's name has happened to you?"

"I don't know," Scarlet whispered back, and then she dissolved in tears. "I don't know what's happened to me." The truth was, she had vowed, driving to Cider Cove that day, that this would be the year she would end things with Alex, and somehow move on. She hadn't seen him since before Christmas, and she'd told him not to call her. Maybe, she thought as she drove south on the Garden State Parkway, she'd even leave New York. But that night, arguing with Lou, drinking too much champagne, she saw that it wasn't going to happen. The next morning, dry-mouthed and queasy, she called him.

Scarlet's relationship with Alex might have continued, in that on-again, off-again way, if the new millennium hadn't brought some surprises, some of them more personal than others, for both her and her parents. What triggered Addie's restlessness again? A stolen presidential election? The threat of greater environmental losses than she and Tom would have even dreamed of, idealistically penning and illustrating *A Prosody of Birds* thirty years before? And eventually the unforeseen, and completely unimaginable, attack on the World Trade Center?

All those things, surely, but this time it was Tom who said they'd better get to work. There were all those dead crows and jays, for instance, that people had begun depositing at their doorstep—having decided, for some reason, that the crazy artist and her bird-loving husband needed to say, or do, something about the sudden appearance of this mosquito-borne malady called West Nile virus. While the bearers of the dead birds would arrive rubber-gloved and even, sometimes, surgically masked, the birds themselves wrapped in multiple plastic bags, Addie handled them indiscriminately. There was no reason to worry about infection, she knew; they were, in all likelihood, dead not from West Nile, but from poisoning by the pesticide sprays coating the fields and streams of Pennsylvania, New Jersey, New York. Chemicals like Dursban, diazinon, ethyl parathion—all aimed at killing mosquitoes, mosquitoes that would then be eaten by birds that were soon falling, dead, into suburban backyards throughout the Northeast and the mid-Atlantic states.

And so Addie was at work again, quietly this time, in her charnel house. Here, by early 2001, she spent her afternoons, after mornings spent, once again, in the field with Tom, stuffing a seemingly endless series of crows (the jays, birds she'd always hated, she had less use for— even dead). She used models of these crows in her last major assemblage, titled *River Nile*. This river of black birds, flowing through a spare white room, was a surprisingly beautiful and moving work, especially in the wake of the September 11 attacks. And especially for those who knew, by the time *River Nile* appeared in her New York gallery, that Addie was ill once again, the cancer filling her womb and making its way toward her lungs.

And what was Tom doing? At first he was broadcasting the news that, one morning in May 2001, he had spotted a rare cerulean warbler on a wooded ridge near his and Addie's home. Then, when news of this sighting of such a rare and splendid species was barely noted at Burnham College, he was keeping strangely mute when Addie claimed, a few days later, to have spotted a Cuvier's kinglet. A bird that had never been seen before, except by John James Audubon (assuming he had been truthful). A pretty little bird very close in appearance to the ruby-crowned kinglet, except for a head stripe that, Addie insisted, more closely resembled that of the golden-crowned kinglet. Tom kept quiet, as well, when Addie went on to call for a change in this species' status, from either long-extinct or— in most people's estimation—a myth to a so-called hypothetical: a species whose existence in a given region is open to question because of the lack of an actual specimen, or a "bird in hand." But also a bird whose sighting, by a serious enough observer, merits its inclusion in official checklists as a possible, or hypothetically present, species.

Interestingly, Addie claimed to have spotted the Cuvier's kinglet on the ridge above Nisky Creek the morning after the developer Bert Schafer made an irresistible offer to Burnham College, for three hundred acres of college-owned land, including this very ridge. Here he planned to build his largest housing development yet, along with a "minimall" holding a supermarket and several other stores. Addie and Tom's hope—a feeble one, to be sure—was that the college might be shamed into resisting the sale of this land, or at least the portion of it immediately surrounding Nisky Creek, on the grounds that Schafer's planned development would imperil one or possibly even two rare species of birds.

And finally, on the afternoon of September 11 came Bobby's reappearance in Scarlet's life—this time knocking on her door, shell-shocked and trembling. He hadn't gone to work that day, he told her that afternoon between rounds of inarticulate sobbing. In fact he had been fired the week before. He was on his way to clear out his desk, and he'd just stepped out of a subway station several blocks away from the World Trade Center when the explosions happened, and the world fell down around him, raining death and ashes.

Scarlet also learned that Cynthia had, by then, kicked him out of the house. That he'd been staying with friends on the Upper West Side, just two blocks away from her apartment, since being fired. And that this was the first time, that week, that he'd been sober for more than a few hours.

He told Scarlet these things, that afternoon, while she held him, trying somehow to calm his uncontrollable shaking, under a pile of blankets in her bed. "I don't know where to go," he'd said, when she'd opened the door to find him standing there, covered in dirt and ash. "And I can't get warm. Could I please just come in long enough to get warm?"

Outside it was a balmy, sunlit day. Though by that time, the acrid smell of smoke had already begun to wend its way toward upper Manhattan, to the air outside Scarlet's building.

Hours later, when Bobby finally slept, Scarlet turned on the television and, like everyone else in the country (except Tom and Addie, who were, at that point, trying desperately to reach Scarlet via the impossibly over-taxed New York telephone lines), watched the footage of planes crashing into the buildings and exploding—and bodies flying from the high win-dows, floating through the sky like desolate black birds—over and over again.

V

hypotheticals

eighteen

TOM'S HANDS, GRIPPING THE big metal steering wheel of the Cider
Cove Seafood House's refrigerated truck, are soothingly familiar to Scarlet. When she looks down at her own hands, she is struck by the similari-
ties—the same long, bony fingers, nails narrow and blunt.

"Who do you think I look like?" she asks. "Addie always said Grandma
Sturmer when she was young, but taller. I can never see that when I look
at pictures. Do you think I resemble anyone from your family?" She has
only met one aunt from Tom's side of the family, one of his older sisters—a tiny, white-haired woman who, when she visited them in Burnham years ago, seemed ancient to Scarlet.

"Thinking about such things now, are you?" he says with a laugh. "If
it's the source of your height you're looking for, I don't have an explanation. Though I'm told my father was tall, by the family's standards—
around six feet or so, they said." He takes a sip of coffee and checks the
rearview mirror.

Between them, on the torn vinyl seat, is a nearly full thermos and a
basket, packed by Cora that afternoon, filled with enough food for a day-
long journey, though they are only making the two-hour drive from Cider Cove to Burnham.

"I don't know where you're going, though I can guess," Cora said as
she handed the basket to Tom, in the deserted parking lot behind the Sea-

food House. "At any rate, there's enough food here to get you to Scranton, if you happen to see reason along the way." She looked tired and worried when Scarlet stepped up to hug her good-bye.

Lou chose not to come along to the restaurant cooler, where Cora helped Tom and Scarlet slip Addie's body into the simple cotton gown, free of any buttons or zippers, that she'd just finished sewing. Before they left, after sleeping through the afternoon and into the evening, Lou gave both Tom and Scarlet brisk hugs. "Be sensible, Tom," was the last thing she said.

As they pulled out of the parking lot and then drove along the silent street, passing by Cora's one last time, Scarlet realized Lou was there, hidden in the shadows on the porch, watching them. She could see the red ember of her cigarette.

Now Dustin travels behind them, driving Tom's car. They are, Tom says, "right on schedule"; they should reach Tom and Addie's cottage on Haupt Bridge Road by ten.

Which is when the real work will begin. So, Scarlet decides, now is the time to start asking Tom some questions.

She has started with the easy one. So her height *might* have come from her Irish grandfather—no great revelations there. Presumably the same could be said about her reddish hair, though Addie "thought maybe" she remembered Uncle John's hair being sort of red when they were young. It is amazing, and a little frightening, how little Scarlet knows about her extended family; she's been thinking about this often, since her first prenatal appointment a week ago.

"Do you think Cora knows, Tom?" she asks next, unconsciously patting her stomach.

"That you're pregnant? I thought you said you told her that much at least."

"I did tell her that. You know what I mean."

"Well, neither Addie nor I told her, if that's what you're asking," he says. "Addie felt the news should come from you."

"No, it's not that—I didn't think you'd told her. It's just that . . . I don't know. Sometimes over the last few days I just felt like she *knew*. She almost didn't seem surprised when I told her I was pregnant, and she never once asked me about the father."

"I'd imagine she thinks it's Alex, wouldn't you?"

Scarlet sighs and shifts in her seat; the springs are practically poking through the ancient vinyl. "I suppose so," she admits, disappointed in herself, now, for not taking the opportunity to tell Cora over these last few days. As she'd told Bobby she would.

"Of course she *does* know that Bobby stayed the week with you last fall, after the attacks. I imagine she knows you've been in contact with him since he checked into the clinic—though perhaps she hasn't realized quite how close that contact's been."

He laughs, a nervous little laugh, and they exchange a quick look before turning their eyes away, Tom's back to the highway in front of them, Scarlet's to the dark woods, and occasional glimpses of the river, out the window to her right.

"Shouldn't *he* be the one to tell her anyway?" he finally asks.

"He's afraid to," Scarlet says.

Tom shakes his head. "I think you both underestimate Cora, Scarlet."

"It's not that he's afraid she'll be angry. I think he's afraid she'll be angry but she'll pretend she's not. He thinks she's never been entirely honest with him about what she feels. About him, about Richard. About everything that's happened to them."

"What do you think?"

"I don't know, exactly," Scarlet says; what she doesn't tell Tom is how awkward it all feels to her, to be caught between her dear old friend—the grandmother of the little mass of cells she's carrying—and this strange, old and yet new love. She isn't sure what she thinks, and she feels vaguely disloyal to both Cora *and* Bobby now.

"I don't know what she's thinking sometimes," she goes on. "Jesus, I feel that way about all of them—Cora, Lou, Addie. They might get each other, but I sure don't get them sometimes—" She catches herself, realizing suddenly that she hasn't yet figured out how to speak about Addie in the past tense.

"Did you feel that way about Addie over these last weeks, Scarlet?" Tom asks then, slowing down and looking at her.

"No," she whispers. "Not at all."

"Neither did I," he says as the Delaware River sweeps into view, filling the windshield for a moment before the road curves sharply north. "I found her less mysterious and more open, in the last year or so, than I had for years, really since I first knew her."

For a moment Scarlet is afraid Tom might cry. There isn't time for tears, she thinks. They have too much to do before the sun rises. And she has several questions she still needs to ask, while they are here, in the strangely timeless and anonymous cab of this big, noisy truck, with Addie's small, quiet body riding behind them.

But instead of crying he laughs. "You know," he says, "really, the only times we *aren't* mysterious to one another are probably when we're first falling in love, and then when one of us is dying. New love blinds us for a while, to all the things we don't know. Wouldn't you say?"

He smiles at Scarlet and she smiles back, aware that this last remark is surely directed at her and her current situation. She clears her throat and mumbles, "I suppose so." Before she can think of something else to say, Tom slows down and turns to her again.

"*Do* you love Bobby, Scarlet?"

She takes a deep breath and exhales slowly, knowing this question had to come. "I think so," she says. And then she turns to look out the window, at nothing she can actually see.

"Because you know," Tom says, "I'd support your having this child, with or without him."

Scarlet looks at Tom, who's watching the road intently. For a moment she is seized by an urge to reach for him, to curl up in his arms like she had as a child. But then she pictures Bobby, his face when she told him she was pregnant, crumbling with such a strange mix of joy and fear and everything in between, all those feelings registering in his eyes, the way he held his mouth, like some high-speed film of the sky, the weather. Like a mirror, a picture of her own wildly varied feelings. A map of her.

Instead of reaching for her father, she only nods toward him. "Thank you, Tom," she says.

With or without him, she is thinking.

Does she love him?

She thinks she understands him.

She knows she wants to have his child.

When she makes love to Bobby now, she feels like she's been given another chance at something. But she has no idea what that is.

Do these things add up to love?

At first she hardly recognized him when he knocked on her door. With his bloodshot eyes and his uncombed hair and his week's growth of beard, he looked more like the old Bobby than the gray-suited businessman she'd met for drinks five years before. Except for the dust and ashes.

"Bobby?" she said, incredulous. She thought she might have been hallucinating. The whole day had been like that, after all, from the moment she'd turned on the television and realized, gradually, that the scene she was seeing—a plane flying into one of the World Trade Center towers— was real.

"I've been walking since this morning," he said. His teeth were chattering. "You can't believe what it's like out there, down there. . . ."

"Oh, my God," she said, reaching for him and pulling him into her apartment, leading him to the sofa. "Bobby, were you *there?*"

He looked at her, then closed his eyes and shook his head as tears streamed down his face.

"I was three blocks away." It came out as a whisper, pained and desperate. "I'd just climbed up from the subway."

He opened his eyes, then gripped her hands. "I wanted to try to get there, to look for people—everyone I worked with would have been there, on the 102nd floor." His face collapsed again, and he shuddered. "They wouldn't let anyone get near. 'Just keep walking,' they said. 'Head uptown.'"

He shuddered again, and his whole body shook. That was when she noticed how thin he was. It dawned on her then too that he wasn't dressed for work on the 102nd floor of the World Trade Center, in his flannel shirt and torn jeans, below his businessman's overcoat—too heavy for a warm day in September. Had he somehow known he would turn cold, she wondered, so cold it seemed that nothing could warm him, all that day and the next?

"I just started walking, with all these other people, just walking and walking, heading uptown, fast. At the corner of Varick and Canal people had stopped. They were looking back toward the towers."

He stopped then, for a moment; he hadn't opened his eyes the whole time he spoke, but now he squeezed them tighter, and Scarlet's stomach clenched, knowing what was coming. She'd been glued to the television all day.

"When I turned around I saw three bodies, floating down. . . . It seemed like they took forever to fall." He opened his eyes then, and stared at her. "I have no idea how long I stood there," he said. He looked shocked at the thought, and he kept staring at her, though it seemed to her he was seeing something, or someone, else. Floating bodies? Richard?

She reached for him then. "Oh, Bobby," she said, crying too as she pulled his head to her chest. She wove her fingers through his dirty, tangled hair and rocked him. "Why have you had to see such horrible things?" He wrapped his arms around her waist and held her so tightly she could hardly breathe.

"I knew this was your building," he said. "I've walked by it lots of times, but I never had the nerve to buzz you before." He was still crying, his voice and his breath both ragged, harsh. "I didn't know where else to go."

"Shhh," she said and stroked his hair, his wet cheeks. "Of course you came here. I've been waiting for you to come here."

She had no idea where such a remark came from. Yet when she said it, it felt so clearly, undeniably true that it stunned her. He pulled his head up and looked at her then, and they stared at each other for a long time. Finally he kissed her, and his mouth felt so warm and familiar that Scarlet forgot, for a moment, where she was. She shuddered then, and he took off his coat and wrapped them both inside it.

They lay down on her sofa, curled together. At times they talked, whispering like children—or like their teenaged selves, in a booth or on a blanket inside the old Cider Cove Diner—about their lives in the five years since they'd last seen each other. And then, for long periods, they were silent, listening only to their breath, watching the light at the windows turn dark, whether from night or from the raining of soot and ashes, they could not have said.

Sometime that night Scarlet warmed the bathroom as much as she could, letting the steaming water run for ten minutes. In that small, hot room she undressed Bobby and herself slowly, then stepped with him into the shower, where she washed the dust from his face and hair. Now and then he stopped her, reaching for her hand, holding it to his face, his mouth.

Later, as she dried and combed his hair while he sat at her kitchen table, slicing a loaf of bread, it shocked her to see strands of gray that hadn't, in fact, been streaks of ash that washed away. Only then did she let herself remember: They weren't teenagers anymore.

That night she piled extra blankets on her bed, and he clung to her, again, as they slept. For two days she didn't leave his side.

She can't recall, now, what she was feeling then. She wonders if anyone remembers what they felt for those first few days. She remembers watching Hollywood stars taking phone contributions, an odd assortment of members of Congress singing "God Bless America." She talked to Addie and Tom, who wanted her to come home to Burnham. And the whole time she kept her eyes on Bobby, who had showered and shaved, but still couldn't quite get warm.

Mainly she felt confused, and worried. She tried to talk to Bobby in a soft, soothing voice. They left the apartment for short spells, to walk in the park or pick up bread or coffee on the corner. Everyone they met looked as unreal as they felt. Everyone greeted each other, asked after each other, looked at each other with concern. Did you know people there? Are you okay? Are we okay? Is it going to happen again?

Most of Bobby's former coworkers, he said, were surely dead. When he tried to call the friends he'd been staying with, the phone rang and rang.

They watched television obsessively, staring blankly at images of police and firefighters, the mayor, the president, all just a hundred blocks downtown. Bobby spoke to Cora several times, assuring her he was all right and asking her to let Cynthia know this too. Neither of them told their parents they were together.

On Saturday, five days after Bobby arrived at her apartment, Scarlet went out on her own for a couple hours, to get some groceries and run a few errands. When she got back to the apartment Bobby had nearly finished a bottle of vodka he'd found in her freezer. He wasn't a scary drunk, or an angry one. Just a cold and sad one. Once again he cried and cried. That night they watched TV in silence, tears streaming down both their faces. In the morning he was up and dressed before she was. She walked out of her room to find him quietly inching open her front door.

"If you go out to get more to drink," she said, "you can't come back here." As soon as she said it her stomach tightened in fear. Did she really mean this?

He closed the door as slowly and quietly as he'd opened it. He stood perfectly still for a while before he turned to face her. "All right," he said, nodding but looking down, not meeting her eye. And he opened the door and left.

The apartment felt, suddenly, cold and cavernous. She tried to watch television but couldn't stand it anymore. There was a hollow ringing in her ears that wouldn't stop. She realized she had no idea how to reach him. Would Cora know? But she couldn't call Cora to ask her that. Would she have to go searching for him in all the bars in her neighborhood, like some sad, neglected wife in a bad old movie?

Four hours later her buzzer rang, and then he was there, in her doorway again. He had flowers in his arms—three big bunches of deep-blue baby orchids. And at that moment, his curly hair falling over the collar of his flannel shirt, he looked like he'd looked when he was sixteen. When he'd watched a ladybug traveling the length of her belly on the beach, tracing its path with his finger. When he'd kissed her sweetly, and made love to her so gently, on the floor of the Main Street Diner.

He still had the same haunted eyes. Looking into them then, as he stood there, watching her watching him, all her memories of Cider Cove, of Bobby and Richard and Cora, and Addie and Tom, all of it came back. Suddenly it seemed that those days of burrowing together in her dim apartment, clinging to one another desperately, made sense—and now they were over. Somewhere, somehow, someone had lifted a curtain or opened the blinds.

"I didn't know what kind of flowers to get," he said. "I don't even know what you like."

"Those are fine," she said.

"I never really thanked you for taking me in."

"You know you don't have to thank me."

She reached for him then, and for the first time since he'd rung her buzzer a week before, *his* arms, not hers, felt like the strong ones. She let go of something then. She let him hold her up.

He dropped the flowers and pulled her face to his. "I read your poem about Richard, after I met you in the bar that night," he said. " 'The dark boy alone,' " he whispered, his breath warm and wet at her ear, " 'while the others cycle through the graves.' "

She pulled back to look at him. "You remember those lines?" she said, scanning his face for any hint of irony.

"I know the whole thing by heart," he said. And then he recited it, line by line, word by word, while he took her hand and led her to the bedroom, and this time he undressed her, as slowly as he had years before, and wrapped her in his arms.

"I think I may love Bobby," she says now, to Tom. "And I do think I want to have this baby with him."

Tom nods. It's clear he is skeptical.

A few days after he brought Scarlet the blue orchids, Bobby went home to spend time with his daughters, and then to visit Cora. Much as Scarlet hoped that day had somehow cured him of his need for a drink, it wasn't quite that easy. He was drunk, in fact, when he came back to her apartment after his visit to New Jersey.

In October he checked into a clinic, and Cynthia filed for divorce. Eventually, when he was free to leave the clinic on occasional weekends, he stayed with Scarlet. "I'm going to stick with this," he told her one weekend near Christmas, "for my kids. For me, for you."

During those weekends when he stayed with her, Bobby refused to watch television or read the paper. Once he saw a picture on the cover of a magazine Scarlet had left on the coffee table, of a little boy's face, peering out from under a bed. He was the son of a man who'd died in the World Trade Center attacks, and he'd hidden under the bed when a reporter had come to talk to his mother. Which didn't stop the photographer who came along, apparently, from tracking him down.

"I understand that kid," Bobby said. "Sometimes you just wanna hide under the bed."

Scarlet was curled up to next to him on the couch. Now she looked up from the book she was reading; remarks like that worried her.

"I read somewhere that all the birds near the towers flew away just seconds before the attack," she said to change the subject, yet not exactly.

Bobby said nothing.

"Addie and Tom used to talk about all the birds that flew into the glass of those towers and died. Someone they knew was doing research on that. I wonder what they're thinking about all of this. I'm kind of afraid to ask." Still no response.

"Listen," she said then, turning to face him, "I've been thinking. I think I'd like to have a baby."

He stared at her, wide-eyed, openmouthed.

"With me?" he said.

She tried to sound lighthearted when she laughed. "No," she said, "with one of the other guys who hangs around here when you're gone. Who do you think?"

He nodded, slowly, then seemed to scan the room as if he were looking for a way out. For a moment she feared she'd really set him up for a bender now. But then he looked at her and smiled, almost shyly. "Okay," he said. "We could try that. Want to start now?"

"I can't really explain why I'm pregnant," she says to Tom now, assuming this is the real question he wants her to answer. "It just suddenly seemed like the right thing to do." She turns to him and shrugs. "That's worse than a cliché, isn't it? Everybody started getting married and having babies after September 11. I guess I'm just one of the horde."

Tom smiles as he looks over at her. "It does just seem like the right thing to do, Scarlet," he says. He reaches over to stroke her hair. "It certainly was, for us."

She leans closer to him, longing to hear more of his soft voice, more of that low, soothing rumble in the impossibly loud cab of the truck. Of course there's more to say, she thinks. But the rushing air, the noise of the road below them—it's all screaming around her now, and she can't hear a thing.

"God, it's like some kind of wind chamber in here or something," she says, closing her eyes and pinching back the tears.

Then Tom says the very thing she would not let herself think, and things grow suddenly still. "We were both losing our mothers when we decided to have a child, weren't we, love?" He reaches over to take her hand and she nods, staring at the darkness. And then she lets herself cry into the stillness.

Later, as they approach the house on Haupt Bridge Road, Scarlet's cheeks are tight from her drying tears. Look how far she's come, she thinks to herself, from dreams of a summer house on Nantucket, to an organic garden in Vermont, then a literary life in New York City. Now here she is, nearly two months pregnant, preparing to have a baby with her teenaged crush from New Jersey, an unemployed alcoholic in rehab, with no clear picture of where, or how, they are going to live, approaching her childhood home with her mother's body in tow. Daughter of the infamous Addie Sturmer Kavanagh and her besotted husband, Tom, on the day after her mother's death. Pulling into the drive behind her parents' home, a cottage still decorated with her earliest crayoned scribblings and her mother's lovely early paintings, preparing to dig a hole and bury her, in this land she loved and sometimes hated, on the ridge across the creek.

She laughs out loud at the thought.

Tom glances over as he turns off the engine. "What's funny?" he asks.

"Nothing," she says, "nothing," and she waves her hand in front of her face. It just feels like too much, suddenly, now that they've arrived.

Finally she takes another breath, then turns to face Tom. "Do you think I'm being foolish?" she asks.

He takes her face in his hands for a moment, then says, "I know you, Scarlet. You'll figure out how to make it work."

Then he pushes open his door and steps out into the moonlit night. The sound of the tree frogs is almost deafening; she had forgotten about that sound.

"Come on," Tom says as he waves to Dustin, who is stepping out of the car behind them. "We've got a lot of work ahead of us."

Tom busies himself with gathering shovels and pickaxes, then disappears into his and Addie's bedroom for a while. Scarlet takes Dustin into the cottage and points him toward the bathroom. When he emerges a minute later, she is in the kitchen making tea. Looking at Dustin's tired face, she realizes that he's older than she'd thought—maybe not that much younger than she, in fact.

He accepts her offer of tea, sitting down at the kitchen table. She tries to make conversation—Was the drive all right? What did he think of the river road?—getting little more than one-word answers from him.

"It's really nice of you to help us with all this," she finally says, stuttering a bit with the awkwardness of it all, frustrated at knowing so little about him. "It must all seem kind of strange to you."

He looks puzzled. "What must?" he asks.

She points toward the back door, in the direction of the truck where Addie's body lies waiting, in Dustin's rough-hewn coffin. "Well," she says, "all of this. Driving my mother's body back here under cover of darkness, getting ready to bury her secretly, nowhere near an actual cemetery . . ."

Dustin smiles at her then—such a sweet, soothing smile; he reminds her, at that moment, of Bobby, and she feels a pang of longing.

"No, it doesn't seem strange. In fact this is a pretty easy burial. Tom worked everything out ahead of time. I've done plenty that were harder than this one."

"You mean you've done this before?" she asks, still trying to absorb his words.

Now he looks puzzled again. "Of course," he says, "lots of times." And then, to Scarlet's astonishment, he hands her a card. "Dustin Lamott, Alternative Burials," it says, with nothing else but an e-mail address in the lower right corner.

"I'm sorry," she says, handing the card back to him. "I just assumed you were one of Addie's friends or admirers. She had a lot, especially among activists and"—she stumbles for words, finally pointing back at the card—"alternative people."

"Well, I did admire your mother," he says, sipping his tea. "Your father too. And I guess I'm kind of an activist too. I guess you could say I'm active in the effort to subvert the funeral industry." He smiles as he says this, then tips his teacup in Scarlet's direction.

She tips her cup back. "I had no idea," she says, "that a natural burial was so difficult to arrange."

"Most people don't have any idea," he says. "And by the time they find out, it's too late. Some funeral director's already got them signed up for a ten-thousand-dollar casket and has shot their mother or their husband full of formaldehyde and started painting on the makeup."

Scarlet shudders, imagining Addie's body being handled this way. "So how did they find you?" she asks.

"I don't know," he says. "Word gets around. Internet, maybe. Tom e-mailed me a couple months ago, and I drove over to Scranton to get the barn siding. And then two days ago he e-mailed again and said it was time to load up the wood and drive to Cider's Cove."

"Cider Cove." She corrects him instinctively, as this bit of background slowly sinks in.

He rises from the table then, carrying both of their cups to the sink. "Like I said," he continues, "Tom took care of everything in advance. He'd already worked things out with the guy who owns that farm now. He said he was planning to tear the barn down anyway—he told me to help myself to all I wanted. And I did too; siding from an abandoned barn is good for what I do—lightweight and already starting to rot, and it hasn't been painted or treated with anything for years, so the coffin's not going to add any more unnecessary toxins to the soil.

"It's not the easiest wood to work with, of course," he continues, returning to his chair. Suddenly, it seems, they've hit on something Dustin likes to talk about. "It tends to fall apart when you hammer or sand it. Fortunately I had plenty to work with for Addie's casket."

Scarlet nods and tries to look interested. But she is still reeling from the things Dustin has just told her. Tom and Addie have been planning this burial for *months?* So all that drama two weeks ago, when she first arrived at Cider Cove to help with getting Addie comfortably arranged in Cora's studio—Addie's insistence that they bury her on land owned by the college, then Tom's apparent hesitation to do anything quite so outlandish—was all of that some sort of *ruse?* she wonders. If they both knew all along what they planned to do, what in the world was the point of all that?

"So you're saying Tom and Addie arranged all this with you months ago?" she says.

"Well, as much of it as they could. But you know, most deaths don't allow you to plan every last detail. You don't generally know when it's going to happen, and when it does happen, you have to move fast. I have to be ready to pick up and go at a moment's notice. Kind of hard on my wife and kids sometimes," he says with a laugh.

"I can imagine," Scarlet says. Thinking meanwhile, Ah, yes, of course this is who he is: another committed ecowarrior who's married to the work of saving the planet. No matter the strain it puts on his marriage, his family. Of course this is who Addie would find. As soon as she thinks it, though, she feels a stab of guilt. What's a parent supposed to do, abandon any and all passions the moment her child is born? "Keep writing," she hears Addie saying to her last night. "That will keep you going."

"But there is one thing that's different about this particular burial," Dustin says then, as he rises from the table and leans on the doorjamb, crossing his arms.

Only one? Scarlet thinks, trying to imagine what he has in mind. Transporting the body in a seafood truck? Burying Addie in such an audaciously illegal place?

"What's that?" she asks, dreading his answer.

"I still don't have any idea where we're going to bury her. Do you?"

Walking outside, they find Tom climbing slowly up the steep hill behind the cottage, flashlight in hand. He is, he tells them, trying to step off the boundary lines for the little piece of land he bought, along with the cottage, thirty-seven years ago.

"I had to dig around forever to find the damn deed," he says. "I've never given the property lines a thought. But obviously we can't bury her down here, near the house."

"No, not on a flood plain like this," Dustin agrees. "We'll have to find a spot that's far enough from the creek, and also from your well."

"Right," Tom says. "But we don't own all the way up to the top of the ridge, and even if we did, that's getting a little too close to being in sight of some of the buildings at the college. And that hillside's steep and wooded; I can't quite imagine how we'll find our way around all those roots."

Dustin reaches for the flashlight. "Show me where you think the lines are," he says. "I bet I can find a spot that will work." He disappears into the darkness of the hillside, and for a while all they hear are his boots tramping through the brush. The beam of his flashlight weaves back and forth as he moves slowly up the hill.

Scarlet opens her mouth to say something, but no sound emerges. She reaches for her father's arm and looks into his eyes, searching.

"But this isn't what she wanted, Tom," she finally says.

Tom looks at her tenderly, then pulls her into his arms. "Scarlet," he whispers in her ear, "this is one of the things Addie and I talked about in that last hour before she died. I didn't see any reason to tell Cora and Lou about it, and I assumed *you* were assuming all along that we'd just bury her here, on our land."

She pulls her head free to look at him. "What are you talking about? *What* did you talk about before she died?"

"About where she wanted to be buried, love. In the end I persuaded her to let us do it here, on our land. Someplace quiet, without all the other complications." He reaches over to smooth Scarlet's hair, an instinctive gesture, something he's done since she was a child.

"It won't do a bit of good now, to try to stir up trouble like that," he goes on. "We all know it, Scarlet. There's too much money involved; something like an inconveniently buried body isn't going to make anyone at the college change his mind."

"That never would have stopped Addie," she says, her aggrieved voice surprising her; since when did she think like Addie? "She never cared about the odds."

"Well, that's true, Scarlet. But this wasn't about the odds. This time it wasn't about her anger, or all that's wrong with the world. It was about something that's right, finally, about you, and about your child. She held my hand last night and said, 'All right, Tom. Let's just rest now. Everyone needs to rest, Scarlet especially.'"

He reaches for her hair again. "She was thinking of you, Scarlet, of you and of her grandchild."

But something about this makes Scarlet pull away from him. *Stop trying to control my goddamn* hair! she suddenly wants to scream.

He's closed his eyes now, and his words are broken, choking. "'We'll find a place you'd love, Addie,' I told her. 'Near the cottage, near us.'" He draws a long breath, then looks over at the hillside, where Dustin is stomping and probing with his flashlight and shovel.

He shakes his head and clears his throat. "I don't think either of us was thinking too clearly about root systems at that point, surprisingly enough for a biologist and his environmentalist wife," he says with a sad, quiet laugh.

Scarlet steps over to face him. "I don't believe you," she says.

He looks at her as if she's slapped him. "What do you mean? Why in God's name would I lie about such a thing?" he says.

"She was so *passionate* about this!" Scarlet says, still staring at him. "I mean, I can't believe you talked her out of it! And come to think of it, why *wouldn't* you lie to me about that? Why would this be any different from any of the things you've somehow failed to tell me?" And then she starts, ticking off a list of her resentments from the last year: "First, that her cancer's back. Next, deciding to call Dustin here—why wasn't I in on that conversation?"

She walks away and starts to pace along the creek. Dustin has returned from his trek along the hillside but chooses not to interrupt them; instead he retreats to a respectful distance, standing behind Tom's car. Part of Scarlet, somehow detached from the strangeness of this moment, watches him from the corner of her eye, wondering if he's used to scenes like this.

Tom walks over and reaches, again, for her arm. She turns to face him. "And while we're at it," she says, "how about this whole plan of dying in Cider Cove, with strangers taking care of her, instead of here at home, with you and me? No one discussed that with me either, ever."

She is choking now, coughing and sputtering. She's as surprised by this outburst as Tom is, and not even sure she means any of it. A month ago, when she'd heard of Addie and Tom's plan for her last days, she'd come to see Addie's choosing to die in Cider Cove as reasonable, and right. But now, preparing to place her mother's body in the earth, suddenly, it seems, she is also resentful of that.

"*I* could have cared for her," she says then, whimpering now, wiping snot and tears from her face with the back of her hand. "Here, at home."

Through all this Tom has stood silently by the creek's edge, watching her; in the dim light from the back porch Scarlet can see his pained look. Now he walks over and takes her into his arms again. She relaxes there for just a moment, considering the possibility of just letting all of this go now, leaving everything to him. But then she pulls away.

"And one other thing," she says. "You never told me that you slept with Lou."

He steps back and stares at her for a moment, then sighs as he runs his hands through his long, uncombed hair. He walks a few steps away, into the shadows between them, then stops and leans against the back doors of the Seafood House truck.

"That's true, Scarlet," he finally says, his voice hoarse and tired. "I never told you that. But I didn't think of that as lying; I would have said something more along the lines of protecting you from something that, believe me, I wish had never happened.

"All these things you're listing," he goes on, waving an arm toward the creek, "I wouldn't have thought of any of them as lies. We were only trying to protect you, trying not to burden you with all these details. Trying to do what we thought was best for everyone. And you know, you were being pretty cagey yourself through a good part of the fall."

Scarlet winces at this memory, of phone calls she didn't return for days, visits she canceled at the last minute. She was so confused about what she and Bobby were doing, so sure no one would understand. *Left-over teenaged obsession,* she imagined them all saying to her, shaking their heads. *Classic female rescue fantasies.*

"I know," she whispers. "I know I kind of dropped out of sight. I'm so sorry about that now."

They both turn to look at Dustin, who's stepped from the shadows and cleared his throat. "I did find a spot that should work," he says. "Should I get started?"

Tom sighs, and reaches a hand toward Scarlet. "Maybe we were wrong," he says. "I'm sure we should have included you in more of these conversations. But I'll venture to say you might make a mistake or two with your own child, Scarlet. It goes with being a parent."

He looks so old then, so old and tired. He already looks like a grandfather, Scarlet thinks. Why, she suddenly wonders, is she doing this to him?

She walks over to take his hand, and she holds it to her wet cheek. "But we can't bury her here, Tom," she says. "You know we can't." She is stunned by how strongly she feels this.

She looks into her father's eyes. "Not to protect me, anyway," she says. "Why in the world would Addie suddenly decide I needed protecting? *You're* the one with something to protect here."

He'd said it himself, when Addie had proposed the idea. Having to disinter a body before Bert Schafer's crews could start building—maybe it really wouldn't be enough to get Schafer and the college to interrupt their plans. But it might be enough to finally get him fired.

Scarlet turns and leans against the truck now, next to Tom. "If that's what we're concerned about here, if you're worried about losing your job, I'll listen to you, Tom," she says. "But not if it's about me somehow, about giving me some sort of protection I didn't even ask for."

Tom sighs, then looks down at his hands. "Well, at this point I'm not concerned about getting fired," he says. He looks over at Scarlet and smiles a weary smile. "It's probably time I retired anyway. Might as well go out blazing." He pulls her hand to his cheek for a while before he speaks again.

"But Scarlet, you must know this is true: before she died, Addie said it to me quite clearly. 'Just bury me at home,' she said. 'For Scarlet's sake, for her baby's sake.'"

Scarlet nods then, remembering. Two weeks ago, when Addie first told them she wanted to be buried on Burnham Ridge, on the college's land, Scarlet still wasn't sure she was pregnant. And she felt afraid, for some reason, to tell Addie and Tom that she might be. She waited until she went back to Cider Cove three days ago, with confirmation from the hospital lab, to tell them. And that was when Addie told her she'd be a wonderful mother.

Oh, Addie, she thinks now, why do I have to do this without you? She buries her face in the handkerchief Tom hands her while he stands by silently, his arm around her again. Finally she says, "If you're willing to go through with it, I want to bury her on Burnham Ridge. I want to do what she asked two weeks ago, when she still felt like fighting." She looks at Tom and tries to smile. "I want my child to know that her grandmother held her ground against that bastard and never flinched, not even at the end."

Those words sound slightly foolish, Scarlet knows, coming from her—as if they don't quite fit her mouth. Does she even mean this? Yes and no. She would fight differently, she thinks. By not refusing to try chemotherapy one more time, for instance. You might have fought harder, Addie, part of her is thinking. For your grandchild's sake.

Not that she'd timed her pregnancy particularly well, of course.

Does she even mean this—that she'd never have refused another round of chemo? There's no possible way to know.

It's not easy to maneuver Addie and her coffin to the spot on the ridge that she had in mind. There's an overgrown dirt road that would get them there a lot more easily, but Tom says it's too risky to drive; it's too dark to find their way in without headlights, he says, and someone in one of the houses below, on Haupt Bridge Road, might see the car lights and call the campus security office, assuming they're drunken students.

For the first time the strangeness of this difficulty strikes Scarlet. Why a coffin at all? And not just any coffin: one made from the wood of her father and mother's barn. Was this the Addie she knew, this woman with a sudden wish for a symbolic link with her past, with her childhood home, like this? *Did* she know her mother at all?

In the end Dustin pulls a makeshift wooden wagon with old bicycle tires that Tom and Addie used for hauling compost out of the shed. Somehow he and Tom manage to secure Addie's coffin to it with a strand of clothesline and several bungee cords, and together they steer this awkward contraption, first across the rickety footbridge over the rushing creek, then up the winding switchbacks to the crest of the ridge.

Scarlet herself feels helpless and lame, trailing behind with a small shovel and a pickax, but Tom refuses to let her help them; it's all she can do to get him to let her carry a few tools. When they reach the crest and find the spot Addie suggested to Tom—a tiny clearing deep in the woods with two old oak trees on either side—he and Dustin drink some water and rest for only a few minutes before they start to dig.

Both of them are shirtless and coated with sweat and mud by the time they lift the coffin and begin to lower it carefully into the grave they've just finished digging, and there are hints of pale gray light at the horizon. Scarlet stops them for a moment, just long enough to kiss the worn siding from her grandparents' barn and whisper good-bye.

It's remarkable how perfect it feels, and sounds, when Tom hands her the shovel and she throws in the first few scoops of dirt. The scratch of soil on the rough wood makes a weighty sound that she feels in her chest. When she hears it, and feels it, it's as if all the tension in her arms, her back and neck, everything she's been holding over these last few days, falls away from her, filtering down with the dirt.

This is absolutely right, Scarlet thinks. How could they have considered doing anything else? Addie is no phoenix; to cremate her would have felt so wrong. Her birdlike bones belong here, in the earth that she loved. Heavy now with certainty, weighed down with dirt—her body beginning the long, slow process of feeding the trees and mosses and ferns above her. Not reduced to ashes, floating on the waves and the creek, fleeting and ephemeral in a way she herself certainly never was.

Scarlet would like to stay here longer, talking to her mother, asking her for advice. Would you call my feelings for Bobby love, Addie? she could ask her. Is this anything like what you felt for Tom? But she knows they are running out of time, and so she steps away, leaving Tom to throw in a next shovelful of dirt and have his own time, now, with Addie. She steps back next to Dustin, who's waiting with his own shovel, looking out toward the river.

Tom throws in one shovelful of dirt, then falls to his knees and starts to sob. Scarlet can't bear to see it, and she makes a move to reach for him, but as she does Dustin gently takes her hand. "Let him grieve," he says quietly, still looking toward the river. So she turns to look with him, her heart heaving, while Tom weeps for his sweet Adeline.

The sky is pink when Tom and Dustin finish packing the sod over Addie's new grave. The birds have been singing for a good hour. As they make their way wearily down the path, Tom and Dustin steering the clumsy wagon, they pause for a moment, listening to a plaintive dove in the trees overhead. At the edge of the creek, a great blue heron, disturbed by their arrival, lifts off, its vast wings only a few feet from their heads.

Dustin takes a quick swim in the creek before leaving to drive the truck back to Cider Cove, refusing Scarlet's offer of breakfast. "Better get on the road," he says. "Your neighbors might wonder what this seafood truck's doing in your driveway." Before Scarlet can point out that it hardly matters now, he's on his way.

While Tom showers, she cooks eggs and toast. When he returns to the kitchen, he is dressed in a completely uncharacteristic jacket and tie; he plans to arrive at the office of Burnham College's president promptly at nine, "in full mourning attire," he says, with the news of where Addie is now buried, and the quiet suggestion that perhaps the college might want to preserve a portion of Burnham Ridge, at least, from Bert Schafer's bulldozers.

"He wouldn't listen about the cerulean warbler—or the Cuvier's kinglet, for that matter," Tom says, shrugging, his mouth full of scrambled eggs. "I'll tell him he left us no choice."

Scarlet spreads some of Addie's blackberry jam on her toast. "You don't think she *really* saw a Cuvier's kinglet up there, do you?" she asks.

He takes a drink of coffee, watching her over the rim of his cup, then wipes his mouth with his napkin and rises from the table.

"I'm a scientist, and also an optimist, Scarlet," he says. "What do you think?" He smiles at her then—a mischievous smile, she thinks, though she can't quite read it—and walks out of the room.

A few minutes later, on his way out the door, he hands her a black loose-leaf notebook. It is Addie's last field notebook, Scarlet realizes as she pages through it, and Tom has marked the last completed page, dated May 10, 2001—a year before she died—where Addie has drawn what is, apparently, a Cuvier's kinglet.

nineteen

WHEN TOM ARRIVED AT the president's office, the secretary raised her eyebrows, but said nothing, when she saw his shirt and tie; she was new this year, and someone Tom did not know well, fortunately—and so she asked no questions about Addie. When he saw the president hurrying out to greet him, he feared for a moment that news of her death had somehow reached him already. But then he saw his happy, beaming face.

"Tom, Tom—perfect timing. Come in, come in. We have something very interesting to talk about!"

When he stepped into the office, there was Lou, seated across from the president's desk, beautifully and expensively dressed, looking quite composed and, Tom thought, more smug than usual.

"Hello, Tom," she said. "I thought I might meet you here."

"Good, good," the president nearly shouted; "then the two of you have already spoken about this. Marvelous." All the while he bustled nervously around the room, arranging chairs, jumping up to refill Lou's cup of coffee. Normally rather reticent, he grew positively gregarious when there was talk of financial gain for the college. I smell a new donor in the room, Tom thought. He had no idea, though, just how large a donor he was seated next to.

"Spoken about *what?*" Tom asked suspiciously, looking not at the president but at Lou.

Ten minutes before he arrived, Tom learned, Lou had presented the president with an offer—more than twice Bert Schafer's—for the three hundred acres of land surrounding the college. All of it: Rising Valley to the northeast, Sunday Woods to the south, and all of the deeply wooded Burnham Ridge, towering above Nisky and Kleine Creeks—land that extended north as far as the east-west interstate, and east all the way to the Delaware River canal path. Her conditions for the purchase were simple: that the land be maintained as a nature preserve and wildlife refuge—untouched, for perpetuity, except for the construction of a series of trails and a few inconspicuous blinds for bird watchers. It was to be called the Addie Sturmer Kavanagh Preserve.

She suggested, but didn't require, that the college use some of the funds to establish a new undergraduate program in environmental studies. To be directed by Tom—if he wished. At the president's suggestion that some of the funds might go toward a new art center as well—also named for Addie, of course—she readily agreed. The president was beside himself with joy, and a degree of disbelief. "I certainly never expected to have a day like this when I left the house this morning," he said when Lou finished describing her offer to Tom.

Tom, who hadn't said a thing while Lou laid out her plans, simply laughed. "Neither did I," he said. And, turning to Lou, his palms spread in front of him, he said, "You win."

She looked steadily at him then, serious and unsmiling for the first time that morning. "It's not a war, Tom," she said. "Or if it is, it's not about us. It's about Addie."

The president, tactful—and unspeakably grateful—fund-raiser that he was, chose this moment to excuse himself to go ask his secretary to put in a call to the college's attorney. When he left, Lou smiled, her tone light and airy again as she went on, "And maybe now Addie can finally rest from all *her* wars, Tom—wherever you and Scarlet have put her."

Tom smiled back at her. "Well," he said, "she's not where I'd expected her to be. All I'll say is that her daughter seems to have acquired some of her mother's fighting spirit."

"She's had it all along," Lou said. Then she added, "And you know, I do understand why. I have to admit I like having an enemy." She leaned closer to Tom as the president walked back into the office. "It's nice to have a new one," she whispered.

"You mean our illustrious local developer?" he asked.

She shook her head. "No, no; he's small fry. I'm going after your slow-witted, sanctimonious senator next. My friends in Washington have already suggested a few worthy opponents I might get behind." The president cleared his throat then, shuffling some papers on his desk, and she turned to face him with her practiced smile.

twenty

ADDIE HAD TRIED, BUT failed, to read Proust. *Swann's Way* from *Remembrance of Things Past*—so ungodly long, and only the first volume! But this had been a final suggestion from Candace, her friend from the library. They'd had lunch together in March, a week before Addie and Tom would pack the car and drive to Cider Cove to meet the hospice workers and "set up camp" (Tom's words) in Cora's studio. When they'd discussed the arrangements by phone, Cora had insisted on that room, with its wraparound porch, its east windows with distant views of the water, and its south windows open to several seed-filled maples between Cora's house and the one next door. "You'll see and hear more birds there than anywhere else in the house," she'd said.

Addie didn't argue; it seemed so important to Cora to give her the studio. Never mind that her feelings about birdsong had changed in recent years. What she didn't tell Cora, but did tell Candace at lunch that day, was that over the last few weeks, as her energy had begun to flag and she'd found herself, once again, too exhausted to go on working, suddenly she was lost in her own mind, barely noticing anything outside her window—awash, instead, in memories, incredibly vivid ones: of places. Their colors and textures, the quality of the light and the way the air felt, on her skin and entering her nose and throat. And their smells.

In fact, after years of scoffing at bird-watchers and their life lists of every species they'd seen, she'd begun a life list of her own—of smells. Not all of them were, strictly speaking, the smells of the natural world,

but all were connected with places she'd loved, like the woods on her
parents' farm or on Burnham Ridge, the green back roads of England
and Ireland, the salty marshland between Cape May and Cider Cove.
And new places too, where she'd traveled with Tom in recent years. She
hadn't written them down; she felt no need to do that. Instead she carried
the list in her mind, running through each item, calling every smell to
mind, several times a day:

The electric smell of must and mold before a Pennsylvania
thunderstorm.

Hay in the eaves of her father's barn, at war with the reeking manure below.

Bacon frying.

River mud.

Diesel exhaust from an English bus.

The water-stained covers of old books.

Cedar bark and damp, clotted leaves outside the door on Haupt
Bridge Road.

Wood smoke.

Traces of rotting fish at low tide on the New Jersey shore.

Turpentine, borax, glue.

Hot, sun-baked pine in the hills along the northern California
coast.

Piñon and sage one spring in New Mexico.

Slippery mangoes on a Costa Rican beach.

Bay rum aftershave on Tom's neck, rusty tang of sweat on clothes
he wore for days in the field, a salty, trickling stream of his se-
men on her inner thigh.

Her own skin, on her chest and arms, brought back to life by the
sun on the first warm day of spring—the way she'd smelled
every May for as long as she could remember—some kind of

nameless blossom, barely open, its scent gone the moment she sensed it.

When she told Candace about her list that day at lunch, Candace had said, "Well, then maybe you should read Proust next." But once past Marcel's memory of his childhood in Combray—the taste of the madeleine, the longing for his mother's kiss—she'd found her mind wandering. An hour would pass, and she might doze, or fall into a kind of waking dream, a memory of her own. Nursing Scarlet in the rocker in the sun. Those fevered days of painting up in Maine, soaking the canvas with pink and orange and green. Kissing Tom on the slippery rocks of Nisky Creek, where she'd fallen back deliberately, knowing he would catch her, desperate to know the taste of his lips and tongue.

She'd look at the clock and see that several hours had passed. She might have read, at most, three pages.

Well, she'd never really been all that literary. Even in her days as an English major, hadn't she gladly thrown aside her Wordsworth and Keats for a chance to consider Audubon at Miss Smallwood's first suggestion? Those plates had filled her with something that no poem ever could, it seemed.

Even Scarlet's poems baffled her at times, though she'd tried to be open to them. She'd held on to certain lines like life rafts, repeating them to herself like the lyrics from familiar songs as she painted or stuffed or mounted her birds.

"In all this bilge and ruin, Mother Kollwitz, will you find us?"

"This rough music, murderous chords of singing bombs . . ."

"And sick with certainty we soldier on."

"The bittern blows out air like it's drowning . . ."

"The dark boy alone, while the others cycle through the graves."

Were her poems about *specific* things? she'd ventured to ask Scarlet last year at Christmas in Cider Cove. Bobby had been there with Cora—

thinner since his divorce and the hard weeks, since September 11, without alcohol. But alive in a new way too, just as, she could tell, Scarlet was. Of course, she'd thought, though she'd said nothing about it to anyone: Of course he and Scarlet had found their way back to each other.

Or, she went on, were the poems meant to call to mind many questions, many moments—unanswerable and disconnected, except for the moment when one read the poem? Because that was how she experienced them, at times (at other times, she simply gave up, but she didn't tell Scarlet this).

"Well, yes, Addie, that's it exactly, I'd say," Scarlet answered. Later that night, Addie thought maybe she'd caught a piece of the memory— "sick with certainty"—something they'd been discussing one morning at breakfast. *Had* it been the Gulf War, then? Wasn't that what the poem was about? She forgot to ask Scarlet about it later.

Of course the Kollwitz references, those she thought she might take a little credit for.

But she truly wasn't literary, and—increasingly, it seemed, since the cancer's return—she was also unable to muster much of her former anger, her "righteous indignation," as Tom called it. And so through that fall and winter she'd mainly sketched and, only occasionally, painted. Whatever birds she happened to see. As if she were a love-struck, bird-struck girl again, but calmer now. She felt almost serene, drawing then.

Not literary and, truthfully, probably not much of an artist either. True, she'd felt compelled to make the things she'd made—and it amused her, now, to think that her assemblages had actually brought her a kind of fame. Because she had never once, she knew, captured what she was seeing in her mind's eye. Even Peterson said as much: "There's a difference between illustration, which is a teaching device, as in my field guides," he wrote, "and painting that's evocative of your emotions. I'm envious of certain painters who have achieved that." He wished he could have made paintings with a more "Audubonesque quality," he said. It comforted her, reading that.

Maybe she *had* made work that was somehow "evocative of her emotions." But now she wondered what, if anything, she'd accomplished by doing that. And now too, with this sudden rush of memories, first throughout the winter in Burnham, and now in Cora's studio in Cider Cove, with everyone hovering and fussing—how she wished she could somehow capture *this*, the unbelievable clarity of her memories of all these places.

Maybe that was all it came down to, really, in the end. A kind of nostalgia fueling everything she did. A longing for the past, for places where she'd been so young and full of yearning, a full and melancholy kind of yearning, that she'd forgotten about until these last months. A need to somehow freeze those places in time, to preserve them, to protect them, and thereby keep the lost world of her youth intact.

Still, she *did* wish she could have done something about the woods on Burnham Ridge. That she might have had the last word there, at least. But of course that was a bit ridiculous. Tom and Scarlet and her grandchild deserved a little peace now, surely, a rest from all those worries.

It did pain her that she would never know her grandchild.

It pained her too, that she had never managed to make a painting of the Cuvier's kinglet, for Tom.

Journal—Field Entry

10 May 2001
Thursday

Burnham Ridge (Small clearing fifty yards or so off the trail leading up from Nisky Creek, probably a homestead from the last century, flanked on either side by two perfect oaks)

Time: 5:30–9 A.M.
Observer: Addie Kavanagh

Habitat: Primarily these two oaks, and the mosses below; some attention to a stand of pines and a handful of residual crab-apple trees farther west along the ridge. Bloodroot, spring larkspur, Cora's favorite anemones.

Weather: Overcast and cool, damp with the previous night's rain. Temperatures rising from 58 degrees when I left home to 65 degrees by the time I'd returned.

Remarks: I wish there were a way to convey this *stillness*. That alone will be a terrible loss.

SPECIES LIST
In the pines and crabapples:
American Robin 4
Black-Capped Chickadee 5
Hermit Thrush 1
Chipping Sparrow 2
Baltimore Oriole 2
Scarlet Tanager 1
In the taller oak at southeastern edge of clearing:
Cuvier's Kinglet [hypothetical?] 1

Number of Species: 7; *Number of Individuals:* 16; *Time:* 3½ hrs.
Comments: No sign of the cerulean warbler this morning, I'm afraid. But there it was again, Audubon's wren, on a branch of one of those towering oaks. It isn't possible, yet there it was. A ruby-crowned kinglet, but with a golden-crowned's head stripe. The Cuvier's kinglet.

10 May—An optimist, and a magician—I half suspect you of rigging up a mechanical ruby-crowned kinglet and dabbing on a little paint to make that stripe (Don't I have a stuffed one somewhere in the shed? To be honest, I've lost track; you and Scarlet can have fun cataloging them all when

I'm gone). After all these years I probably could have been fooled, still, as you know.

I'm ill again, Tom. I know the cancer is back. I'll tell you in another week or so. But I want nothing to do with the usual treatment.

I believe I'd like to die in Cider Cove. Cora has made a kind of peace with death; she's had to, of course. You and Scarlet will too, but I don't want to drag you both there by dying slowly on the banks of your beloved creeks. Cora and Lou can help out at first, and you can escape to the light-house or the marsh whenever you need to. If it drags on, our insurance should cover hospice care, I'm told; if that isn't enough, go ahead and sell *River Nile* to the Driscolls or the Lloyds, or to Lou if she insists (I expect she will, though God knows why. Well, God and the two of you.)

I'm concerned that Scarlet will think she needs to be the one who cares for me as I get worse. Please encourage her to visit when she can, but don't let her try to do this. Tell her to stay busy with her work and her life in New York.

I hope I do have some time, to travel a bit more, maybe. To keep going with you into the field. To spread our blanket below the trees and make love, as if it were 1965 all over again. This morning in the cottage you looked and smelled and felt to me exactly like you did back then.

It's funny what I've been remembering lately. Not the sorts of things you'd expect. I've been thinking a lot about my mother and father, how all Mother wanted was to live in town—or, if she wasn't going to get to live there, to be buried there. And I've been remembering my dad, tend-ing to the graves in the middle of the field next to my parents' little strip of land. Remember when I showed it to you? Just five or six flat, old little gravestones, and a crumbling old statue of an angel in the middle, right in the center of a cornfield.

It drove Mother crazy that he fussed so over those graves—pulling the weeds that grew around them, sweeping off the dirt. "Crazy old Slo-vak, dusting off the graves of some poor old German family he never even knew," she used to say.

But I admired him for it. I often wished there'd been a way to bury him there too. But of course Mother never would have stood for that. And it wasn't even their land, of course. Still, it does seem like a person should be able to rest, finally, in a place he's loved.

Strange, isn't it, how sentimental I've become! Like when you first knew me, I suppose.

If you'd like, give my notebooks to Scarlet when you've read them. Apologies to Joseph Grinnell, but I don't think I'll write any more entries in here.

Here is my sketch of the kinglet. Maybe it's enough to go on; maybe I'll manage to paint it too.

I love you more than ever, Tom.

twenty-one

IN THE YEARS FOLLOWING Addie's death, a core group of avid environmentalists and fans of her work, both early and late, have persisted in their impassioned belief that she is buried somewhere on the nearly three hundred acres of the new preserve surrounding Burnham College—that at the time of her principled death she chose to have an equally principled and simple burial. Rumors spread quickly among this group of true believers—about a refrigerated truck being spotted near the Kavanagh home shortly after Addie's death, about Tom's claiming to have lost the New Jersey certificate of death when the Pennsylvania authorities came to inquire.

Most days a handful of Addie's followers—a couple of Birkenstock-wearing members of Greenpeace here, a few pierced and alienated admirers of her assemblages there—can be found wandering the trails of the Addie Sturmer Kavanagh Preserve, in search of her grave.

Others, more rational types for instance, like the bird-watchers, both amateur and professional, who also frequent the preserve, consider the notion that Addie is buried there a myth, urban lore of a sort—rather like the oft-told story of Addie's having spotted a Cuvier's kinglet somewhere along Burnham Ridge. Still, when they visit the preserve early in the morning during nesting season, many, if not most, of these more rational types scan the woods of Burnham Ridge with their high-powered binoculars and scopes, half believing they might spot a four-and-a-half-inch bird with a vermilion patch on its head, and a faint stripe from its eye to the back of its head.

On her walks there with Tom and her daughter, Scarlet has yet to spot either a cerulean warbler or a Cuvier's kinglet. But often, as she sits on the fallen log beside Addie's grave in the early morning, she listens to the call of the wood thrush, and she remembers her parents, together and singing.

acknowledgments

My reading as I worked on *In Hovering Flight* was as wide, eclectic, and rich (not to say undisciplined) as that of my characters Addie and Scarlet. Among the works that were helpful, inspiring, or both were Roger Tory Peterson and Virginia Marie Peterson's edition of *Audubon's Birds of America (The Audubon Society Baby Elephant Folio);* various editions of the Peterson Field Guide to *Birds of Eastern and Central North America;* Richard K. Walton and Robert W. Lawson's sound recordings, *Birding by Ear, Eastern/Central;* the Library of America's *John James Audubon,* compiled by Christoph Irmscher; David Sibley's *Birding Basics;* various publications of the Cornell Lab of Ornithology; Maurice Broun's *Hawks Aloft: The Story of Hawk Mountain;* Judy Pelikan's illustrated adaptation of F. Schuyler Matthews' *Field Book of Wild Birds and Their Music,* titled *The Music of Wild Birds;* Duff Hart-Davis's *Audubon's Elephant: America's Great Naturalist and the Making of The Birds of America;* George Miksch Sutton's *To a Young Bird Artist: Letters from Louis Agassiz Fuertes to George Miksch Sutton;* Roger Tory Peterson and Rudy Hoglund's *Roger Tory Peterson: The Art and Photography of the World's Foremost Birder; The Diary and Letters of Kaethe Kollwitz,* edited by Hans Kollwitz; Martha Kearns' *Käthe Kollwitz: Woman and Artist;* Elizabeth Prelinger's *Käthe Kollwitz;* Bruno Bettelheim's *The Empty Fortress: Infanitle Autism and the Birth of the Self;* and Richard Pollak's *The Creation of Dr. B.: A Biography of Bruno Bettelheim.* Also helpful was a March 2005 lecture in Santa Fe,

New Mexico by Ami Ronnberg, Curator of New York's Archive for Research in Archetypal Symbolism—a lecture that enriched my understanding of the powerful place of birds in historical and contemporary art, and that made me aware of the work of Kiki Smith, whose "Jersey Crows" is a clear inspiration for Addie's "River Nile."

For the love of birds and birdsong that is this book's deepest root, I want to acknowledge, and thank, my father, Lynn Hinnefeld, and my brother, Steve Hinnefeld. For his lectures, field work, answers to my many questions, and patient reading of the book in manuscript, I am deeply grateful to Dan Klem, Sarkis Acopian Professor of Ornithology & Conservation Biology at Muhlenberg College.

My friends and fellow writers, Mark Harris and Ruth Knafo Setton, read this manuscript repeatedly and with such kind and intelligent devotion; I am thankful to them, and to my other writer's group members, Paul Acampora and Virginia Wiles, for their wise insights and wonderful humor. For thoughtful readings, and for advice on birds, art, writing, and other matters, I am grateful to Ursula Hegi, Joanna Scott, Alix Ohlin, Billy Weber, Martha Christine, Dana Van Horn, Stephanie Anderson, and Pat Mansfield-Phelan and Tom Phelan.

For providing beautiful spaces and quiet, uninterrupted time—as well as delightful conversation—I thank Ann and Preston Browning of Wellspring House in Ashfield, Massachusetts, and the staff and students at Pendle Hill in Wallingford, Pennsylvania. For their enthusiastic support of my work on this novel I thank Moravian College's Dean of the Faculty, Gordon Weil, and the Chair of the English Department—and my good friend—Theresa Dougal.

For her faith in this book and in me, I thank my agent, Liv Blumer, and for his good sense, insightful editing, and clear commitment to this book I thank my editor, Fred Ramey. Thanks also to Caitlin Hamilton Summie and Libby Jordan at Unbridled Books.

My daughter Anna Hauser, artist and singer, though she was only six as I finished work on this novel, has been a vital inspiration for the character of Scarlet—particularly for Scarlet's sensitivity and independence. My husband Jim Hauser is my wisest editor, my most thoughtful adviser on language and art, and my steadfast solace; my deepest thanks go to him.